LOVE SEX AND TIME TRAVEL

Could you. Would You?

www.stanrogers.co.uk

Welcome to Love Sex and Time Travel. The characters, events and places in the book are either fictitious or if based on real people etc are disguised with name changes to protect the innocent. The novel is very loosely and I stress loosely autobiographical.

Thanks and dedications are due to the Lovely Elaine, my Mum and to all of the characters from down in 'Cardinals Stratford'. But the biggest dedication is to my Dad who passed away peacefully on 29/12/2007 and who will now never get to read the finished book.

Also thanks are due to my gal pals Karen, Jen and Tracy for their comments on extracts of the manuscript sent to them and to the good people of 'Falconer Plastics', you all know who you are. For updates on the book go to www.stanrogers.co.uk

Stan Rogers February 2008

Forethought.

I feel such a great sense of personal sadness at the many times and opportunities that I have wasted in my life. So many of them I think sadly. The things I would have done differently if only. Yeah I know. If only? I know life is full of 'if only's' and 'maybe's' but do you ever think to yourself what if I could get the opportunity to go back and do it all over again? Go back and put things right, or try to do things differently. Could you face down those fire breathing demons of your past again or would you just invent them all over again to face in your future? Would it be a good thing or would it just negate your life? Would you be any happier? Would getting everything right the second time around just lose you the experience of messing up and all the inherent benefits of the learning process? Or would it be your own personal nirvana, answering life's many questions with a crib sheet, as it were? Pre-warned is pre-armed if you like. Would you change things? Could you change things?

Chapter 1. Saturday Night.

Everything started for me normally enough that evening. You know how it is. Yet another uneventful Saturday night at home is drawing to its inevitably boring conclusion. A few too many whiskies and cigarettes as usual. Parkinson has just finished, there's nothing much else on the TV and so I click on the remote control. Channel surfing I find that Top of the Pops 2 is about the only thing I can find to even slightly stir my interest. I am fascinated by all the old nostalgic pop videos from the 1970s and 80s and I think; oh my God I wish I was able to live those times again. Wouldn't it be really great to be young and back there again, knowing the things I know now? That was it, nothing more. Totally innocuous, a fleeting whisky fuelled wish. We all have them sometimes.

A little about me? Well Ok then. I'm Matthew Spears, aged fifty something, and married for the last nineteen years to the lovely Elaine who has given me the unedifying pleasure of three teenaged kids, little darlings one and all. I'm an average 5 feet 8 inches tall, fair haired, blue eyed, not as slim as I used to be but looking on the bright side at least I still have all my own hair and most of my own teeth and everything else still seems to be in fairly good working order. I work shifts in a local factory as an injection moulding machine and robot setter, pretty mundane I hear you say, but secretly, apart from wishing I could be 21 again, I want something more exciting from my life. I want to be a rock star, a martial arts expert, a male supermodel even, just anything more exciting than the dull life I am leading now. Nothing strange about that, I would think that probably most people over fifty have the same dreams as me. In fact I know they do. Who wouldn't want to be young again?

I'm struggling in my unexciting life, really struggling. Trying to keep below 200 lbs and give up the cigarettes and I just know I should ease back on the booze as well, but forever asking myself what direction can I take in my remaining years, how can I get some much needed excitement back into my life because that's how it gets you in your mid fifties. You start to realise that in not much more than a decade you will be retired and pensioned off and totally washed up apart from an inadequate pension and maybe some grandkids to dote on. The clock of life is ticking faster with every year. The idols and heroes of your childhood all seem so old or are dying off at an alarming rate so it seems. Life finished then except for descent into old age, death and peaceful oblivion. Game over. I seem to have so few years left and what am I going to do with them? I look at my lined face in the mirror and it seems to be slowly sagging and disintegrating in front of my eyes. I'm metamorphosing into my grandfather it seems. Still, that's life I tell myself, we all get old and then we die. Life's a bitch. No second chances. No going back.

Enough about me then and back to my strange tale, to a warm summers Saturday night. It's late and as I said I'd probably had one or two too many whiskies. I'm slobbing it in just my shorts and flip flops due to the heat of the evening and reclining back in my favourite chair sipping a scotch, cigarette in hand. The kids are staying over at their friend's places and my wife Elaine had just said a very definite NO to a portion of unbridled lust and has disappeared off to bed leaving me downstairs on my own watching old music videos on TV from the 70s and 80s. I get the feeling I should go to bed as well but what's the point I think? I'm just Oh so comfortable sitting here alone and feeling unloved and hard done by. I try hard to imagine a better past. The 1970s or 80s will do, I'm not fussy. Top of the Pops 2 finishes and so still in the mood for times past I put on my wireless headphones, wind up the computer and external hard drive and look for some music that reminds me of those long lost times. After a quick search I decide on Human League's 'Dare' album. That will do very nicely I think. I relax comfortably back in my chair, turn up the volume slightly and start to drift away to the music. The first track is aptly called, 'The Things That Dreams Are Made Of'. As I'm reclining back comfortably listening to the song I try to remember the words to sing along to and I think of the times when it first came out. About 1981 I think. A great year I tell myself trying to remember it clearly but I yawn and, well you probably know the feeling yourself, the eyes start getting heavy, you feel no pain, and then you are fading away knowing that you are going to wake up in the morning still in the chair with a nice little hangover throbbing away in your brain and the threat hanging over you to mow the lawn or to do something else productive. Lovely Elaine always manages to find me something to keep me occupied. Sometimes you dream, sometimes you remember them but mostly you don't.

Chapter 2. Discovering The Past.

Slowly coming around but strange feelings disturb my dream. I feel as if I am deep under water holding my breath and needing air badly. The water is comfortably warm but my lungs are bursting and I look upwards and see light above me through the blue shimmering water. I strike out for the light, pushing myself upwards towards it kicking wildly and eventually breaking the surface to take great lungfuls of life saving air. Then I fade back to my darkness again.

Slowly coming too again and I can see through my half open eyes a bright shaft of sunlight angling across the bed through a gap in the curtains. Birds are twittering outside the window and I can smell a roast dinner cooking. It smells absolutely delicious. I roll over languidly, stretching my legs, yawn, and scratch my balls. Doze again, thinking about the water and my dream. But then it slowly sinks in that I've come to in bed instead of the armchair. Hmm how did I get here I think curiously, I don't remember making it up to bed last night? I've got a bit of a hangover but still feeling remarkably good anyway, certainly better than I deserve to I think. Then it slowly dawns on my slowly waking mind that this is not my bed and where the hell am I? No quilt, just sheets and blankets covered with a light brown bed cover. I feel myself roll over slowly and instead of my digital radio alarm I can see an old red wind up alarm clock ticking away and telling me its 11:45. This is getting rather weird now I think to myself. I scratch my balls again and think about this, I must still be dreaming? But no it all feels too real, as if I am awake. Then I hear myself shout "Mum how about a cuppa I think I'm dying of dehydration here." I must be dreaming I just must be; I know that I never said that although it sounded very much to me like I did. I try to get up but can't move of my own accord and then a few seconds later the bedroom door opens and a woman comes in with a mug of tea in her hand. "About time you got up you lazy little sod she says putting the tea down on my bedside table, it's almost twelve o'clock." My brain seems to flip as I realise it's my mum but looking one hell of a lot younger. This must be a dream I think yet again, but then again it just seems so incredibly real. I really don't want it to end either as I look around because I can see that I'm in my old bedroom at my parent's house from the early 1980s. It's fantastic beyond belief, I recognise my old Akai stereo, and there's my black and white telly propped up on a chair in the corner at the foot of the bed with its aerial hanging from the ceiling. That old Athena poster Lovelight is tacked to the wall above the bed. A stack of twelve inch vinyl albums are lined up beneath the stereo and an opened pack of 20 JPS cigarettes sit on my bedside cabinet with one sticking out of the pack. It looks tempting and I watch as my hand snakes out from under the covers to slowly to take it then light it with an old Ronson Variflame lighter. My mum picks up last night's clothes to wash and leaves my room grumbling something I don't catch as I feel my body lifting itself onto its side then taking a swig of tea. I can taste the sweetness of the tea and the feel of the welcome smoke of the first cigarette of the day in my throat. That is so damned good I think. Damn this is a great dream but I just know it's going to end, I'm gonna wake up any moment now; you know you always do in good dreams just before the best bit it seems to me. It is just so surreal though, I can see and taste and smell but I can't control my movement. I seem to be looking out from inside someone else's body, a younger me, but unable to influence anything, just an observer in another body so it seems.

I feel myself getting out of bed and making my way to the toilet, and WELL now that's a novelty. I don't pee with power like that nowadays anymore; a stream of piss seems to explode into the toilet bowl with a gorgeously loud splashing sound. I think sadly that the old pipes must be furring up a little by 2007. I even recognise that I'm wearing my old leopardskin pattern briefs. Then I watch as I pad barefooted back to my room to pull back the curtains to allow the sunlight of a summer's day to brighten the room. I sit on the bed and allow a large yawn to escape. It's funny but as I watch myself flicking ash into the ashtray I realize that I still have it now, a stainless steel one that I bought in Denmark in 1977, it cost me a packet too I remember. I watch as I see myself select an album from the large pile by the stereo and deftly flip it on to the turntable. Then I'm listening to Rush, 'A Farewell to Kings' booming from the speakers, a great album from the 1970s and Wow the memories that brings back. Then my Mum's voice from downstairs, "You can turn that rubbish down right now." "Bloody hell mum. I hear myself say and then I ease the volume back a tad. What times dinner mum?" "About two o'clock when your father gets back from the pub." comes the reply so I hear myself shout back, "OK I'm going down the pub as well. Can you put mine in the microwave please?" "What's a microwave"? My mum shouts back. Now this makes me think because obviously I would know little of microwaves then, in those days, they were invented but no-one had them yet, so it seemed a bit odd to say it? "OK so put it in the oven then and I'll be back later." I must admit to being a bit sad at that as it smells just gorgeous and I wouldn't mind some right now and I do remember those old Sunday roast dinners of my mum's were delicious. Always roast beef as my dad wouldn't eat anything else on a Sunday, always had to be roast beef. I can even remember my mum dishing up roast pork once and how it ended up in the bin courtesy of my good old dad. Next I watch myself as I don a pair of old faded blue denim jeans and a brown check shirt after having a quick wash and brushing my hair. I can see myself in the mirror as I do this and it is definitely the younger me. A slimmer me with an unlined face looks back at me from the mirror smiling cockily, "You handsome beast." he says and laughs blowing himself a kiss. Deodourant and a splash of Tabac aftershave comes next even though I haven't shaved. But the most wonderful thing was putting on my old pair of brown leather cowboy boots. Mmm, the smell of that leather, I loved those old cowboy boots. I'm up and away downstairs grabbing my black leather bomber jacket on the way.

"Romilly rang." said my mum as I was heading towards the front door. I mentally froze at her words, although my old self kept on going. "She said she will see you in the Old Crown." "OK mum." said the younger me as I strolled out of the front door. Now Romilly was the love of my life at the time and eventually my first wife and I was going to see her again as she was then? How amazing. The memories came back to me like old familiar friends, of the love Romilly and I had together back then and how it all ended so disastrously in my crash and burn in 1984 but that doesn't matter now, I was just totally gobsmacked as even more memories unfolded in front of my eyes. At what I could now see parked before me on the driveway. A true automotive classic. My old mark three Ford Cortina parked there on the drive, 1600cc of heaven clad in metallic Roman Gold coachwork. I used to love that car. I mean I REALLY loved that motor. I remembered buying it in 1978 while working at the local council. It had cost me top dollar and I wondered at the time how on earth I would ever keep up the payments of 26 pounds a month on it. I'd spent even more on it by fitting a decent stereo radio/cassette player along with black furry seat covers, very chic I thought in the early 1980s. It was a gloriously hot summer's day and I smiled proudly as the sunlight glinted blindingly off of the cars polished chromework. Why do cars no longer have chrome bumpers I thought sadly? Had proper chrome hubcaps too, none of these imitation plastic modern ones. I watched as I unlocked it with a key, no remote central locking for me in those days, and after throwing my jacket onto the back seat I eased myself comfortably into the driver's seat. Starting it up my old self donned a pair of aviator style sunglasses while enjoying the smooth purr from the engine and reversed out of the drive then put his foot down allowing just a tiny little squeal from the back tyres as we headed off into town, Hollywood tyres, I laughed. My old self pushed a cassette into the player and the sound of The Beat, an old 1980s ska revival band permeated the Cortina at full blast. I heard myself singing along to 'Mirror In The Bathroom', now that's great music as well I think as my other self lights another JPS and pulls deeply on it, then winds down the side window to allow the smoke to escape, no electric widows then either for me, but I thought, what the hell, the exercise would do me good. I relax in my young body listening to the music and the purr of the engine. Total heaven or as close to it as can be imagined anyway.

Chapter 3. Meeting Romilly.

The old 1981 Matt sang enthusiastically along to the cassette on the way into town, badly too I couldn't help noticing, passing and tooting the horn at a couple of nice looking girls on the way. The lovely twosome laughed and in a very unladylike manner gave me the old two finger salute. Oh well can't win them all I thought to myself and I felt my old self returning the gesture to them. A few minutes later and we pulled up outside the Old Crown pub and I thought this dream was just getting better and better by the minute as brushing the cigarette ash from my jeans I locked the Cortina and walked into the pub. Ahhh the good Old Crown, the scene of many of my finest times, tatty and even a little run down but a pub of such great character in those golden days. A few of the guys were there that I recognised from 1981. "Mornin all. Lovely day aint it." I grinned as I entered the public bar and the place looked just as comfortably scruffy inside as I had fondly remembered it. Bob was behind the bar and that brought a mental tear to my eye remembering that he must have been the best landlord ever and he was to die so young not so far in the future from cancer. After acknowledging them my old self headed off into the saloon bar and there she was.

Sitting on a bar stool in the saloon bar talking to Dot, Dot was Bob's wife. Romilly held a drink in her hand with one leg crossed casually over the other tapping her toe in time to the jukebox music. She was a perfect vision of loveliness and my heart seemed to rise into my mouth. My lovely Rommy, tight blue denim jeans encasing her sensuously slim legs, a plain white t shirt and her gorgeously sexy shoulder length honey blonde hair framing her beautiful smiling face, just as I remembered her. In fact it seemed to me that sitting there at that moment she looked even more beautiful than I had ever remembered her. Romilly was all smiles as she rose from the barstool and came over to hug me warmly. I put my arm around her small waist and bent down to kiss her waiting lips. "Allo sexy, she says Got up at last have we?" "Yea, I laugh, hugging her tightly, I needed beer badly. All that sleeping has given me a thirst." I've worked out by now that this must be 1981 about July I reckon or maybe June. I'd have been 27 and Romilly was 17, and we'd been together since the previous December, a bit of an age difference I know but it didn't seem to bother us at all at the time. We just loved being together so much and had some great laughs not to mention some great loving along the way too. Then just as I am reveling at seeing her again my vision starts getting hazy, the room starts to spin and I feel as if I'm blacking out, everything dims and sounds seem to pass into a dreamlike distance, everything starts to fade out. Typical I think, just like I said, all dreams seem destined to end at the best bit.

"Ouch, I feel a hand lightly slapping my face, Bugger off will you." and the next thing I am awake in my armchair while Elaine is saying to me, "Wake up you piss artist the lawn needs mowing and you promised to finish off painting the toilet today." Good old Elaine, I think, that's the wife, was busy organising my day for me. But I felt so disorientated, one moment I was enjoying a gorgeous 1980s dream and now I was awake in the cold reality of 2007 again. Why couldn't Elaine have just left me to enjoy my dream a little longer I thought miserably? It was a lovely summer Sunday morning in 2007 and I had my hangover as expected. My head was throbbing, my mouth tasted like the proverbial Turkish wrestlers jockstrap and I had woken up with such feelings of disappointment at having my lovely dream so rudely curtailed as well. I lit the first cigarette of the day and inhaled the smoke deeply. Oh well I thought, coughing the first cough of the day as well, just a dream although it had been so vivid. That was the thing. It had been so magnificently real, as if I'd actually been there but I could only put it down to a dream although wishing it could have lasted a little longer. I staggered out of the recliner heading off to the kitchen for the kettle and a much needed mug of tea before beginning a hard hours toil behind the strimmer. The garden's not really big enough for a mower. "Hey maybe we should get a sheep I jokingly tell Elaine, we could flog the strimmer then and I'm sure it would be more environmentally friendly you know." "Yeah, laughs Elaine, and the next time you're feeling randy you can put a splash of mint sauce behind your ears and see if your lucks in." "Baaaaa." I bleat and then tell her to go forth and multiply and I prepare myself to start the strimming thinking, maybe I'll name the sheep Pauline, after her mum.

I kept on thinking about the dream for the rest of that morning, trying to imagine how it could have continued although to be truthful all of the scenarios involved extremely sensual rudery with my lovely Romilly. Oh yeah and consuming vast quantities of 1981 ale in the Old Crown as well. Something did keep nagging at me for the rest of that day though, apart from the wife that is but that's normal and I just ignored her as usual by putting my mp3 player on as I was working. Why in my dream had I asked my mum to put my dinner in the microwave? They were invented back then but were as rare as the proverbial rocking horse droppings. Was it just a quirk of my dream state mixing up the past with the future? Was it my modern day self breaking through into the dream just a little? In the end I put it down to being a lovely if ever so slightly odd dream, and I had put it to the back of my mind. By the time I had I started painting the toilet I had more or less forgotten it anyway and I started humming along to a song I remembered from my childhood as, hangover now gone, I merrily splashed paint over the walls along with lots on me. The song? Oh yeah it went something like this.

When Father painted the parlour
You couldn't tell Pa from paint
Dabbing it here! Dabbing it there!
Paint was getting everywhere
Mother was stuck to the ceiling
The children stuck to the floor
I never knew a blooming family
So 'stuck up' before.

I smiled at the memory and stopped for a ciggy break as Elaine came and examined my handiwork carefully and passed comment on the small bits that I had missed as she pointed them out to me helpfully. I smiled again imagining how she'd look wearing a paintbrush inserted in an uncomfortable place. "What are you grinning like an idiot for." she smiles sardonically and I just laugh and tell her I'm going to name our new sheep Pauline. "Very droll Matt and I am sure my mum would be very amused about that too. Now how about finishing the painting like a good boy eh?" I finish the cigarette and get back to the job in hand. Good old Elaine, she is one in a million.

After eventually finishing the painting I get changed from my paint spattered clothes and making myself a nice strong mug of tea I fire up the computer. I start playing some Editors through the headphones, the first album, I think it's my favourite, and entering my pictures folder I find some old shots that I had scanned in years before of Romilly and myself taken in the 1980s. Yep I thought looking at a picture of me in Capfield Forest taken by Romilly as I blow a kiss at her cheekily, that was the face looking back at me from the bedroom mirror in my dream. I looked so young and happy, so carefree. I noticed that in all of the photos of

Romilly and me that we are smiling or laughing and really seem to be enjoying life together. Young love eh? So wonderful to behold. Such good times we had as well I think back nostalgically. Such a shame it all ended so bitterly one cold day in January 1984. I still remember the day she left me not knowing at the time that she would never return. It had been a Sunday afternoon, cold as I said but quite sunny. We had been to the pub at lunchtime with my dad and we had even made love that morning together in the lounge. Everything seemed to be getting better between us after a recent bad patch. I had been working so hard to try to please her. We had a roast chicken cooking in the oven but somehow an argument started between us about God knows what, I can't even remember now but it was probably something trivial knowing Romilly, but it all gets out of hand and the next thing I know is that she is ringing her parents and asking them to come and pick her up. I had tried to pull out the phone line to stop her in my desperation to make her stay and sort it out but they must have caught some of it and so a short time later her Dad had turned up at our front door. And that was it. She left me. She just walked out of the door. I was totally bewildered and thinking why? From such great love to hating me in just three short but event filled years. Could I really have been that bad? I supposed I must have been. I had asked her to come back. Even pleaded but it all fell on deaf ears and so it all ended there finally between us in January 1984. We met for the last time in March 1984 on her 20th birthday. It seemed to be going so well. I talked to her about us and she seemed initially enthusiastic and we went out for a meal together. I took her back to her parents and we even made love in the car together but it seemed that the fire died that day as that was the last time we had any kind of loving contact. After that she became distant and even returned the birthday presents I had sent her. The next thing I knew was that

I was receiving divorce papers full of lies and half truths about me. But hey that's solicitors for you.

I did see Romilly a couple of times in the next year or so. Once driving past in a car and once with some dodgy looking guy in the local DIY store, both times she looked so bloody miserable and I asked myself at the time what had happened to the happy Romilly? But we never spoke again and I have never seen her again till this day in my dream. So why all of a sudden now do I start dreaming of her? Who knows I think to myself sadly and go on to look through some more old more pictures on the computer? Back to the 1970s even. A long time before Romilly came into my life. Pictures of Heather, Agnetha from Denmark, Tracy, all the old loves of my life paraded before me that Sunday afternoon on the computer screen as Elaine sits back watching her TV behind me. So why have I not started dreaming about them? Again who knows? And so turning off the computer I sigh inwardly and go to watch the TV with the lovely Elaine.

Chapter 4. If You Go Down To The Woods.

That Sunday night in bed I had a few flashbacks of the
dream while I slept but nothing like the first occurrence.
I kept dreaming of Romilly's inviting lips coming to
meet mine but they never met, and I also had a few
memories of driving in my old Cortina, but nothing
more than flashes until the following night. A miserable
wet Monday it was too. I had developed a terrible cold
in sympathy with the weather and felt so lousy that I
had left work early in the afternoon after the shift
supervisor Warren Slack, seeing how rough I looked
told me to go home to bed. I invested in some whisky.
Purely for medicinal purposes of course. Any old excuse
will do for this fella. To be honest I got pretty rat assed
that evening and dozed off in the chair again listening
to my music as usual and all of a sudden I am back
there again. No watery journey this time, just straight
back there. Back in 1981, almost exactly where I had
left in my last dream. The Old Crown and I am kissing
my Romilly at last, our arms wrapped around each
other, my hand stroking her slim back. Such bliss, her
lips were so silky soft and her eager tongue was probing
my mouth. I wanted it to last forever; I could have died
happily in her arms right then but after a few seconds
my old self pulled away and said "C'mon Rommy. What
are you drinking?" "A Cinzano and lemonade please
Matt." she smiles in reply and the memories all came
back to me. That was her favourite drink back in those
heady far off days. I ordered it along with my usual pint
of lager and taking our drinks we headed over to a
window seat and I listened to my old self talking to her
swigging beer between sentences. I wanted to talk
myself but as much as I tried I couldn't, I could just
hear my old self prattling on about things such as music

and last night's drunken antics which seemed to be so banal to my 2007 self now. Damn what did she see in me I thought as I heard us talking about music? I was still re-acquainting myself with Romilly and my present surroundings while only vaguely listening to the conversation when I heard us talking about Joy Division a band from the late 70s who I loved at the time and still do now, they later went on to become New Order, but then my ears pricked up when my old self said. "I just love The Editors too." WHAT? Wait a minute, The Editors? They are a band from the 2007 future? What is going on here? Shivers ran up and down my back but then doubled as Romilly looked at me strangely and said "Yeah the Editors are cool but I prefer Snow Patrol don't you?" Now things in this dream were entering the realm of serious weirdness at the mention of two bands whose members probably weren't even born then, twinkles in their father's eyes as it were. Perhaps I could have some influence on my old self after all through my dream but how could this old version of Romilly know about Snow Patrol? I tried mentally concentrating on us being alone and whether or not it worked I don't know but the next thing I heard was my old self asking Romilly if she fancied going over the forest. "Yeah Ok she said it's a lovely day, so why not." I remembered spending many blissful Sundays over Capfield forest in 1981 and 82. Laying back in the grass soaking up the rays with a few beers and maybe a joint or three, happy days indeed, and so linking arms we said goodbye to the guys in the Old Crown and leave amongst much ribald humour and the next stop was the off license for vital supplies, those being beer and fags and then we make our way over to Capfield forest.

The Cortina was stiflingly hot as we set off towards Capfield forest but with the windows down and a cold beer apiece we were soon nicely chilling down and listening to Tom Petty and the Heartbreakers on the car stereo. I listened idly to their conversation as I enjoyed 'Refugee'. It was mostly about my job at Wembley Plastics. I worked there in the 1980s and I would have been there only for about three months in July 1981. I listened to myself moaning about the really low rate of pay I was getting for doing a very monotonous boring job in a plastics factory in Enfield. "I'd get almost as much on the dole I continued especially if I flogged a little dope on the side." "Stop moaning Spears, grins Romilly, at least it's a start, you'll do better I know you will." And I did do better I thought smiling inwardly. I eventually made it from working on the shop floor to being the department manager there by 1985.

It was a gorgeously hot summer's afternoon, the sun beating down from out of a cloudless blue sky and after arriving at our favourite secluded spot we were laying in the cool shade of a tree, drinking beer and smoking. Then my old self rolled a joint and lay back with his Romilly just enjoying the moment. Now that was an old familiar taste I hadn't had in many years, the pungent taste and smell of cannabis. I lay back beside Romilly savouring the taste of the joint but then looking into her eyes my old self said "Romilly I'm thinking of jacking the stupid job in and just going off to bum around Europe again for a while." I was totally surprised at this as I certainly did not remember this conversation ever happening then at all, and the look of disappointment on her face almost wrenched my heart out. You bloody idiot I thought before I realized I was talking about myself. I knew I had spent the previous spring and early summer of 1980 bumming around in Holland but I had no recollections of going back there in 1981, perhaps this was just one of those daft conversations you have when you get stoned. I sincerely hoped so at least.

I watched in total helplessness as Romilly was reduced to tears by my comments, I wanted to take her and hold her and tell her that the fifty four year old me wanted her so much but nothing I could do would get through, so I just had to sit back and watch angrily as my old self gave his reasons for wanting to give it all up and disappear off to Europe again, the job was crap, I was bored of England and perhaps we should just make a clean break, but then her face running with tears she grabbed my old self's hand and said, "How can you say that you idiot?." She kissed me and I tasted the salt of her tears and I yearned so much for her at that moment. Then she said "We can't split we have to talk about our future babe, because we do have one even if you don't realise it yet and things will get better with your job believe me Matt." My old self laughed at this dismissively but she continued "We will talk about this Matt, we really must." With her words then I felt all of my old love and desire for her returning and realising that although back then she was ten years my junior she was years ahead of me when it came to sense, but as I did I felt myself gradually fading out again and trying so hard to see as if through a mist and remember her lovely but tear stained face as I came out of my dream state and firmly back to the present day.

6:30 Tuesday morning, back to my wife Elaine shaking me awake. "Must have been a good dream Matt, she said, you were rabbiting away to yourself like a good'un." Then the hangover hit me and feeling my head pounding with the effects of the alcohol and the cold and the taste of bile in my throat I raced to the toilet where I coughed my guts up. Eventually the sickness passed and I made my excuses and after making a cuppa I made my way up to bed pleading illness. "Self induced." I heard Elaine muttering. "Can you ring work I ask her, tell them I'm still not well and that I won't be in today? She says yes grudgingly as I disappear up the stairs, a totally confused mess by now.

Lying in my bed full of cold and with my hangover to keep it company I tried to analyze my dreams, they were no ordinary dreams that was for sure, and now I had experienced them twice. They were as clear as any real event that I could remember, as if I was really there but as an observer and so unlike anything I had experienced in dreams before. I could feel, smell and even taste in them. Yes they were disturbing and I even worried that I might be going mad or hallucinating but still I so wanted to go back there again and I tried in vain to sleep in the hope that I could continue the dream but nothing; I dozed but no return to that golden past that I so yearned for. I lay there in bed full of cold and nursing my hangover and think of 1981 and wanting to return to my dream. I thought of my old self and Romilly's conversation in The Old Crown saloon bar about Snow Patrol and the Editors. What was happening there? I thought, and what about our conversation in the forest where she had pleaded with me to talk. Very strange and not quite like the Romilly that I remembered so fondly.

Chapter 5. 1981 Life.

And so how about 1981 then? What was the real 1981 like? I think about myself in the original 1981. Assassination was in the air in 1981. John Lennon had been tragically gunned down in December 1980. The first Beatle to die. The Pope and Ronald Reagan, who was the U.S president at the time both narrowly escaped assassination attempts and later in the year Anwar Sadat the President of Egypt was not to be so lucky. Prince Charles and Diana were not so lucky either as it was the year that they married, I remember we got a day off work to celebrate it. Maggie Thatcher was our Prime Minister and the Falklands war was still a year away in the future. The music of the time was in a state of flux. Punk rock was almost dead giving way to new wave and the New Romantic scene. 1981 was the year bands like Adam Ant, Human League, Duran Duran and others started to come to the fore. The UK had even won the Eurovision song contest that year with Bucks Fizz.

It was also a time of great change in my life which had started in 1980. 1980 started on the day I had broken up with my girlfriend of three years on and off duration, Heather. I had a steady responsible job as a local government officer. I was also getting into harder drugs in a big way, mostly speed and acid but also everything else in between. The old slippery slope indeed you will agree and by March 1980 I just gave up my job and set off to bum around in Holland. Arnhem to be precise, living in a squat above a row of dope shops in the delightfully named Spijker Kwarter along with a couple of mates. But by the summer of 1980 I was back in England with no job, no money, and no girlfriend and with a nasty little affinity for the temporary pleasure of drugs, particularly speed. I just drifted; my life was a long way off track. I lost all of my self confidence. Yeah

I know I was in a bad way and I could see no future for myself. The speed was destroying me. I knew it. I was a wreck. I even wrote this sad short poem at the time while contemplating suicide as a possible way out.

BLUES COMEDOWN

Midday Saturday 15th November 1980

I'm trying to sleep, I want to but can't
I'm grinding my teeth and my head feels aslant
I just want to sink into a warm black hole
Got blues comedown again, killing my soul
Up all night again, did lots of those pills
Speeding and boozing, a night full of thrills
It adds up to losing and that's what I'm doing
Feels so great when I'm up there, flying so high
Everything's right but it's only that way
Till the end of the night, the beginning of day
This morning's cold dawn really brought me down
Couldn't get off again, from my blues come down
I'm trying to rest, please get me out of this rut
My eyes won't stay open but I can't keep them shut
I know that my brains only firing on three
It's all out of time; it's not part of me
I wish I could sleep, just keep moving around
Tossing and turning with blues comedown
I say to myself No never again but tonight's a new night
And I'll speed just the same
And enjoy it because it's all part of the game
I'll feel like a king and just boogie around
But then comes tomorrow
And the same blues comedown.

But instead of suicide I decided to put all of my effort into turning my life around. I didn't give up the drugs totally but I stopped letting them rule my life. And that's how I found myself a week before Christmas 1980. John Lennon had been murdered a week or two earlier and I found myself in the Old Crown listening to his music on the jukebox. Pretty stoned but with a purpose in my life now. The pub was packed out that night. Well it would be wouldn't it just a week before Christmas. I'm sitting talking to some of my old mates in the public bar and having a great time when I notice a lovely girl slide in between the jukebox and the table I am sitting at ending up directly opposite me. Tight blue denim jeans. Gorgeous mid length honey blonde hair, tatty old blue woolen jumper. I instantly forget all that is going on around me as she smiles at me. Now I suppose that love at first sight is an overused and underrated expression and probably even a cliché nowadays but that was how I felt at the time. I have to get to know this girl I thought, my heart melting at her happy smile. Something must have clicked as we started to talk to the exclusion of everybody else in the bar. She told me her name. It was Romilly, of course. And she told me she was 19, although I later found out that she had added three years to her age and we find ourselves leaving the pub at closing time together hand in hand. I pay for a taxi home for her and get her phone number promising to ring her the next day. The next day, a Saturday comes and I ring her with the expectation of a rebuff but to my great surprise she wants to see me again. That was the beginning and by the start of 1981 we were truly an item. Life for me had truly started again. With my Romilly.

Chapter 6. Truth and Doubt.

I'm back in 1981 for the third time. Such depth in those lovely smiling eyes; so much behind them, they can read my soul, I know they can and so does Romilly and they are staring right back into mine, seemingly questioning my innermost thoughts. I come too with a jolt like an electric shock when I realise I'm back and gazing into Romilly's beautiful eyes. We are still in Capfield Forest and I'm laying on my back looking up at her. "You dozed off ya wally." she smiles. I look at her face and I think to myself that some people might like symmetry, some might swear by it, oh it's perfectly symmetrical. But not me. I like asymmetrical, I adore her perfect imperfection. From my story so far you must think Romilly is a beauty. She is most definitely a lovely looking woman but even so her legs are a little too thin, her feet are a little too big. She's never going to be a model. Her nose is a little too beaky too but all these and other small imperfections add up to total perfection to me. I can see her abundant inner beauty, the way her mouth crinkles up at the corners when she smiles and the expressive way her eyes sparkle with hidden mischief when she laughs, that is her beauty to me. Just the way her hand automatically finds mine, the way we fit so well together, we know what each other wants without saying anything at all. As I said, Perfection is asymmetrical.

"You are awake then my sleeping beauty?" she says smiling that old enigmatic smile at me. "Yeah and just so bloody glad to see you again Romilly after all these years." I reply before realizing it's my 2007 self who is speaking now and not the old 1981 me. Somehow I seem to have taken control of my young body for the first time I realise with joy as I am able to push myself up to lean on one elbow and speak to her. "And so who am I talking to?" she says mysteriously while watching my face for a reaction. Good question I think and say so, unsure of her reaction, I tell her that this is a dream that I'm having and I am sharing it with her. "Aha, she grins, I was right. It is you isn't it? Are you finding this as weird as I am? What year are you from then. Tell me." I tell her 2007 and looking at me and nodding she says "Yeah me too." Then we start to talk, really talk about our situation. I'm still not sure if this is a dream or not but it turns out she is getting much the same experiences as me, like some massive hallucinogenic flashback to the past. "So what do you think Romilly, is this a dream we are sharing or are we really back in 1981? Can we visit here when we want?" "Not always, it comes and goes, she says, it can be days and then I find myself back here again. But as to whether it's a dream? Well I just don't know the answer to that one, but it seems too real for me to believe this is not actually happening." "Yeah I know what you mean. I tell her, it's just all so real." She smiles at me and picking some blades of grass sprinkles them in my hair. "But if this all for real and not a dream then I want to know is why is it happening and why to us?" "I get the thing about our Editors and Snow Patrol conversation now, I say, you already knew didn't you?" Romilly lies down on her side next to me and pulls out two of my smokes. Lighting them, she passes me one and slowly blowing out the smoke she says, "Well not at the time, I thought I was alone here in the past but when you mentioned the Editors I thought I'd mention Snow Patrol to see your reaction, see if it sunk in and seeing the perplexed look on your face I think it did, and I thought well if I can do this then there's no logical reason that you can't either. I was so glad at the thought of you being able to come back as well. I wanted someone to share this with. Someone to tell me I'm not just dreaming or going insane."

By now I'm full of questions. "Can we control this I ask her?" "As far as I know, no she says, it just happens, sometimes I'm like an observer but then other times I'm here fully talking and reacting, it is just mindnumbing. But every time I come back it seems to be for longer periods and it seems to be getting easier to do all the time." She laughs and sits up cross legged next to me, "Have you noticed it's like a foreign country here?" "How do you mean I ask?" She stretches one of her legs out and rubbing her bare foot against mine says, "Well it is so different from 2007 here; no CDs or DVDs not even many videos yet, just vinyl records and tapes, no computers. She goes on, counting down on her fingers. No playstations, only 3 channels on the telly. No A.I.D.S , no Al Qaeda although the IRA are still up to their old tricks and people just seem more open, you know less afraid to open up and talk. AND, she stresses, no mobile phones." Unconsciously I reach up to my shirt pocket for my Nokia but of course it's not there. "O My God how can I exist without my mobile?" I grin. "No unleaded petrol and fags only 50p a pack too." she laughs. Then her face turns more serious. "Matt, she pleads looking deep into my eyes, this is so weird and why is it happening to me? To us now, it's actually quite frightening?" I sit up and put my arm around her shoulder comfortingly, and pulling her closer to me I say "Romilly I just don't know but being with you here is so bloody wonderful. I mean here we are young again back at the start of...I look for the word.....US?" " Yeah but you know what happened to US don't you Matt. It all ended so badly for US, didn't it? Is that all going to happen again too?" Then she begins to cry, just little sniffles at first but then I can see the tears at the corner of her eyes and before I can help it I crack up too and we are sitting there holding each other tight and sobbing our hearts out remembering the way our relationship had ended. Two people lost in a joint past together not knowing why and remembering all the good times we had shared and all the hurt we inflicted on each other. I wipe her tears away with my fingers and tell her, "No Romilly it's not going to end like that again, not if I can help it."

Why am I feeling like this I think? By rights I should hate Romilly. She had left me all those years before. Betrayed me even. I knew I hadn't been the best of partners but for all of my mistakes I had loved her deeply and would have stood by her through thick and thin. I had tried to stop the rot with her, I really had. I had changed my ways to please her even. But when it came down to it all her honeyed words of love were meaningless in the end. She had deserted me. And now I feel myself falling in love with her all over again? Why for God's sake? I ask myself. I suppose that despite all that she did to me that a part of me never stopped loving her. "Get your head read Spears; she will only do it again. You just know she will." I tell myself. But I know I can't stop my heart overruling my head. It's another of my weaknesses. It's my nature. Act now and think later that about sums me up. I suppose that I never learn.

We lay together in the grass on an old tartan car rug I had found in the boot. I had taken off my shirt now and could feel the hot July sun's rays warming my bare chest as in between our talking it happened. We have been apart for 23 years since that acrimonious parting of the ways in 1984 and this shouldn't happen. Should it? Logically she should still dislike me too but suddenly we start to exchange small kisses, tentatively at first, just the light barely touching kisses of lips to lips and cheeks. Teasing each other with our lips and our fingers. And yet we exalt in the simple joy of being together again and after so many lost years apart. The small intimacies of those light kisses take on a whole new pleasure. And with such great pleasure in holding each other's hands, fingers intertwining and now laying down in the warm grass face to face, body to body, making love to each other with those gentle kisses. We are comforting each other with those kisses. I pick a blade of grass, and run it around the features of that face I realise I have loved and missed for so long now, tickling her nose and making her laugh with innocent pleasure, her eyes crinkling up with her smiles. I stroke her lips with my fingers and she runs her moist tip of her tongue over them, making me laugh along with her. As we talk about our situation she plays with the fair hairs on my chest, twisting them and curling them between her small slim fingers, and then picking more grass and pushing me gently on to my back she sprinkles it on to my chest playfully. We laughed aloud like a couple of young kids sharing a secret rude joke, and the next moment our lips meet and meld together in full union. Our tongues play together, and I open my eyes briefly to see her face totally lost in that kiss. Her arms wrapped gently around the back of my neck and I could feel her fingers stroking the hair on my neck. My lips leave hers to explore her ears and the soft skin of her throat, causing her to sigh in sheer delight, and she brings her hands around to stroke my face lovingly. Cupping my cheeks in her hands she looks deeply into my eyes and mouths the words, "I want you." I returned her questioning gaze and hoarsely whispered. " And I need you."

She gently pushed me on to my back and I closed my eyes, as I felt her small delicate fingers rubbing small circles on my chest and then running down lightly over my stomach to unbuckle my belt and unzip me. Her hand slipped inside my briefs caressing my hardness. Her tongue described small circles on my face and neck as she stroked me. "Ohh Matt " she breathed as I in turn rolled over and eased her gently on to her back. I stifled her soft moans of pleasure with my lips as I slowly pulled her jeans down freeing her lusciously sexy legs and then removing her knickers I felt the warm soft inviting wetness between her legs. I lifted her white T-shirt off over her head and removed her bra. Teasing her breasts with my lips and tongue my hand returned to the soft wetness between those lovely slim legs turning her on with my fingers as I used to do so many years before. Her back arches pushing herself against my hand as my fingers caressed her most intimate region causing her to reach a climax by my touch alone. Then she pushed me onto my back again, and while shading my eyes from the sun with my hand, I can smell her delicious musky woman's scent on my fingers. She knelt beside me and passing one gorgeous slim leg over me, she lowered her soft inviting wetness on to me. So much ecstasy, such pleasure as I felt my hardness slowly entering her so easily, so luxuriously, even after all this time we just seem to fit together so perfectly. I had never before made love before like we did then. We made love almost savagely at first, biting, scratching, squeezing each other's lust wracked bodies as if we wanted to make up for the 23 years of being apart in one torrid lovemaking session. We rolled over and over each other in the warm summer grass crying and laughing with sheer naked wanton abandon, but slowly our initial heat calmed down to gentle tender movements trying to give each other the maximum pleasure, now seeming as if those 23 years didn't matter after all. It was as if we hadn't been apart at all now, our bodies becoming one again so naturally and so passionately. As we made love now I did all the favourite things she had liked me to do. I was kissing her eyelids, the crook of her neck, her earlobes. Running my fingers so lightly up and down her spine as we enjoyed each other's bodies anew. We climaxed together, a gorgeous soaring of souls. A complete and tumultuous cementing of our re-union. An affirmation of our being together once again. Sweat rolled from our fulfilled bodies as we lay together on that perfect summer afternoon. We held each other tightly as our sweaty naked bodies stuck together and as our breathing returned to normal we dozed in the warm sun, happy to just be together again. Just to be sharing the same space in time together was enough for us at that moment. The sun was lower in the sky now and looking at my watch I saw several hours had passed and lighting us both a cigarette I propped myself up beside her and admired that post lovemaking glow of hers, her face looking so happy and content. She yawned and stretched lazily and taking the cigarette from me I saw the tip glow as she pulled deeply on it. "Damn I hope no-one saw us Spears." she chuckled. "I don't know Rommy; I replied innocently, some people would have paid bloody good money to watch that performance." I just managed to avoid her answering slap as we both burst out laughing again. Then she turns serious and looks at me and I can see it, that look, the look in her eyes that says, "I love you, I want you." Lovelight was in her eyes and I suppose it was in mine too at that extraordinary moment in our lives. Then I feel the pull, dragging me up and away from her it seemed, pulling my heart out as well it felt. "I love you Romilly." I cried as everything faded out and I felt myself passing out of consciousness and 1981.

Chapter 7. Of Time Travel.

I began to re-awaken back home in 2007 in my chair with feeling of a warm wet tongue on my face, but no my luck hadn't changed unfortunately, it was my dog Pepper letting me know he wanted to go out by giving me big wet tongue licks. He looked expectantly at me wagging his tail as I came awake fully. "Yeucchhh!" I tell him and he has to make do with the garden. I said a while back that I'd almost given up hope of returning to Romilly in 1981 but this visit had happened totally unexpectedly on the following Saturday afternoon with Elaine away at her mums with the kids till Sunday. I had recovered from my cold and returned to work on the previous Thursday. Being on my own I'd had a few beers up my local pub that lunchtime to relieve the boredom. Beer at lunchtime always makes me sleepy nowadays and coming home I had dozed off in the chair listening to some music on the headphones, when all of a sudden I had woken up in 1981 again to Romilly's lovely smiling eyes above me and to discover that we were both travelling back and were able to take control of our bodies back there and to end up making such wonderful love with her. This had all occurred in the few hours I had been asleep that Saturday afternoon as I noticed it was still only just after 5 o'clock. And now a feeling of devastation hit me, no perhaps desolation is a better word I think. I wanted so much to be back with her in 1981, to make love to her again in our favourite forest spot. I felt bereft and lost without her as if my heart had been ripped from my chest. I think I would have given up everything to go back right that minute but on the current record it could be days if at all. I dissolved into tears and cried my heart out that Saturday afternoon for a love lost then re-found, then lost again. There's no distance like time I thought to myself bitterly.

I am having some seriously weird dreams and I tried to analyse the situation, how could I tell if this thing I was experiencing was some kind of reality or just a fantastic series of dreams. Was I hallucinating or going mad even? Will I go back again? I guess there were no answers, so finding solace in a large scotch, I dozed in my armchair again till about 7 o'clock and after taking the dog for a half hour's walk to clear my head and get my thoughts into order I sat down in front of the TV alone. Of course I was hoping to go back to Romilly as I hoped now that this was more than a dream. It had to be but if not a dream then were Romilly and I actually going back in time to meet in 1981? If so, how? I sat there drinking scotch and smoking watching nothing in particular on TV just wanting to pass out and go back to Romilly. Eventually I passed out but no visit back this time to my great disappointment. Just a few jumbled mixed up dreams about nothing in particular. I woke at 3:15 in the morning disappointed that I hadn't gone back and after letting Pepper out in the garden for him to pee I decided to make my way up to my bed. I was alone that night and the large empty bed reminded me of another song I used to play back in 1984 after Romilly left me. 'The Beds Too Big Without You' by the Police. And it was.

The next morning I awoke with the expected throbbing head but in my sleep I had resolved to do something concrete about the situation and having taken advantage of the fact that Elaine was away with her mum and the kids till that evening I decided to do two things. Firstly I would try to find the present day Romilly; I knew I couldn't try to contact her parents as they would be very unlikely to speak to me, I wondered if they still lived at the same address still. Secondly I decided to research my current dilemma of whether this was a dream I was having or was any kind of time travel possible as unlikely as it seemed. And what else?

I of course used the internet. I've had a computer since 2001 and from being a total PC illiterate then I have turned myself into a bit of an expert, even taught myself Html and C++ to hack the occasional program and design my own web pages. I searched Friends Re-United for Romilly, I googled for her but all to no avail, almost every lead turned out to be false leading to a total dead end until finally I did find out by searching the marriage indexes that she had married again in 1987 and the name of her husband but that was as far as I could get at that moment. I must admit I felt sad that she could marry again so quickly after leaving me. But what would I do if I did find her and all this was just a dream. Try explaining it to her and they'd soon be carting me off to the funny farm so I gave up searching for her for the time being to turn to time travel. Ah yes, as to time travel? That was a different matter. There was plenty of information on time travel. I tried to stay on the reliable sites ignoring the obviously crackpot fringe ones. It seems to be a scientifically proven fact that in theory at least time travel can happen. It all comes down to Quantum mechanics and superfast particles. Oh and M Theory. Google it yourself if you don't believe me and no I don't pretend to understand it either. Most of it all went way over my head but some of the basics made sense.

Originally it was believed inconceivable that time travel was possible, as any action back in time would cause a paradox. The classic explanation quoted is that if you go back in time and kill your grandfather before he met your grandmother then your father would not be born and you could not therefore be born to travel back in time to kill your grandfather. I supposed that this could also apply here too with Romilly and I. If Romilly and I changed history by getting together and not splitting up this time then I wouldn't marry Elaine and be where I was in 2007 to go back to meet Romilly.

Nice little explanation of a time paradox that, but quantum theory allows for a multiversity of infinite universes side by side all branching out from each other and taking different paths from each different action taken and even rejoining as they come back into line. So if I go back to kill my grandfather then I will cease to exist in that universe but in another I don't kill him and so go on existing and don't go back to kill him. Two new universes then exist, one with me in it and the other without. It gets a bit trickier to understand after that, but it seems these different time universes called 'branes' by the scientists can theoretically co-exist physically as little as a millimetre or even less apart and there are an infinite amount of them too. By infinite I mean never ending and not just a very large amount . I read about quantum computers which we are apparently only a matter of time away from building. They are no faster than an ordinary computer but by using quantum mechanics they can dash off into hyper space and perform their calculation returning instantly with the answer a billion times or more all at the same time, time is irrelevant to them which is going to get a lot of governments worried as no passwords will be safe with them. For example say you have a 10,000 number password protecting your files or even a million then it won't matter to a quantum computer. It can try every one of the millions of different combinations instantly and simultaneously. Don't take my word for it. Look it up, it's all on the internet.

But if any of you budding Doctor Who's out there think it would be a cool Saturday morning's work to nip out into the shed in the back garden and knock up a quick Tardis so you can nip back in time to place a bet on the lottery after getting the results, forget it, because although at least possible in theory to build one it would need the power of a black hole to power it up. It aint gonna be going nowhere on a few quid's worth of unleaded I'm afraid. Also who can say if these universes have the same lottery results either? But anyhow sitting there mulling these mindboggling thoughts over I started to think about dreams, another subject full of theory as to the mechanics and meanings of them. I even remembered reading many years ago about astral projection, which basically allows for the idea that by training the mind to enter a trance state the mind can leave the body and travel around at will. If different but similar branches of the same universe could be so close then maybe in a dream state couldn't we maybe step from one to the other? In fact couldn't dreams or even astral projection actually be that sometimes? Insights into a parallel universe that is right beside us. Little sleeping mind trips to a different universe or reality? Could that be what I was experiencing, not a trip back in time but just a small step to a close but slightly different reality in another time universe? My head tried to get around it but just found it so hard to understand it all. Also for instance if there were infinite numbers of universes co-existing would it not be a pretty small chance that Romilly and I had met up in the same one. Wouldn't that make it statistically impossible I thought? But by following the theories through I realized that all I had just researched allowed for an infinite multiplicity of Romilly's and even of me's. Statistically impossible becomes possible maybe even probable. It's like the old chestnut about being given an infinite amount of time a group of monkeys could type the entire works of Shakespeare. O My God I needed a drink to even start to get my head around that one. But was there any way I could test the theory myself? All of a sudden it came to me. Maybe there was. Just maybe there was a way that I could. But I would need to be back in 1981 to do it first.

I had by now worked out that all the times I had the dream or was it a trip? I still didn't know which, were mostly whilst sleeping in my armchair after a few drinks, so no problem there... I would try again that day. I doubted that the chair mattered but perhaps the alcohol was relaxing my mind enough to go back, or was that sideways? I just didn't know. Perhaps yoga or meditation would have the same effect but knowing little of either I would settle for the booze, an onerous task I know but someone has to do it I smiled. I grinned to myself again and thought that all the years of training some people put into meditation and yoga were wasted. They should just get pissed instead, yeah tantric whisky if you like. First I popped up to the local Londis to top up the time travel juice. That's whisky, and then home again to the armchair and hopefully 1981 again that evening. I spent the afternoon being a good boy for the lovely Elaine. I strimmed, I did washing and hung it out to dry; I even vacuumed the house and changed the bedding. By six I had had enough of earning brownie points and after making myself something to eat and a mug of tea I put some music on. Something from the real old days even before the eighties. And so Jefferson Airplane it was and I settled down to eat. One song particularly stood out from the early days of the 'Airplane', Come up the Years. It's a sad bittersweet little ballad about being in love with a younger girl and was particularly appropriate for Romilly and I due to our age difference and I think the words of that short little song just about summed up in totality my feelings for her at the time we were together all those years ago.

By eight pm Elaine and the kids were home from her mum's, but Elaine was tired and she was in bed by nine pm. Jamie and Beth stayed up for a while watching TV but they disappeared up to bed just after 10:30 and so then I was alone and winding up the hard drive and slipping the headphones on. I sipped on a nice malt whisky, some ice clinking in the glass while listening to

Journey, an old seventies rock band, the track was, 'Look into the Future', typical Journey I thought to myself. Lovely slow vocal build up leading to a great rock song, a classic rock guitar lover's track of over 8 minute's duration with some lovely organ keyboard work in it too. I was by now experiencing that feeling you used to get when you used to be young on the night before a long looked forward to holiday. Want to sleep, need to sleep. But can't sleep due to the excitement of the thoughts going through your mind, but after a few more scotches and what seemed like hours my eyes slowly began to droop and before long my mind started drifting away.

Chapter 8. Good Old Romilly.

I was back in 1981 driving the old Cortina home from the forest, Romilly was sitting beside me dozing and looking wonderful as usual. We had the cassette player on playing some long forgotten 80s rock, it may have been Saxon. I couldn't remember but it sounded good to me. We'd left the forest and were on our way back to my parent's house, the late afternoon still warm and sunny. Romilly yawned and opening her eyes took two of my cigarettes and lit them for us as I admired that face I had once loved so much. "Well babe it took a few beers and some CDs but I'm back from the future" I grinned. "What are you talking about you fool? She replied yawning again. What's a CD?" Now I'm confused and say "Don't you remember us talking earlier about why we are here?" "Ah philosophy was it" I must of dozed off, I usually do when philosophy is on the menu" she grinned. I realize now that I must be with the 1981 Romilly. Briefly I wonder what's happened to 2007 Romilly as I so wanted to talk to her about the events of that day from 2007, but I think Oh well what the hell. We drive on for ten minutes to eventually pull up the drive at my parents place. "Wake up dopey " I say to Romilly who has dozed off again, digging her in the ribs and grinning. "Hey you. You will pay for that." she says laughing and getting out and chasing me around the car. By now I am laughing so much; I just can't believe how good I feel. "Let's go in, I'll see if I can scrounge us some grub, I think I probably have us a burnt dinner on offer." I say. " Where have you been? Says my mum as we walk in, your dinners ruined, and... Oh Hello Romilly." " Can Romilly have some too? I ask, she really likes burnt offerings." Romilly takes her turn to dig me in the ribs. "Ok I'll see what I can do. Go and sit in the lounge." groans my mum returning to the kitchen.

We go through to the lounge and I switch on the TV while my mum busies herself in the kitchen, Oh My God I think, only three channels on TV and no remote control, but who cares anyway I think as I sit down and pay full attention to the 1981 Romilly. I watch as she takes her jacket off and then I pull her gently to me on the sofa and kiss her passionately on the lips lingering over her taste and enjoying the smell of her, the glorious smell of her sex still mingling with her perfume and reminding me of our earlier lovemaking on the forest grass. I notice the newly acquired grass stains on her top and smile. Pulling away I look her in the eyes and tell her I love her. "My god you are being very loving today Matt, Are you feeling Ok? She giggles. But please don't stop, I like it Ok." Then she pulls me back to her and kisses me on the lips, a long slow loving smooch. I feel her tongue exploring mine as her arms wrap around my neck, then pull away quickly as my mum comes in with two plates of what was once Sunday lunch. "Don't look at me like that, she says, it's been sitting in the oven for 3 hours." "Where's Dad?" I ask stuffing my face with overdone roast beef and realising I haven't seen him yet. "Matt you know its Sunday and he is having his weekly bath as usual. He'll be down soon I expect." replies my Mum grinning. We eat our dinner but Romilly gives me a hard time when I proceed to scoop my gravy up with my knife and lick it off. "Spears, you are so uncouth and I am not going on holiday if you do that again you pig." she laughs. I remember then that we have a holiday booked on a cabin cruiser on the Norfolk Broads in a couple of week's time.

About half an hour later I hear my Dad descending from upstairs, singing, having finished his weekly ablutions. He puts his head round the door after asking my mum what is for tea. "Hello you two, he says, and to what do we owe the pleasure of your presence today?" He looks so young I think, My God he still has dark hair, but then I realize that he is only a few years older than I am back in 2007. Hiding my incredulous look I tell him, "Well old-timer, me and the little lady here was hungry and thought we'd take advantage of the first class comestibles that come so highly recommended in this establishment." I can feel Romilly stifling a giggle next to me and jab her lightly in the ribs with my elbow. "Cheeky bastard, replies my Dad with a smile on his face, just make sure you are up early in the morning for work. If you aint up by 6.30 sharp I'm leaving without you." He disappears back to the kitchen to chivvy my Mum up into making his tea. The rest of that Sunday evening was spent watching garbage on 1981 TV and talking about our forthcoming week away on the Norfolk Broads until my parents went for their usual drink at 9.30pm. As soon as we heard their car drive off we were all over each other, kissing, touching, and then making love frantically to each other on the sofa. One thing I remembered about the old Romilly, she loved her nookie, and she could wear me out even in those days sometimes. Afterwards we sit naked my arm draped around her shoulder, I light us cigarettes and clasping her hand in mine I kiss her lovely finger tips and ask her about the afternoon over the forest. "Yea it was great, she says grinning, a bit blurry though. I suppose you got me drunk just to take advantage of me. I smile and ruffle her hair lovingly. "Yeah right, since when did I need to get you drunk first Rommy?" "Must have been the dope then Spears" she says looking all innocent and trying to suppress a chuckle." "C'mon beaky, I joke, I'd better be getting you back home or I'll have your old man on my case again. She picks up her scattered clothing and dressing says to me with a twinkle in her eye "And less of the beaky, big ears or you are history." I aim my hand at her ass as she bends down to pull her jeans up and hear it connect with a nice meaty slap. I sit back looking pleased with myself and admiring the nice handprint I can see has appeared on her butt. She turns around and with a large grin on her face advances on me slowly doing her belt up. "You are gonna pay for that you know Spears." she smiles. I'm still naked and putting a shocked look on my face I cover my wedding tackle protectively with both hands. "That won't help you one little bit." she giggles and her hand shoots out toward my chest. I make the mistake of raising my hands in protection and her hand changes direction, tapping me lightly in my now exposed privates. The crafty cow I think proudly as I collapse in mock pain on the sofa. "Omigod I scream that's the Spears family tree finished now. I'm destined to be childless after that you cruel wicked woman." "And why should I care when you are so horrible to me?" She grins mischievously. "Well at least you could kiss it better?" I say hopefully. She thinks about it for a few seconds then, "Naaa, if I do that we both know what will happen and I will be late home again and if you think that hurt then wait till you see what my dad will do to you." "Point taken I say sadly, I would like to keep it I suppose. Hang on I'll get the car keys." " Yea and putting some clothes on first before we go might help too." she laughs throwing my briefs at me.

Chapter 9. Meet The Wife.

The next day I wake up and I am still back in 1981. This is a first. It's the longest I have stayed back here in one visit. My old red wind up alarm clock is ringing itself off the bedside table as I blearily come to. The early morning July sun is shining through the thin curtains. Its 6am and I can hear my dad downstairs rattling cups and coughing as he makes tea. I groggily push myself out of bed to face the 1981 day alone. Washing and then dressing in my work clothes I go downstairs. My dad is sitting there sipping tea and he looks at me above his glasses as I enter the kitchen. "I've made you a tea you've got ten minutes to drink it and then we are going." he growls. "Ok mein Fuhrer lead on." I grin giving him a Nazi salute. We leave the washing up for my mum and at 6.30am prompt we are in his company car heading off to work, always a stickler for time my dad. His driving leaves a lot to be desired I remember as we narrowly miss clipping a lorry as he weaves in and out of the early morning motorway traffic causing it to swerve and flash its lights madly at him. As we reach the end of the motorway he is still doing 80 in the outside lane and braking sharply he nips in between two cars causing one to brake dangerously. I'm gripping the car seat in terror as the car he's cut up toots its horn. My dad just gives it the old two finger salute in the rear mirror and carries on. The last three miles into work takes longer than the first thirty due to the weight of traffic but at least we are not in any danger of killing ourselves I think gratefully, and at 7 15am we arrive at work. Wembley Plastics, my workplace for the next 5 years in the old 1981. I eventually worked my way up to manager after my dad took early retirement and I moved them up to the north east of England when they relocated in 1985 but on this sunny July morning in 1981 I was still a new boy operating machines in the finishing shop. Bloody boring stuff too, sitting in front of a lathe or hot foil printing machine getting your allotted amount of work out, or even a little more if you wanted some bonus. I enter the factory with a look of gloom on my face at the thought of the eight hours of drudgery ahead of me. But my dad? Well he's a different man here, he loves his work. He has a smile on his face and a spring in his step as he heads off to his managers office. I just let the old 1981 Matt come to the fore and get on with his boring 1981 work turning out plastic components on an old fashioned lathe, even for 1981 this lathe is ancient I think. It is quite fun seeing all the old faces again but by 2007 I think most of them must be long dead. Some of the women working there are in there late sixties at least so they'd be in their nineties now if they are still alive but they were a great bunch and a right laugh to work with. I just looked forward to seeing Romilly again that evening, hopefully the 2007 Romilly, but on arriving home at 5:30 my mum told me she'd had a message from Romilly saying she wasn't well and would see me tomorrow. Bugger it I thought, what now? I really needed to talk to her about the previous day's exploration of the internet and my findings. I was also thinking I had been here for over a day now, my longest visit yet. So OK then I think, while I am still here I'll pop out and visit the old haunts. See some old faces. I'm slightly annoyed that Romilly can't make it out but I get changed anyway, putting my best jeans and shirt on and I decide to visit the Crescent Moon. I know it will probably be dead on a Monday night but I think Ok so what the hell. The Crescent Moon used to be my local up till 1980 with Heather but I'd used the Old Crown instead lately after we had split up. I walk in and a couple of guys say Hi but I only vaguely remember them so nodding to them cordially I take up a solitary position at the bar and order a lager. I suppose I am on foreign territory now and even the landlord has changed. I put a pound's worth of change in the jukebox, pound coins weren't around then and we still had the old pound notes, and select some music to cheer myself up with. Santana's Black Magic Woman starts playing and I sit back to watch life go by. Two pints later Bruce Springsteen's 'Born to Run' is finishing and the saloon bar is totally empty, but all is not lost as I hear laughing in the public bar and decide to pop my head in to see what is going on there. I push open the saloon bar door and stroll up to the public bar. There are another couple of guys at the bar I don't know and a group of people in the corner by the dartboard, all laughing and obviously on a good night out. One laugh amongst the others stands out and immediately I recognise it. I realise with a shock that it's Elaine, my wife from 2007, well the 1981 version at least. I pop myself on to a bar stool and prop up the bar listening to this group laughing and enjoying their selves. I order a large scotch, had to be a Famous Grouse in those days. I remember we called it a 'low flyer' and I'm sitting at the bar slowly sipping it and listening to Elaine and her group chatting and laughing, when one of the group, a small bearded guy comes over and asks if I fancy a game of darts? Ok what the hell I say and ordering another large Grouse I mosey over to the group in the corner to join their darts match. There are two guys and three girls including Elaine and although one couple seem tied up Elaine and the others seem to be unattached. Elaine looks great in a white frilly blouse and a blue knee length skirt. Her dark blonde hair falls loosely about her shoulders. This could be interesting I think saying hello to the twenty four year old Elaine. She says Hi back and tells me that I'm to be her partner for a doubles match. I laugh at that thinking "If only she knew. I'm going to be more than just her partner in a darts match." I have never been much good at darts but I soon learn that Elaine is even worse as I duck from one of her darts missing the board completely and rebounding back towards me. "Oops sorry." She grins.

Before long we have lost our match abysmally and I'm sitting with her chatting and laughing. We are sitting so close that I can smell her perfume. Although she is still so young at only twenty four I can see my future wife in her laughing eyes and buying her and her friends a drink and a large one for myself we engage in a great conversation and I start to feel that old devil called lust stirring my loins at the sight of her. What the hell I think I can hardly commit adultery with my wife now can I? Even if I haven't married her yet. Eventually it's just me and her as her friends move on to pastures new and we seem to be having a great time together. Elaine has knocked quite a few back, well so have I, and is obviously enjoying my company. If only you knew I think again. I feel myself lean forward and taking her hand in mine I kiss her lips and ask if she wants a lift home. "OK, she says I live up on Thurley. "I know I say, conspiratorially, Marley Hills?" "How did you know that? She slurs. "I'm psychic." I tell her. I take her arm and we leave the pub together. "Nice car." says Elaine on seeing the Cortina. We head up towards her home but I drive straight past and pull up on a small track leading off to some woods, one of my old favourite nookie haunts off of Thurley Lane. She smiles as I put my arm around her and then start to kiss her. I start by probing her mouth with my tongue then kissing her ears and neck and the next thing is I have my hand inside the frilly white blouse caressing her ample breasts."Be gentle, she giggles as my hand works its way round to the clasp and unsnaps it, they are very sensitive." Next I ease her skirt off and pull her lovely flowery knickers slowly down below her knees and off over her ankles along with her shoes. She opens her legs slowly for me to allow me to start playing with her. I can hear her breathing deeply as I take one of her gorgeous soft breasts and start to suck on its warm full nipple, while massaging the other one with my eager hand; she truly has a splendid pair I think to myself knowing sadly that by 2007 they would have headed south considerably. Then my fingers start working between her legs again. I can smell the musky aroma of her sex as I slowly stimulate her moistness with my finger. Then I work my way down her body, using my mouth and lips to explore all of the places of interest on the way, until my tongue is working its old demon magic between her welcoming thighs. By now she is soaking down there with her excitement and she is going wild, her hands on my head pushing me against her. I kiss my way slowly back up her sweat soaked body and with a little positioning I slide easily into her inviting moistness as our mouths lock together sharing the taste of her sex on my tongue. We make love enthusiastically for about half an hour before I feel myself reach climax and release my seed deep inside her. "Oops sorry about that Elaine. I hope you are on the pill." I smile, panting from my exertions. "A bit late to worry now so it serves you right if I'm not." she laughs squeezing me tightly to her as my manhood softens slowly inside her. After we get our breath back I light cigarettes for us both and we lie back in the reclining seats chatting and just enjoying the afterglow of our passionate lovemaking. "Come on Elaine, I say eventually, flicking the cigarette out of the car window; I had better be getting you home. I've got work to go to tomorrow." But she wants to play a little longer does my Elaine and she starts to kiss me passionately again. Her hand is on me arousing me to renewed vigour and she looks at me gratefully as I enter her. "Mmm that feels good." she breathes in my ear as my hardness fills her again. This time the lovemaking is slower and more relaxed and she cups my face in her hands and looking into my eyes asks me if she will see me again. This is a bit awkward but I tell her, "Yes I'm sure you will." I just didn't say when but I wasn't lying was I?

She gives me her phone number and I drive her home with a smile on my face. We kiss as she gets out of the car. "Well Night then Matt. Don't forget to ring me will you." I blow her a kiss and assure her that I won't and then I head for home and bed. I am pondering on whether I have been unfaithful as I settle down in my old bed, happy but tired from our lovemaking and I turn the question over in my mind. Have I been unfaithful to the Elaine of the future by making love to her younger self? Probably not I think. Have I been unfaithful to Romilly? Certainly I been unfaithful to the old Romilly, but have I been unfaithful to the 2007 Romilly? My head spins and as I slowly doze off trying to work out the conundrum.

About my Elaine? My present wife in 2007? I met the lovely Elaine only seven months after Romilly left me in the original 1984 and I guess I owe her a lot. I was in a bit of a state about losing my Romilly. Well actually I was a total mess but then all of a sudden this lovely sexy happy girl knocks at my front door one August evening, all smiles and wearing 'screw me' shorts delivering the weekly football pools. Well lust prevailed, and as I've said before I can't resist a lovely lady and so before long a very pretty girl is missing her shorts and knickers and we are at it like knives together. She more or less moves in with me shortly after, spending more time at mine than her own place. But she was a great and true friend and stuck by me when lots probably wouldn't have. I missed Romilly tremendously still and I often told Elaine so. It must have hurt her I know but she stuck with me thankfully and before I have time to think about it we are married and on the way to having three children, the aforesaid little darlings. Don't get me wrong I do love Elaine, I always will and it's a good solid love. But I love both her and Romilly although in entirely different ways. My relationship with Elaine has hardly any of the fire and passion of Romilly and myself. But then again Elaine is a person who is 100 percent behind you all the way. Solid and dependable that's Elaine. I would trust her with my life if it came down to it. And I spend the next twenty years or so wondering what could have happened in different circumstances. Should I have worked harder to win my sweet little Romilly back or should I have just accepted that it was all over? Elaine and I never had much in common in our lives, it's the she likes coffee I like tea thing but I suppose. She hates any music that I like. I hate all the TV shows that she likes but 23 years later we are still together so it can't be all bad. Dependable that's the word for Elaine, a better woman to have in your corner I can't think of. She has stood by me through thick and thin. Probably more thick than thin I think sadly looking back on our past. And I think ironically that is more than Romilly ever did. And so it's my lovely but older Elaine that I wake up to that Monday morning back in 2007.

Chapter 10. Night Shift.

"Wake up you lazy little git. I need to go shopping so cough up some readies please." "Ok, I groan painfully passing her my debit card, draw some cash out you know the number." "How much can I draw out only the freezers a bit low?" "Ok take out 30 quid." I tell her jokingly. "Piss off I need more than that you bloody tight sod." "Ok for god's sake make it 40 then, not a penny more." "Ok tightwad we'll call it 50 then Ok? I nod thinking that I would have gone up to 60 and count myself lucky at saving a tenner. I'm on night shift this week so I don't need to go to work till midnight, but before I work my way up to bed via the kettle I look at Elaine and think the years have not been kind to her, she still looks younger than her 50 years but has piled the pounds on over the years. She used to be a fine figure of a woman, always a bit chunky around the thighs but she always had breasts to die for. They say, look at the mum and see the daughter in 30 years and this is the case. Her mum is a lovely woman too but the pounds have not been kind to her either. But no-one will say a word against my Elaine to me, not if they want to keep their looks anyway. I think of explaining to her what I'm experiencing at the moment but then I think no. She would never believe me and just tell me I'm obsessed with Romilly. She has always known that Romilly was the love of my life I suppose and accepts it and I wonder how she puts up with it. I wouldn't to be truthful. So Elaine goes off to Sainsbury's with my card to stock up for the week, and I am left alone to think about what is happening. I make myself a mug of tea and instead of going to bed I go about tidying up and then put some washing on. Elaine arrives back about eleven with the shopping. "Blimey you've got enough here to feed an army." I tell her helping her to bring it in from the car. "Yea well tell me when they turn up I might get lucky." She replies sarcastically. Elaine has a couple of days off work so at least I get my dinner cooked before going to bed ready for the night shift.

I lay there in bed thinking about my last visit to 1981. Certainly extraordinarily erotic I grin to myself, having made love to my first and second wives in just one trip. But if it came down to it which one would I chose from them? Did I even have to? Why couldn't I just continue this as it was, visiting 1981 for some fun but carrying on my life unchanged here in 2007? I knew the answer; I was at heart a one woman man, always have been. I've enjoyed a few affairs while I've been with Elaine but not many and I always finish them to stay with her. While I was with Romilly I never had any dallyings to speak of and even if I had I would never have left her either, so I think I knew deep down that if this continued I would end up having to make a decision one way or the other between the two of them. It would hurt I knew as I loved them both in my own way. I eventually drift off to sleep but the first evening of night shift is always a pain. The slightest noise wakes me up and so I don't get too much sleep and no 1981 visits either. I get up at 10:30pm feeling like death although my shower helps a little to revive me and then it's time for work at midnight at good old Falconer Plastics.

I've been telling the people at work about my experiences but only from the perspective that I'm writing a novel. They would never believe it if I told them it was really happening and I suppose that's why I started writing this account. Partly that and partly because maybe writing it down would put things in perspective a bit for me. Two of the women on my shift, Julie and Noreen, seem quite interested in my story, so I tell them about my supposed fictitious escapades back in an imaginary 1981. Luckily it's a fairly quiet night at work and the machines keep running sweetly, the robots throw no wobblies so I can take it easy and think. I suppose work is Ok, we all moan about it don't we but then I suppose everyone does that and to be honest we do have the odd laugh there. Old Dillip Patel makes me laugh with his sense of humour. He has christened me with a new name from an old 'Carry On' film he has seen and so I become Gladstone Screwer. Very flattering I don't think. 'The bastard.' I laugh to myself. In an earlier time he would be getting a slap but nowadays I just laugh at his oriental humour and christen him Uncle Fester instead due to his rotundity and folically challenged head. Warren Slack who is the shift supervisor has a night off, so while keeping them all busy I enjoy a fairly quiet night.

At last 8:00am comes around and the day shift arrives typically looking only half awake as usual and I can gratefully make my way home to my nice comfortable bed. First I have to do the shift changeover report with the dayshift supervisor and the managers. "Busy night?" asks Larry Maddison the technical manager looking over my shoulder at the shift report. "No. Very quiet Larry, I tell him, and I've managed not to break anything for you so that's a result I suppose."

Elaine is up and on the computer when I get home. "Hiya babe's. Where's me breakfast?" I ask cheerily as I walk in. "In the fridge, she says, you can cook it yourself." Damn I think it'll have to be muesli again then. I prepare it and a huge mug of tea then retire to bed for the day. "Don't wake me unless we declare war or you fancy a bit of fine loving." I tell the lovely Elaine on my way up. It's another hot day so I sleep naked with the quilt off and the fan on. I'm almost straight off to sleep and before I know it I come to back in 1981 again.

Chapter 11. A Night at Bazza's.

A Friday back in 1981. Romilly and I had spent the night at the Old Crown. A great night as it happens. People had come and gone as usual. Beers had come and gone. It was one of those nights full of old friends and laughter. The pub was a loud and raucous smoky haven. I had proved again I was the master of the Pacman table beating all comers. I laughed as I saw another contender for my throne dispatched, throwing my 'magic hands' into the air and letting out a war cry. Romilly had talked to some of her own friends as I had to mine. What was once history was now the present, it seemed so vibrant and I was just so glad to be alive? Every time I looked towards Romilly she was laughing and looking towards me mouthed the words "I love you." I had been talking to an old friend Theresa while I was dispatching sad pretenders to my throne on the Pacman table and I knew she fancied a bit of a closer relationship with me but my woman was Romilly so I just laughed it. But Romilly noticed what was going on and soon reacted as only she could. I was starting another game with Theresa cheering me on when Rommy jumped in grabbing Theresa by the arm, pulling her up to face her. "Theresa that is my man you are trying to pull and I would appreciate it if you took your bloody hands and eyes off him Ok?" The whole bar went quiet at this and I watched as Theresa tried to bluff her way out of it then backed down at Romilly's icy glare and ran from the bar in tears. Everyone started to cheer as Romilly sat down beside me. "You little bugger I told her, I am so glad that you are on my side cos I'd hate to get on your wrong side babes." " She deserved it, says Romilly, she has been giving you cows eyes all night and it had to be nipped in the bud." I let my latest opponent win as I take her face in my hands and kiss her. "Rommy why do you worry so much? You know it's only me and you. Don't you?" "It had better be Spears unless you want to be wearing your bollucks as earrings." she smiles menacingly.

We ended up in the saloon bar later that evening feeling no pain with Bazza and a few other close mates. "Well Baz, I said, back to yours for a session I suppose mate." Bazza was a great mate of mine back then. With his long brown hair a full beard and dressed in denim he was one of the well known faces around Cardinals Stratford in those days. Don't get me wrong I wouldn't have trusted him within an inch of my wallet or my woman, a few too many drinks in them or me and he would take his chance, but our friendship went back to 1975 and we had shared a few brilliant escapades together, got into a few scrapes too. If anyone could make you laugh with his chat it was Bazza. We all took the piss out of him but some of the finest moments I spent in the 70s and 80s were shared with Bazza and we could talk about most things. We probably wouldn't remember them too well next day but hey ho such is life, drugs and alcohol have such effects we found.

Now in the late seventies up until the time I had met Romilly I had become a bit of a druggie. Ok, very much of a druggie. Even a few friends had expressed concern about me back in 1980 as I explained earlier. I remember my ex Bev even changing the words of the David Bowie song 'Ashes to Ashes' on my behalf. 'We know Major Tom's a junkie' became, We all know Matt Spears the junkie.' Speed was my poison along with LSD. Cannabis was an essential of life and there weren't many drugs I hadn't at least tried. You name it; I tick the yes box Ok. You get the picture, I'd done them all and I'm not proud of it now but at the time it was in vogue and I grabbed the bull by both horns as usual. The only thing I stayed clear of was injecting. The thought of needles made me cringe, always did, always will so perhaps my cowardice was the saving of me. I certainly did my fair share of heroin but only up the nose. But by 1981 I was in starting to ease up a little on the drug use and was starting to wind down just a little from it, but I still had the occasional session and a night at Bazza's without drugs was like bread without butter.

There was Romilly and me, Bazza, Pete Pierre and Bev, who was a gorgeous blonde ex of mine. I suppose we got back there around about midnight; the pubs all shut at 11 pm in those days and the first thing was to sort out the music. Bazza put a Santana album on and we all sat back just enjoying the vibe as the joints passed around freely. About 12.30 a knock on the door and another couple of old friends turned up, Ian and Mouse, and the party really started. The joints started doing the rounds at double speed and I enjoyed another nostalgia moment as I made my first joint for 20 odd years, perfectly I might add. I was always proud of my joint building. As usual built on a good old fashioned 12 inch vinyl album cover. Three Rizlas licked with love and anticipation, the breaking of the cigarette and sifting the large lumps from the tobacco till I had a lovely bed prepared. Then the large lump of Lebanese Red cooked slowly till it just flaked off nicely into the joint. My rule was always make sure there's enough in there and add half as much again before rolling it just right. Not too tightly because it gets too hard to draw on. Romilly watched critically as I made it, she was almost as good as me in the joint making department in those days. How do they manage it nowadays on a Cd cover I wondered with a smile? Romilly and I curled up on the floor my arm draped comfortably around her shoulder as I torched the joint and passed it to her for her approval.

We lay back against Bazza's bed and enjoyed the taste before passing it on. Hunky Dory by David Bowie was playing on Bazza's stereo by now. I have to explain here that Baz had a small bedsit on the second floor of a Victorian converted townhouse just off the town centre. Hardly palatial but we all loved going back there. It contained a large double bed a few armchairs, a sofa, a stereo and a small kitchenette. The toilet/bathroom was shared with the two other flats. I whispered to Romilly "Damn I really miss Bazza's place so much." "You would you druggie" she whispered back, her eyes smiling at me. "You can talk." I laughed back. We all settled back listening to Bowie and talking until Baz pulled out his secret stash. For Pete's Sake I thought, Blues. A whole damned bag of French blues. There must have been 200 at least. "Sweeties anyone?" chortled Bazza. Now as I said back in the 80s blues were my favourite drug and I gratefully swallowed half a dozen. Romilly surprised me by taking the same as me. Everyone else took lucky dips. Now if anything can make you talk it is blues, they are amphetamines. You tend to grind your teeth a lot too but that's by the bye. But although you have a great time on speed the comedown can be horrific. Within half an hour the conversations had ratcheted up a notch, mostly about total crap but that's the way with blues. Even the price of potatoes becomes interesting. You can talk about total nonsense for hours on end. Romilly me Bazza and Pete formed a close little group beside the bed and of course I steered the conversation around to time travel with Romilly's help.

"So Bazza, I said with a smile, what would you think if I told you I'm from 2007 along with Romilly here" "Yeah perfectly possible, he said, I always knew there was something strange about you two. "He collapsed in a heap guffawing on the way. "Why's that Baz?" said Romilly squeezing my leg. He sat up again and looked at us strangely, seemingly straight for a brief moment. "Because you two are just too perfect together to be from here? Have you looked at yourselves lately? You are like a couple of limpets, he laughed, never apart. Always clinging to each other." "Really, says Romilly, how do you mean, I mean I've never been compared to a limpet before have I? " She looks at me and winks; I used to call her my little limpet sometimes as a joke as she clung to me in our early days together. Bazza relaxes sitting cross legged and looks at us both. "You both seem to glow when you are together; I have never seen two people so happy with each other or so perfectly matched. The perfect couple, he laughs but you just be careful Ok." Romilly frowns and I feel the need to hold her hand tighter. "Because with such a great love comes danger. It can be so incandescent that it can burn you out and leave you destroyed so you two just be very careful Ok?" I feel Romilly squeezing my hand so hard it hurts. I whisper to her, "Well maybe he is right there babe."

After this the mood lightens a little but Romilly's and my initial euphoria is gone at Bazza's words as I suppose that is what actually happened in the real 1983 causing our split and my crash and burn. The night wears on and Romilly and I end up on Bazza's bed together totally stoned. We lay beside each other leaning on our elbows face to face pulling funny faces at each other and talking the nonsense that amphetamines induce. I pull the cover over Romilly and we try to doze a little, a pretty hard job after speed, but eventually we drift in and out of sleep. I'm laying awake at about 4 am, Pink Floyd are playing, 'Dark Side of the Moon'. Romilly is snuggled up beside me snoring lightly but as I pull her closer to me I feel movement beneath her T-shirt in her chest area. Pete is lying behind her and the dirty git is feeling up her breast under her T-shirt. I raise up my head to look at him. He looks to be pretending to be asleep, so I gently raise Romilly's T-shirt enough to put my hand up and sure enough his hand is cupping Romilly's breast. I can feel his hand massaging her lovely breast, her bra raised above it. I slowly take his hand and remove it, then gripping two of his fingers in my hand I squeeze gradually increasing the pressure; he comes awake with a jolt. I look at him in the dim light and say to him. "This is just a reminder Pete, his eyes are watering with pain now, you might be a mate but if you touch my woman again like that then next time I will break them, OK?" This seems to get through to him and he rolls off the bed sullenly and onto the floor.

I can see Bazza is still awake, a cigarette in his mouth and his eyes are slits behind the smoke and taking this all in. Romilly is still sleeping so I ease off the bed after re-arranging her clothing and sit beside Bazza, my back against the bed. "Nasty, he says, you can be a vicious little bastard when you want to Matt." I nod. "I can't help it Baz; I will seriously hurt anyone that hurts her, you know that don't you." He looks at me for a moment, then nods and says, "Yep I think you would." Then grabbing an album cover he starts to roll a joint with plenty of dope going in to it I see. Just the right thing to relax you after the blues. "You come across so cool and such a nice guy but I wouldn't want to cross you." he says sagely. "Baz, I say, I'm not vicious, never have been. I've never hurt anyone that didn't deserve it but I don't like people taking the piss. If you let them do it once they will keep on doing it. I just teach them that if they do it to me or my woman then it will hurt, Ok." He rips a bit of card from my JPS pack for a roach to finish the burner. Everyone else is dozing by now. He offers it to me and I light the blue touch paper and retire with caution as they say. I taste the cool blue smoke as I inhale. "Nice one Baz." I cough. I pass it back to him; he inhales deeply and looks back at me through slitted eyes. We pass it back and forth a few times. "Well you've got a handful there mate, he says a smile on his lips looking at Romilly sleeping peacefully on his bed, she will be your making, or your destruction you know that, don't you?" "Maybe I know that already Baz, but I'm really hoping for the good option mate." I croak. He offers me more blues but I refuse them preferring the joint. "Got any Taj Mahal?" I say. He leans over and after riffling through the album collection for a while we are soon listening to 'Corinna'. "So what's 2007 like?" he asks matter of factly putting the Pink Floyd disc away. "Why. Do you believe me then?" I ask." "Maybe he says, tell me about it, are we going to get nuked or anything?" The cold war was a big issue then back in 1981. "Nope you are ok Baz, no nukes; in fact we only have about 8 years left of the Soviet Union. It's all going to collapse in about 7 or 8 years and I remember the TV news showing ecstatic Germans tearing down the Berlin wall and tell Bazza about it. In 2007 half the Eastern Europeans are living over here. You can't move for Poles and Croats Baz, Oh and the Portuguese too. He looks surprised as I suppose I would have been back in 1981 knowing that the USSR would be history soon. I continue after taking a toke and pointing at his old stereo. "You see your stereo there mate? It will be defunct soon as CD's replace it; you see your album collection? He nods. It will fit 3 times over on a gizmo I can fit on my key ring. I can play it back on my PC." "What's a Pc?" He asks me. "It's a personal computer mate, and don't worry you will be alive to enjoy one Baz." We are all going to have personal mobile phones too that you can take photos with and even video. You will be able to keep your entire music collection on an SD card not much bigger than a stamp that just plugs into it." "Well I'll believe it when I see it " he laughs. I tell him about my life in 2007 and the rise of modern technology, and I realise that as Romilly said this is indeed a foreign country to us but eventually the dawn arrives and the sun shines in through the window casting a surrealistic orange glow in the room through

Bazza's curtains. "Look Matt I hope you do get the good option mate, he says, cos she is one hell of a lovely lady." He has seen Romilly is stirring by now and so I say "Morning Babe, Nice kip?" "Mmm yeah I'm hungry Spears." She yawns. "Let's go get breakfast then babe. I say. I'm starving too."

We head off to the Little Chef in Thurley and in the car I think back to my little violent interlude with Pete and sadly remember that I had once been violent to Romilly in the original 1983. We had argued one Friday evening and I remembered it now. Very good eh? Had I had been a wife beater? Definitely not but I had hurt her and at the time I blamed it all on her. I watched as she ate her breakfast and my mind recoiled at the thought I could ever do anything to hurt her and wondered how I could have been reduced to that? Using such violence on the person that I loved so much. But I had and all the reasons I could muster held no excuses. We reached the Little Chef and I ordered our meal, two full English breakfasts with a milk shake for her and a tea for me. So why had I hurt her? Why indeed? I looked at her thoughtfully sucking on her milk shake and then noticing that I am looking at her returning my smile happily and I tried to analyse my mind set at that time in the real 1983. When it came down to it I suppose that was one of the reasons that she had left me, it was certainly a huge contributory factor. I deserved it, I let her down. I abused her trust in me after all. I should not have. I remembered the time we argued about something so stupid that I can only vaguely remember it now. But I had lost my temper with her and chased her to the bedroom as she laughed at me. She pulled the duvet over herself and I jumped on the bed after her but I landed on top of her. I certainly hadn't meant any harm but it was too late for that. Afterwards she had complained that her shoulder hurt. I tried to ease it with witch hazel telling her how sorry I was and thinking it was just a bruise, but I had accidentally broken her collar bone. She kept crying that it hurt and what had I done? I had left her. To go to bloody work for Saturday morning overtime till I received a call from her in the hospital telling me what I had done. Looking back now I think it was the lowest point of my life and thinking of it now still hurts. Incredibly so, believe it or not. How could I have been so careless to do that to her? But I did and its history now. Except history keeps coming back to haunt me and bite me in the ass so viciously even after all these years. But that's not me I think, I'm not violent and certainly not to people I love, but I had been in her case. Even unintentionally, I had hurt her. I caused her harm. Feel good do I? No I feel like the lowest of the low. No wonder she left. So now in our new 1981 timeline I sit and watch her as I feel the last of the drugs influence leaving me and sighed. "What are you thinking about Babe, you look so sad?" she asks me starting to look a little concerned. I told her of my memories of that day in 1983 and she told me not to worry. "For God's sake I do Romilly I say. I hurt you in our past life and that's not me. Why did I do it? How could I hurt a person I love so much?" She looks me in the eye and after thinking for a while says "Ok let's talk about this I think we need to, don't you?"

It's a gorgeous July Saturday morning; the sun is warm already at 8:30 in the morning. We go over to the forest to our favourite spot to talk. Sitting in the car together with my arm around her shoulder I ask her how I could have been violent to her. "I can't answer that for you Matt. Only you can do that." she says. "But no way had I ever hurt anyone I loved before you or after you." I say. "But you did hurt me, she says, and I still have the scars in 2007." But why did I do it? I remembered again the evening it had happened and sitting up I held my head in my hands. It had been a normal Friday evening in our old flat. I was hungry and made myself crackers and cheese with pickled onions. She started winding me up about how I was getting fat and she wouldn't want me anymore. I had endured a bad day and she was taking the piss. I wasn't drunk it was just a normal Friday evening, but I got up and I chased her into the bedroom and caused her harm. Accidentally? Yes. Unintentionally? Yes. Excuses? Yes. And now I recalled Bazza's words. "You can be a vicious bastard when you want Matt." he had said and I suppose it was true. People can fuck with me and I will laugh but it oversteps the mark and I crack. The good thing is people don't expect it of good old Matt and I still remembered a guy smiling at me trying to sell me some crap that was supposed to be cocaine but wasn't. As soon as I realized he was taking the piss I exploded and left him on the floor in a lot of pain, but I hoped I would never do that to someone I loved. The other good thing in the old days was that people didn't tend to fuck with me. But I was normally an Ok guy; I would rather use words than fists. But I had lost it and hurt Romilly. Why. For the umpteenth time WHY?

In my old life in the original 1980s I had loved her so much but I supposed I knew by mid 1983 that I was losing her and as much as I wanted to I could do nothing about it. We met, we loved, and I lost. You win again. I should have expected it. I had exited a similar relationship with Heather in late 1979. Heather and I had a stormy relationship but I had never hurt her never laid a finger on her as I had Romilly. Why? Was it a character defect? I suppose that the frustration of seeing our marriage crumbling around us while I was too stupid to be able to mend it didn't help. I tell her this as she takes my hand and looks into my eyes. "Don't worry she says, I can handle it Matt I didn't help either. I'm to blame as well. I was just as much to blame for us breaking up. You did try to rebuild our marriage at least. I remember even if you don't. But I wanted you to do all the re-building I didn't want to do anything to help." My eyes fill with tears and I say "For God's sake Romilly you were blameless it was me and I promise you I will never hurt you again, Ok?" "You won't, she says taking my hand, I think it was probably a lot to do with the drugs you were doing at the time as well. And I know I used to wind you up which didn't help either but we have both seen life and I can see the man you are now and I totally trust that man. Ok? Have you ever hurt Elaine?" I shake my head. "No never." "There you go then. You are not a violent person are you? If you were then the same would have happened between you and her. Do you understand that?" She pulls my head up till she is looking into my eyes. "Do you?" she reiterates. I nod my head sadly and she pulls me to her holding me tightly. She strokes my hair as I lay beside her. "Look Matt please stop torturing yourself, it was just an accident, I even told you that at the time. We had bad times I know but we had more good times. Don't you remember them? I still remember those little notes that you put in my lunchbox telling me of how much you loved me. Do you remember those?" I smile at the memory of making those sandwiches and the notes I put in with them. "And the time we got a kitten, Gerald? Do you remember him? How you cried when he got run over and immediately bought two other kittens to replace him for me. You could be so sweet so just put the bad memories behind you. Please. I remember the man that looked after me when I wasn't well, looking after me so tenderly. The man who wrote such lovely poetry about me and rang me at work just to tell me he loved me." All of these memories return and I start to cry in her arms again. "Shhhhh she tells me tenderly stroking my face. I remember when we first met and you wouldn't make love to me until it was just right between us. Do you remember that? Until you cooked me a meal at your parents and chose the moment so it would be so perfect for our first time together. Oh yes I know you come across as the hard little git sometimes but I know it's just an act and all the time underneath that you are such a soft romantic. I know that now. I think I knew it even then. Such a shame I didn't appreciate it then. And now I find out from you that through the last 23 years you have never stopped loving me after all of the shit I gave you and you say you feel bad? Spears I am the one that should be feeling bad not you ya wally and you at least have your demons in your past. Mine are in my future."

I am still thinking of our past sadly as we lay there arm in arm that sunny Saturday morning in our favourite forest spot and I vow to her and myself that this time around will be different. But I know that this is going to be a cross that I will always have to bear throughout my life in whatever timeline I am in. We get the rug out of the boot and spread it on the grass to lay and enjoy the warm sun and before long I doze off as the speed has left my system and a sleepless night catches up with me. Romilly told me later that I had been crying out in my sleep and how she had comforted me. I remembered dreaming over and over again about our break up and kept seeing her leaving me back in 1984. But eventually the dream passes and I wake up back in 2007.

Chapter 12. Discussing Time Travel.

As the days went by I realised that my visits back to 1981 were getting easier. I found with practice that by simply relaxing my body and emptying my mind I could return almost at will to 1981. Controlling my actions back then was so much easier too now. I could switch between my old and new selves with comparative ease, although I spent most of my time as the 2007 me, but if need be I could go into autopilot mode as it were and let my old self take over for a while. I also learned to repel my forced returns mostly, although on occasions the instinct to come back was just too strong but fortunately these instances were fairly rare. I had learned this from Romilly who had been doing her travelling back to 1981 a bit longer than me. She told me of the surprise of her first visit a few weeks before me. She had fallen asleep one night, she told me and just thought she was having a really powerful dream much as I did on my first trip back. She had dreamed she was in The Three Ways, another old drinking haunt of ours back in 81, and was surprised to find herself watching her old self talking to me. The old me of course. She told me of the initial shock followed by amazed pleasure at seeing me and all the old faces again, although like me she was only there as an observer at first. Of course like me she had thought this was just a one off really vivid dream, until she had returned again the next night. She had started to be able to take over her old self on her third visit back, while her and the old me were making love in the back of my old Cortina one night in Capfield forest. Her biggest surprise though was to come on the time we had talked in the Old Crown and I had mentioned the

Editors and shortly after in Capfield forest realising she was not alone there but that I had joined her. Of course we talked a lot about how our trips back affected us. While I was back I noticed that I had regained faculties I had not noticed before. My eyesight was a lot sharper for example. The joy of being able to read small print again without glasses was a revelation but even my other senses seemed enhanced. Taste, smell, and even my hearing seemed so much sharper although I had not gained any powers as such I supposed, just regained my young senses. Rejuvenation would be a good word for it.

Also it seemed that time back in 1981 was not relative to modern day time in as much as I could spend a couple of days back in 1981 but when I awoke back in 2007 only a matter of hours had passed, and I could spend a few days back in 2007 but on my next visit back to 1981 I might continue at the same point I had last left it. I of course talked with Romilly about the things I had researched on the internet about time travelling. We had spent a whole evening in my room back at my parents place with a couple of bottles of wine talking about it. It was one of those great evenings we spent alone just talking and expounding all types of theories but mostly just enjoying our re-found companionship while sipping wine and listening to some great music as well. She would lay with her head in my lap, laughing and arguing with Joy Division, Santana or similar playing softly in the background. We would listen to my old vinyl albums just as we used to in the old days and talk until the early hours. Sometimes we would make love, other times we would just sit and hold each other or hold hands drifting away to the music and one of our favourites became Dan Fogelbergs 'Netherlands' album. It seemed nothing could end our newly re-found happiness but by now a worrying thought started to nag at me and I told her of my concern. If in fact the theories I had read about a multiplicity of time universes forever moving and rippling throughout space were correct then might the fact that we were finding it easier to travel mean that they were getting closer? Might that also mean they could eventually move apart again? What would happen if they did? Would our ability to cross over end? Would we be unable to see each other again? Could we get trapped in 1981 even? Or could we find ourselves in a different universe in a different year? I had by now come to the opinion that the multiple universe theory seemed most likely. We had not been going back in time. We were probably just sidestepping into a different parallel reality. Could it last for days, weeks, years? Perhaps millennia even.

All our questions and theories just spawned more theories and questions. Were other people doing this too, we were nothing special so I suppose that if we could do it then others most likely could do it too. Could we find them if they were? I mean we could hardly put an ad in the local paper could we? Perhaps some of the tales you hear about could be put down to this meeting of universes. You must have heard of people getting premonitions such as the person who gets a sudden feeling not to take a certain flight only to hear later it has crashed? Could it be a warning from another universe? What about Déjà vu? Could that not be the result of seeing somewhere in a parallel reality and remembering it? How about ghosts and poltergeists? Or even re-incarnation? Could that be stepping over to a younger self as the old self dies? It seemed to me that the whole multiple universe theory is no harder to believe than so called supernatural occurrences, but then again the whole parallel universe idea is pretty damned supernatural anyway. We agreed on one thing. No-one was ever likely to explain it to us. We agreed that would have to make our own suppositions in this case.

As to my earlier worry about our visits stopping if our universes moved apart? I asked Romilly what she would do if that happened and she had the choice in which timeline to stay in. She was absolutely firm in her opinion that she just wanted to stay in 1981 with the 2007 me. I had asked her why but again she skirted round the conversation saying she had nothing worth staying for in 2007. I asked her about her husband and kids, how could she just leave them without any guilt? She just looked forlornly at me and clammed up and tried to change the subject. If I tried to push her on the subject her mood would change and she'd snap at me to mind my own bloody business. Romilly could always get quite petulant in the old 1981, it was one of her less likeable qualities then and I smiled inwardly thinking she hadn't changed much, although for pure stubbornness she had met her match in me. Then she'd tell me that who in their right mind would not want to be young again and put everything right the second time around. But personally I had reservations. I agreed with her totally about wanting to stay young and put right past wrongs but I did have a life in 2007. A wife, Elaine but most especially three children I would never see again if I stayed. They would not be hurt if our theories were right as an identical version of me would live on in their universe, they would never know the difference. But this version of me back in 1981 would never see them growing up and having children of their own. I would miss out on all that. Not such an easy decision after all eh? But why would Romilly tell me so little of her 2007 self? Why was she so guarded about her 2007 future each and every time I mentioned it? She must have something to hide but I thought that she would probably tell me eventually and so I let sleeping dogs lie for the time being.

Chapter 13. The Ashtray Test.

Later I lay back on the bed in my old room at my parents place in 1981 and pondered the situation. I had taken Romilly home earlier and I turned ideas over alone in my mind alone about how I could prove this was not a dream. I lay back on the bed and flicking my ash in the ashtray I remembered the idea I had back in 2007. It might not totally answer my questions but it could perhaps clear up one thing. I put on the headphones and lay back listening to an old Styx album. My test would be very interesting, I thought, drawing deeply on my cigarette and watching the swirls of smoke rise up to my ceiling. Perhaps I could answer at least one question with what I was about to do. I did what I had to do and kicking my boots off and putting my feet up on the bed, I drifted away listening to 'Babe'.

I was back in 2007 again. I awoke in my chair with a start and immediately lit a cigarette to wake up my brain. As I coughed at the day's first intake of smoke, Elaine walked in and looked at me. "What's the matter?" I said. "Matt, I thought you were giving up those things?" She frowned at me."I know. I coughed again. I will soon, I promise." "Yeah I bet." she moaned and I watched as she fussed about picking up dirty plates and glasses and generally went about tidying up the lounge, "Oi leave my ashtray alone" I said rescuing it from her housekeeping frenzy. I watched as she left the room and I picked up the ashtray, my old stainless steel one from 1977. It was full of my cigarette ends but I emptied it into the wastepaper bin and wiped the inside to peer inside.... Interesting I thought, looking in to the bottom of the stainless steel ashtray. I knew I had answered at least one question, but that still left lots more. Back in my bedroom in 1981 while listening to Styx I had scratched a deep cross into the bottom of that ashtray with my pen knife knowing I still had it and used it regularly in 2007, but holding the ashtray in my hand I noticed the result...No scratched cross. No message from me to myself 26 years in the future. It was as clean and unmarked as the day I had bought it one August day at Amager airport in Copenhagen back in 1977. Mm so I could rule out time travel, I thought. The cross would still be there, but that left me a little more knowledgeable at least. I was either suffering from a series of extremely weird dreams or I was losing my marbles, but the results of the research I had carried out on the internet seemed the most logical I hoped, as unlikely as it seemed. I must be sidestepping into an alternate but almost identical reality. Time in this 2007 reality was unchangeable. It was carved in stone as such. Romilly and I HAD split acrimoniously in 1984 here. I HAD met and married Elaine in 1988. What I had not done was go back in time to visit the original 1981 past. Nothing had changed at all here nor could it. The past here was dead and gone and in some strange kind of way that made me happy.

I sat there and my mind tried to sort out what was happening. I was not time travelling back to 1981 I accepted that now, the ashtray proved that, but what was happening and why? It must be the parallel universe theory that could explain it. I must be sidestepping into that alternate and possibly almost identical universe and creating a new timeline with a different branching out future there. If that was so then theoretically I could start a whole new life there. The possibility was stunning, so utterly mindboggling as to beggar belief, but what if the parallel universes drifted apart? Then I would be stuck in one with the other one carrying on its own sweet way. I would no longer be able to sidestep from one to the other. Would the universes drift apart? Would I know if they were starting to drift apart or would it just happen? Bang and suddenly no more travel? I knew which one Romilly would chose but then which one would I chose? We probably would not actually get a choice. If the universes drifted apart then we would just be stuck in whichever one we were visiting at the time.

Again if my theories were right then no one would even know in 2007 as I would for all intents and purposes be there still, and I could make a new life and timeline in 1981.But would it be better? Would Romilly and I make the same mistakes all over again, or had we learnt from them? Could I even trust her? On her poor past performance then no. Could I even end up alone again but in a different timeline, younger but no happier? I would still have the memory of my kids up until 2007 but in all other respects they would be lost to me forever as if they were all dead. I wouldn't even have a photo of them and I worried that the memory of their faces would fade to me with time. In fact I thought they would be dead to me as they would never even exist in my new life. They would not even be born. Conversely I supposed that if I stayed in 2007 then any children that myself and Romilly might have in the new timeline would become non-existent to me there also. There were just so many possibilities, a lot of which were once again suppositions. Educated suppositions I thought but they could be totally false. Damn I needed a scotch badly.

Chapter 14. Bust up with Romilly.

The next time I go back to 1981 I find myself lying dozing in my bed. It must have been a Saturday morning, and my mum calls up to me "Romilly's here. And before you ask. No I am not making you tea." "Send her up then mum, I'm awake." I shout back. Romilly walks into my room, she is wearing a lovely white dress and looks absolutely drop dead gorgeous as usual to my randy half open early morning eyes and she sits down on the bed beside me. "Allo sexy." she says grinning. I needed tea badly and told her I would love her for eternity and a day if she would go and make me one right now before I died of de-hydration. "Spears you are a lazy little git. Why can't you get up out of your pit and make one yourself?" She tells me this while removing my wandering hand from under her dress where it is quite happily stroking her bare thigh. I look at her pityingly giving her my best 'I'm dying' look and she eventually succumbs and goes down to make me one. I can hear her laughing in the kitchen with my mum as I lay there luxuriating in my soft warm bed and eventually she comes back in with my cuppa. "Awww baby you are the best." I smile and lighting us cigarettes I tell her about the ashtray test. "So your ideas about the timelines were right then and we aren't going back in time at all." She says frowning. "Why though?" I reply. Romilly smiles at me and bends down to kiss me, I feel her hand under the sheets seeking my hardness and then wrapping her fingers around it. I feel it spring to attention as her fingers gently massaged it, but I pushed her gently and reluctantly away. "Romilly I think you need to tell me more about what's happening. You obviously know more than I do. Tell me about your future self." She releases her hand from my now very eager hardness and looks away but I pull her face back towards me. "What are you hiding?" I say. I can see a cloud descend across her face and she tells me not to ask. "For God's sake, I counter, just tell me. It can't be that bad can it?" She tries to rise from the bed but I hold her hand and pulling her to me I tell her "Romilly I love you. Always have, always will. I have never stopped loving you for the last 23 years. It's as simple as that. I trust you with everything so why are you hiding this from me?" "So why did you let me go so easily then if you loved me so much Matt? " she replies angrily. "Because you left me and I tried to respect your decision even though it tore my heart out at the time. When I sent you presents you just returned them to me. Every time I tried to talk to you, you just ignored me or don't you remember that?" I say. I am holding her small hands gently between my own and looking deep into her eyes as I tell her that I love her unconditionally, as far as I'm concerned she has always been the only woman I loved and I deserve to know what's happening. I watch in amazement as her whole demeanour changes, her head lowers and she starts to cry softly, small sobs against my chest, she seems to sink into herself. Her whole body shakes and the tears start as if they will never stop. I hold her to me and try to calm her and then she tries to pull away. But I won't let her. "You are stupid you know that don't you Romilly, I whisper to her, I have loved you from the day I very first met you, I know I made so many mistakes and for that I am sorry, I know I hurt you, but I loved you so much and you left me. I wanted you so badly but you just left me? The vitriol was now pouring out of me; you hurt me so badly, left me for 23 years of pain without a word, without a thought. I've spent all of those 23 years wondering how I lost you and now I'm back with you wanting me so we can start it all over again? Why?" I dissolve into tears also and we end up holding each other bawling our eyes out. My mother's concerned voice calls up. "Are you two ok?" "Yep we are ok mum." I shout holding Romilly's crying body tightly to me.

Shortly after her tears turn to sniffles and I ask her why she had left me? She lies down beside me and snuggles up to me. "Matt I was only 20 when I left you. You have to admit our relationship wasn't good at that time. I felt trapped by you, I wanted to escape, perhaps I overlooked our love but I was young, you seemed so wrapped up in yourself and drugs and yes you did hurt me. I just wanted to escape." "What from, I asked her, someone who loved you so much?" "Yes she says the tears drying on her cheeks; I didn't think I needed love. I wanted my freedom and instead I ended up giving it all away in a dead end relationship. That was when I started to realise how much I did need love and yet I threw it away when I left you. I don't regret my kids, I love them even if...at this she stopped and dissolved into tears again. She shuddered and said to me between tears, "I made such a mistake babe, I want you so much, and I'm never going to leave here again." "I don't think you have a choice; I say to her, I think that we can only visit." "Is that not enough." she says. "No, not for me. I say. Maybe I belong in 2007, maybe you do too?" I feel her body shaking in my arms. "Matt I don't want to go back ever, let's just stay here...we can be so happy can't we?" "Can we?" I ask. "Of course she says, our futures will be wiped clean, we can start again, just me and you together here forever. This time we can get it right I know we can." "O yes and what happens when the arguments start again Rommy?" I ask her, and there is something you are not telling me Romilly don't forget that, it's a pretty ropey start to our new life isn't it if we can't even tell each other everything, if we continue to keep secrets from each other." At this she looks at me so sadly and then she gets up and leaves me. I hear her running down the stairs and out of the front door slamming it behind her. I jump out of bed and throw last night's clothes back on rapidly and follow her down the road thinking to myself that, well I could have handled that better. I catch up with her by the river lock. "Why won't you tell me?" I ask pulling her back by her arm. She tries to pull away from me, breaking into more tears and I say again, "Why won't you tell me Romilly?" She pulls me to the side of the road and grabbing my hand says bitterly "Because when I look into your eyes I want to see someone who will stick with me forever, who never lies to me and who loves me? And if I tell you about my future then maybe I will lose all of that you idiot." I'm stunned, struck dumb and she walks off pushing my hands away, leaving me by the side of the road. I hear her sobs as she walks away and I just sit by the roadside in tears as well. I have never felt as distraught as I did then. So what should I do? "So that's your answer as usual is it, just run away from me again?" I call out after her but she's gone. I walk slowly back home shaking my head in complete disbelief at her total lack of faith in me.

My mum is waiting by the front door looking concerned but I just walk past her and walk up to my bedroom. Emptying my wallet I count my money. Enough to get totally blitzed. I shower quickly and after putting on a fresh shirt and jeans I grab my keys and jump into the Cortina to head off to the Old Crown. The good old 1981 Old Crown, no one minds if you get totally pissed there. Eebs and Nick Pardoe are there sitting at a table in the public bar and I say Hi to them but I hope my body language is enough to tell them to let me be as I'm in getting pissed all on my lonesome mode. I order a pint of lager and lean at the bar drinking and thinking. But Eebs wanders over to me, a look of concern on his face. "You Ok mate?" he asks, looking concerned. I try to look happy and reply, "Yea I'm fine Eebs no worries mate Just feeling a little unsociable today." Eebie is probably my best mate back in the real 1981. He is 6 foot 8 inches tall with long brown hair, a formidable looking guy but a big old softie at heart and he loves a pint or ten. "Looks like woman trouble to me Matt, he says to me smiling, is it Romilly?" "Yea I s'pose so I say, she's not being straight with me." He pulls up a stool beside me and orders us pints of Abbot Ale. "Drink this he urges me, it's better than that gnat's piss lager you normally drink." I take a sip and grimace hoping it will taste better on the second try. "Look Matt if I know Romilly then she has her reasons, I can't see her lying to you without a good reason. She loves you too much mate. You can tell that when you two are together. Her eyes hardly ever leave you, she is totally smitten. And you are just as bad I can see how much you care for her in your eyes. She has changed you for the better and you know that?" "Eebie mate, I joke, I never knew you were so bloody perceptive. I laugh and swig some more of the Abbot Ale and yes it does taste better after the first swig, but meanwhile I am going to get totally rat assed." "You'd be surprised mate. Just give her a chance Ok?" I agree but my mind teeters between staying here and going back to 2007 for good. Do I have a choice? Not really, I have to find the 2007 Romilly even if she doesn't want me to. I know that before long I will have to find out, if not from her then in 2007 before it becomes a festering sore between us. I can't even begin to think what terrible secret she is hiding from me. Surely it can't be that bad that it would make me stop loving her. No I think to myself I will give her till after the holiday then I would find out myself somehow.

It's just one o'clock and I'm just starting my third pint when she walks into the bar. Romilly walks up to me and smiling sadly puts her arms over my shoulders, linking her hands behind my neck. She kisses me full on the lips, a long loving soft kiss, then moving her lips to my ear, she kisses it and whispers "I am so sorry babe; I love you so much." I pull her to me. I notice Eebie smiling at me and giving me the thumbs up sign as if to say I told you so. "No it's me who should be sorry, you obviously have your reasons for not telling me about yourself in 2007 and for the time being I will respect them Romilly but you have to promise me that you will tell me one day." She looks into my eyes, and after thinking for a while she says."Ok I will make you that promise on one condition." "Ok go on then." I say. She makes me promise her faithfully not to try to find out about her in 2007, it was as if she had read my mind earlier but I promised her I wouldn't and we sealed our joint promise with a kiss, before I bought her a drink. "Can I let you into a secret?" She smiles conspiratorially. I nod my head and she says "My house is empty this afternoon; they've all gone to visit relatives down in London and won't be back till later today." "Mmm sounds interesting, what do you have in mind?" I say innocently. "Weeelllll she smirks, I've always had this fantasy you know, about you making love to me in my old bed. We never did it there back in the old 1981 I seem to remember." "You're certainly right about that young lady, so if you would care to knock that drink back a bit sharpish it would be my pleasure to pleasure you there." I laugh and my faith in human nature is restored for the time being at least.

Chapter 15. An Agreement to Marriage.

We head back to Romilly's parent's house her hand on my leg as I drive running her fingers so very sexily along my thigh. To be honest I have not visited her house that much as we normally go back to mine or spend time together in the car. I think I have only seen her bedroom once and was amused and very touched at the time I remember by the stuff she had written about me on her calendar. She had declared her undying love for me at the time on that calendar. We immediately ascend to her bedroom and after putting some music on her small record player she falls back on the bed arms above her head smiling. Oh so seductively she sighs and then holding her arms wide she winks and says "Take me big boy" "You wanton hussy." I laugh and fall into her waiting arms. My jeans and shirt soon join her white dress on the floor along with our underclothes, and I am lying beside this gorgeous 17 or is that 43 year old woman on her small bed totally naked. Our tongues toy with each other and I feel her soft young breast in my hand and Oh so slowly caress her excited erect nipple between my thumb and forefinger. Her hand heads south and she continues where she left off this morning in my bedroom, stroking her slim fingers up and down my manhood. I can feel the tips of her nails against it." Oh shit, Spears she sighs, that feels so bloody good." She squeezes my hardness gently and redoubles the intensity of her kissing. She had put an album on her small hi fi before we start, The Rolling Stones, Emotional Rescue and listening to Indian Girl I am in heaven feeling the wetness below now between her parted legs and her tongue is so deep in my mouth. I stroke her moist pussy gently with light fingers anticipating the heavenly feeling of being inside her shortly. I roll her on to her back, all the time my lips never leaving contact with hers and raising myself on my hands I position myself between her slim legs. The most marvelous thing I think about our lovemaking was that I just slipped inside her with such ease. It was so natural. It was as if we had been designed to fit together perfectly. I started to make love to her so gently, just small movements as we gazed into each other's eyes and unspoken words passed between us as we enjoyed each other's closeness. We did not need to talk to each other then; we each knew what the other was thinking as we slowly made love to each other that sunny Saturday afternoon on her small single bed. I rolled over on my back and watched as she took pleasure in being on top of me, taking control, her hands holding mine tightly fingers entwined, and rising and falling in time to the music playing in the background. She lays back down on top of me and with her with eyes closed tightly started breathing heavier and moaning, "Oh my God, Oh my God." I feel her mounting orgasm and mine as usual together and naturally in perfect synchronisation, my seed filling her with its joyous release as she collapses totally spent upon my chest.

We lay back, my arm wrapping around her sweat drenched shoulder afterwards, totally spent but so happy in our afterglow. She raises herself up on one arm, her breast against my chest, and stroking my face says "So when are you going to make an honest woman of me Matt?" "Are you talking marriage young Rommy?" I grin. "Well yes I suppose I am, she says, I mean we are going to anyway next year aren't we in this timeline?" "Even after what happened between us the last time?" I ask. "Yes in spite of what happened last time. I want us to be together now. This time it will be so different for us. I will see to that my darling. Just me and you and our love, and maybe some kids later on." She may only look seventeen but the words are from the forty three year old within. "So what are we going to call the first then?" I ask her. She lays back and lighting us both cigarettes says, "Ok if it's a girl I want to call her Leah, if it's a boy it's your choice." "That's a toughie I say, pulling on my cigarette, but I think Daniel is a nice name." "Ok she grins so if we have one of each then they are going to be Daniel and Leah." "Yea, I laugh and the third one if she's a girl can be Mildred." Romilly sits up smiling beside me and putting the ashtray between us says, "If you call any child of mine Mildred you are headed for the divorce courts buddy." I laugh and tell her, "Ok we will worry about the third when it comes."

"So if you are serious about this then name the day." I tell her. She looks at me with an exasperated smile as only Romilly can and says. "Spears you bastard of course I'm serious and how about after our holiday?" I roll her on to her back and grin, "So we have the honeymoon first and then we get married. I like your twisted logic girl. I really like it. Won't your parents be pissed off though I mean you are not 18 yet back here and we need their permission don't we?" "There you go again, she laughs poking me in the chest, putting obstacles in the way already. Do you want me as your wife or not you...you.... Bastard." I take her hand and kiss it gently. "I have never wanted anything more, I tell her, and I guess we can handle Will and Naomi." "That's my boy." she says her face alight with pleasure. I start to feel the passion in my loins again and start to kiss her with feeling. She smiles at the feel of my new hardness against her thigh and says. "Haven't you forgotten something you little git?" "Condom?" I grin cheekily. "No, the ring? she says. Let's go shopping." "Awww Romilly. Right now?" I ask looking down at a very eager little chap between my legs. "Yes Matt right now before the shops close." She laughs at me telling me there will be plenty of time for nookie later. And so reluctantly I dress and we head towards the town. I don't have much cash and I have to visit the cash machine. It's a little tricky as I don't know what my 1981 pin is but I let the 1981 me take over briefly to enter it as I note it mentally for future reference. I check the balance in my 1981 account and see it's not too healthy and draw out 30 pounds. We are going to have to find a way of making some more cash I think sighing inwardly. We eventually find a ring in our price range and with Romilly admiring the new ring on her small finger we return to her parent's place to tell the proud in laws. They have just arrived back when we return and so I help Will unload the car as Naomi goes in to make us all a cup of tea. Will and I have never really got on but he thanks me for helping as we unload the last of the stuff and we go into the house together.

Romilly's mum has made us all tea and we all sit in the lounge together. Romilly's younger brother Paul disappears upstairs as Romilly nudges me in the ribs. "Ermm Will, Naomi, I say clearing my throat. They look at me expectantly not knowing what is about to hit them. Romilly and I would like to get married and we would like your blessing. Now the shits hit the fan I think and Romilly looks at me smiling wondering how I am going to handle this. Will splutters as he drinks his tea. "Are you sure about this Romilly?" he asks. Naomi is sitting there open mouthed in surprise. Romilly gets up and shows them her ring. "Dad I have never been so sure. I love Matt and it's what we both want. If you don't Ok this we will wait the few months till I'm eighteen and do it anyway." Will answers, "But you are so young Romilly, why don't think about this for a while first. Don't be in such a hurry." Romilly kneels in front of her dad and tells him. "Dad, Matt and I just know this is right and it is what we want Ok? Please say yes Dad." Will doesn't look convinced one little bit but he looks to Naomi and asks her what she thinks. She looks at me and then at Romilly and says, "Well to be honest I'm not too sure about this either; I mean you have only known each other a matter of months. And you are so young Romilly. You are still not much more than a girl and your ideas can change so much at your age and over the next few years. Don't get me wrong Matt, she says turning to me, we can see in your faces how much you love each other now but wouldn't it be better to put this off until you know each other better?" Will is nodding along to this and looks at me expectantly. I recognise their concerns are justified as these probably were the reasons our original marriage in the original 1980s had hit problems. Romilly's youth and naivety. But I could obviously not tell them what was really going on here as they would think we were insane. I looked at the sad smile on Romilly's face and I could sense her thinking that I was going to capitulate. No way. I lifted Romilly from her kneeling stance in front of her dad and hugged her to me and then looking back at Naomi and Will I did what I'm good at and I proceeded to flannel for England. I told them that I understood their concern as I had also thought about Romilly's youth along with our age difference, which Naomi had tactfully not mentioned. I told them that although we had known each other for only seven months; we had been together continuously through that time and I felt I knew Romilly better than anyone I had ever met. That I wanted to cherish their lovely daughter for the rest of our naturals and would strive to make her happy and them proud of us. About how unhappy we could get when we were not together. I could see my little speech was working as I watched a smile forming on Naomi's face. I finished by saying that their full blessing on us would truly be the icing on our cake. I could see that Will was definitely getting a hint of the smell of bullshit about my speech but I knew we had won as I noticed Naomi nodding and looking a little tearful. Will would go along with her I knew. As always. And I hugged Romilly as I knew the fight was won.

As we left their house with their reluctant blessing and agreement to us marrying Romilly whispered in my ear, "Now I have heard it all Spears. Where the hell did you learn to bullshit like that you smooth tongued bastard?" I pause before starting the car and turn to her smiling. "It's nothing. Us men pick it up naturally after a few years of marriage." Will and Naomi are waving to us from the front drive as we pull away. I hope that the tear in my eye will be mistaken for emotion and not as the result of the jab in the ribs I have just received from my own dearest intended one's elbow.

And so next it's back to my parents to tell them good news. They too voice the same concerns about rushing this and Romilly's age but we convince them and Romilly is proudly showing them her new ring before long. My Dad suggests going out for a meal to celebrate and we find ourselves enjoying a lovely meal at my dad's local that evening. Steak and chips and black forest gateau, all washed down with a nice couple of bottles of a cheeky little Champagne. Cheesy I know but that was a celebration meal in 1981 after all. We tell them that we want to marry after the holiday, nothing big just the local registry office, a few friends and relatives, maybe a meal afterwards. It's what we want we tell them as my dad enthused by the bubbly tries to convince us to have a big wedding. We eventually convince him that in our case small is beautiful and he acquiesces to our wishes. "Can Romilly move in with us till we sort a place out? We want to buy a place but obviously it's going to take a while to sort out a mortgage." My dad agrees but not until we are married he stipulates. He has some quaint ideas my dad but we agree and my dad orders more bubbly.

Chapter 16. A Night at The Three Ways.

It's the Friday night before our holiday, and we are
spending the evening at another favourite haunt of
ours. The Three Ways, an old converted malting. It's
another lovely warm July evening and we sit outside by
the River Strat, me holding her hand, her with her bare
feet in the river, swirling them along with the rivers
gentle flow. She releases my hand and leans back
closing her eyes enjoying the early evening sun's rays. I
light a cigarette and slowly exhale the healing smoke. I
squeezed her hand and said "Romilly I know I'm a pain
but isn't it about time you told me about your future?"
"You never give up do you Spears?" she smiles. "Well it
seems that I have told you all about my future. I take
her left hand and point at the engagement ring on her
finger. And doesn't this mean No secrets between us?"
She sighs and pulling her feet from the river lights a
cigarette and looks at me. Taking my other hand she
lifts up her lovely legs and crossing them looks down at
her lap then up into my eyes. "Matt really really I will
but not yet OK, let's just enjoy these times first." I
acquiesce as usual and leaning back as well I flick my
cigarette end into the river then lay back watching it
lazily float away with the rivers flow, again thinking. "So
why do you think we can do this?" she says smiling that
enigmatic Romilly smile. I tell her again about my
internet research but she doesn't seem convinced. "How
about God?" she smiles. "Isn't that a bit more in your
parent's field?" I say dismissively. They would love this
I think. I remember Romilly's mum taking away my
tarot cards as being ungodly. Well she hadn't admitted
it but they had disappeared right after one of her visits
to our flat in 1982. "Look I say you know how anti-
religious I am don't you? I watch her nodding her head.
The only god I worship is the god of no gods." "But
couldn't this be a religious experience?" She grins so I
know she is not being too serious. "Romilly I know this

is not religious babe so stop winding me up will you ya wally." The sooner we get rid of religion, the better for mankind I think. The sooner we get to lose the priests and the mullahs and realise we have our destiny in our own hands and not the one dictated to us by men in black the better. I despise them all with a passion. They are stifling the human race with their false promises and lies. "I know Matt you know I feel the same. God only exists to let us down with weak excuses." she smiles. We stand up and my arm goes easily around her shoulders. Let's see what's happening inside eh. See what the band is like tonight? Romilly is wearing a lovely knee length blue dress, blue T-shirt and sandals, showing her lovely slim legs off to the best advantage. I'm in my usual scruffy blue jeans and I laugh at a remark she had said earlier. We were at the Nags Head pub having a beer and I'm getting the drinks in at the bar and wondering why she's looking at me lewdly and grinning. I ask her why as I bring the drinks back. "Cos you have such a sexy ass Spears." she grins cheekily. I sit down feeling contented. Rightly so.

Time for a mad Saturday night in The Three Ways, some local band is playing and we mingle listening to them, some pretty bland stuff I can't help noticing. They are trying to be cool playing their version of modern Jazz, badly I think. I watch as Romilly circulates, her ready smile making people laugh wherever she goes and I feel such pride that she's my lady. My mind goes back to our old past and I remember that I missed all this the first time around or at least I did not appreciate it back then, it's amazing what you miss first time around I think to myself. I grab us a seat in a corner after getting us drinks and sipping my nice cold pint think back about to the things we had said about religion. I knew I was certain that this was not a religious experience. No way. I suppose my view of religion is that it is just a throwback to our primitive times when we lived in caves. A caveman's fear of the world around him and especially fear of the dark in a prehistoric world, a thunderstorm could be so easily explained as the gods being angry. And so the priests were born. You must make offerings to the gods or you will die they say and next thing we get from our self appointed priests is, we are gods representatives on earth you will follow our rules or else the crops won't grow and you will all die the death of a thousand boils. What a load of bullshit. Why can't we just lose this superstitious nonsense? There is no god, never was and never will be. I'm not saying there is not a superior being of some sort, I like to keep an open mind but of one thing I am certain. He is not the god of the Bible or the Koran. That is all stuff of childlike superstition. To me the tooth fairy or Santa is as likely as any religious god. Another thing I am certain of is that I place all forms of religion up there on a par with Nazism or tyrannies of any kind. Ask yourself who has killed the most people to prove their superiority and I think Hitler's slaughter palls into insignificance compared to the Catholic Church or Islam's excesses. The sooner we grow out of them all the better it will be. But we humans can be so gullible. Something as innocent as our daily Sun telling us what it thinks so soon turns into our government sponsored Sun telling us what we should think and before long its good old pogrom time again. The men in black always get their way. First it's the outsiders, the immigrants, then the Jews, next the rebellious and young people who don't conform. Eradicate them and next on the men in blacks list are the free thinkers. That's me and you. Don't tell me you haven't been warned as its happening right now. Just look at all the troubles in the world now and think of how many are caused by pathetic religious beliefs.

Romilly slides into the seat beside me and pointing her finger at my almost empty glass says, "Time for another babe?" "Yea go on then spoil me, I grimace, get me drunk why don't ya so you can have your wicked way with my young innocent body later." I feel the wetness draining through my jeans where she has poured the remains of my pint over my crotch and I think proudly, "Oh shit, what a woman" as she avoids my grabbing hand and goes to the bar smirking gleefully back over her shoulder at me to fetch us a refill. I stick my tongue out at her.

The rest of the evening we sit and listen to the music and talked to old friends, Snonky Eebie, Bazza, Mouse, Pete, Ian, and Mick P. They all came and went that memory filled night. The beer even made the music sound better I must admit. It was just a mad carousel of friends and pints, total madness, a smoke filled anarchy but so uplifting as all night I had Romilly beside me whispering lovely things to me and laughing at my stupid jokes. Holding my hand and running her delicate fingers along my thigh, kissing my ear. THIS was the real spiritual experience I thought to myself, total love between a man and his woman; it beats any god you care to name hands down. But eventually last orders come and so it's time for us to leave. "Am I taking you home?" I say." "Only if we can stop on the way for me to ravish your sweet innocent body." She giggles and her face is so alive with the lovelight in her eyes for me. We prepare to leave but not before I pour the remains of my last pint into her lap. "You bastard she squeals laughing, I want a divorce right now." "Tough, I say, we aint even married yet." We leave The Three Ways arm in arm together in our new past.

Chapter 17. First Day of the Holiday.

Up early Saturday morning we take the train to Cambridge, and after several changes we arrive at Reedham where we have about a miles walk to the boatyard and there she is. Our boat and floating home for our week together. She is called Sandpiper and it is the first time Romilly and I had spent a whole week together alone in our relationship. First time around I remembered that the week had its ups and downs including many arguments; we ended up splitting even for a while although we were soon back together again. But this time I had decided I wanted to find out why Romilly was so guarded about her future and why she wanted to leave it behind forever. But for our first day I resolved to say nothing about it and just have great fun together. We stopped at a restaurant near Acle that night and had a lovely meal of fresh Lowestoft fish and chips. "Well Rommy I joked, at least we got here without you shipwrecking us. Your boat handling skills leave much to be desired you know." I ducked to dodge the chip flying in my direction. "Bugger off Spears, she grinned, at least I got us here in one piece didn't I and still remarkably sober too." "Well its traditional to splice the mainbrace on the first day aboard." I replied with a mock drunken slur. "I'll splice something in a minute if you even think of eating your peas with that knife, she laughs and what the hell is a mainbrace anyway?" "Its nautical talk, I say, you landlubbers wouldn't understand it." I proceed to eat my peas with my fingers and 5 seconds later I am nursing a bruised shin from Romilly's well aimed kick. "Medic I cry, I think it's broken. Fetch me whisky at once." "Stop whining before I keelhaul you." says Romilly dissolving into laughter, but I did at least get my whisky. The rest of that evening passed that way, laughing, joking and generally having a wonderful time as we sat there our fingers entwined across the white linen tablecloth. Could things get any better? Romilly's eyes danced in the reflected glow of the candles on our table. So full of life and her love for me. She wore a simple yellow and white dress with a matching band in her hair and I told her I had never ever seen a woman look as beautiful as she did right then. Her eyes started to fill with tears as she said to me, "And no-one makes me feel as beautiful as you do. I love you so much Matt." I reached out across the table to stroke her cheek and wipe a tear away. "Time to get back don't you think Rommy." I helped her with her coat and we strolled back to our boat arm in arm stopping every two minutes to kiss in the cool night air feeling like a couple of kids on a first date.

I watched Romilly as she slept next to me that night. We had made love before she slept and I could still smell the musk of our lovemaking in the small double bed. Her sweet face was surrounded by her tousled hair and she looked so beautiful. She wore no makeup and her eyes tightly shut, she would occasionally stir and a small murmur would escape her lips. She pulled closer to me, her leg draping its way over mine and snuggling up against me and her hand twitched against my chest. I listened as she slipped into a deeper sleep while I watched her and her breathing deepened, I could see the moon outside, full and almost ghostly, a silver orb shining down on us as the river gently rocked the boat. I listened to the night sounds outside, water lapping against the boats side, the plop of a water vole as it entered the river hunting for its food, the hoot of an owl far away, and I wondered how anybody could be happier than me at that moment. I felt such feelings of tenderness and emotion towards this woman beside me. MY Romilly. My future wife. I knew then how true unquestioning love for a person could feel, the sheer heartbursting feeling that this was the person you wanted to spend your whole life with. The one person who's being with you made you so complete, two sides of the same coin as it were. I don't know how long I lay there watching her sleep beside me but eventually the moon set leaving us in darkness and the sounds quietened apart from the flow of the river against the boat, but still I lay awake for a while listening to her rhythmic breathing and feeling her toasty warmth against me, till I too passed into a deep and dreamless sleep myself, her small hand in mine.

I awake to pain. Romilly is shouting at me and pulling my hair. I am immediately awake and notice through my pain that there is a faint hint of dawn outside. A slight lightening in the sky. Romilly is swearing at me horribly and pulling my hair at the same time as she is trying to push me out of bed with her legs. She seems possessed, and I see tears running from her closed eyes as she fights me in her sleep. I push her onto her back as she tries to bite my shoulder, her teeth bared like an animal. I get my arms around her to stop her now flailing fists from connecting with me, then holding her tightly I try to calm her. I whisper over and over that I love her and I need her, and eventually she calms and seemingly awake for a while she looks at me in surprise then starts to sob uncontrollably. "Shhhhh my baby, it's only a dream, I'm here with you. You are safe." As soon as I let her go her arms shoot out around me and pull me tight against her as if she is afraid I will leave her alone in the dark. "Shhhhh, I whisper again, I'm always here with you, never going to leave you ever again." And I watch as she drifts off to sleep again as the sky lightens wondering fearfully about what had just happened. But I eventually fell asleep myself and we spent the rest of that night peacefully.

Chapter 18. Loddon.

I awoke the next morning to the sound of a commotion in the kitchen area of the boat. Pans and crockery were rattling and I could smell bacon cooking. I yawned and tried to fart quietly but failed. A head appeared around the door. "Thank you for that, said Romilly sniffing and pulling a face." "Sorry about that, I said smiling, is that breakfast I can hear you cooking or are you merely trying to wake me up by dismantling the engine out there? "Yes it's breakfast and if you are not up in two minutes I'm feeding it to the ducks." "I'll report you to the RSPCA, I cackle, they can get pretty pissed off if you try to sink their ducks you know." My cowboy boot comes flying through the doorway narrowly missing my most tender area. I take the hint and throwing on last night's shirt I step into the kitchen/dining area. I kiss Romilly and notice she has gone to a lot of trouble with breakfast. Two plates of bacon, eggs, fried bread and mushrooms sit on the table, between them a flower in a glass. "Awww you are so sweet" I say sitting down to tuck in. Beside my plate is a card. "It's not my birthday is it?" I say a surprised look on my face. "Open it stoopid." she laughs ruffling my hair with her fingers. Stuffing a forkful of bacon into my mouth I open the card. To my dearest Matt, it says, thank you for the most wonderful time of my life. It was signed Your Romilly. I almost choke on my bacon as tears start to flow from my eyes. Damn another paradox, why do we cry when we are deliriously happy? Perhaps sadness and joy are close relations, I know I've had both with Romilly. She hugs me and wipes my tears away with a hankie. "Eat your breakfast babe, it'll go cold" So I obeyed and it was delicious. I think about her nightmare that morning but decide not to mention it to her; she probably doesn't remember it anyway.

After washing up we take our tea back to bed and make love, there's no mad thrashing, and no wild sex just gentle caring lovemaking. A wonderful enjoyment of each other's bodies together, more kissing and caressing than anything else, words of love and commitment and joy. We are totally together in the foreign land of our past. We lay there afterwards in a warm glow and I tell her how I feel and start to plan our day. I tell her how lovely she looks to me laying there in a warm glow. She laughs impishly, "More like laying in the wet patch again Spears. Bloody men." I decide to teach Romilly about boating that morning being of a nautical disposition and so we shower and dress and make ready to cast off. "Before we sail off into the wild blue yonder Romilly I need to teach you a few nautical terms." I say. "OK m'dear I'm all ears." she says cheekily. "Right me hearty, I say pointing, that bit of boat at the front is called the sharp end." Turning round I point to the back and say" And us old sea dogs do be calling that bit the blunt end me hearty." Romilly advances towards me with a wicked smile on her face. "The old seadog looks a bit hot, she says, perhaps he might like an early morning dip in the briny eh?" "OK shipmate, I smile, backing away towards the cockpit, enough nautical lessons for one day, lets cast off for new lands." " You cast off, I'll drive." she says. I groan loudly and start untying the boat.

We cruise the river for a few hours before the clouds come over and it starts to rain. I'm having my turn steering the good ship Sandpiper, and with the rain getting heavier we pull up the awning. "Best make for sunnier climes shipmate." I laugh, and so we head to Loddon. Loddon is at the source of the River Chet and as we can go no further we moor up for the day. It seems that as soon as we do the clouds lift and the sun starts to shine down warmly on us. "Break out the grog." I cry happily seeing as we haven't wrecked the

Sandpiper with a little too fast an approach to the mooring. "Righto Skipper shouts Romilly, All hands on deck." We enjoy a chilled can of beer each and then I decide to take a swim in the river and stripping down to my boxers I dive in gracefully; well Ok to be honest it's a belly flop. "Turd at 4 o'clock shouts Romilly pointing wildly behind me. "Dammit where I shout back?" I doggy paddle and look around expecting to see a floater in my vicinity. "You git." I say when I realise she is having me on again. The wicked cow has successfully wound me up again I think and that deserves revenge. I doggy paddle beside the boat looking up at Romilly. She is sitting on the side of the boat in her black bikini covered by a horrendous check shirt, her legs dangling over the boats side. She is looking down at me and laughing fit to bust a gut. I lower my hand below the water and splash her. "Spears you are a bastard." she laughs and then I grab her ankle and before she can pull away I drag her into the river with a squeal followed by a large splash. She surfaces in front of me and spits river water at me. "You are going to die for that Spears." she laughs before I put my hand on her head and duck her under the surface. She looks so gorgeously sexy with her wet hair around her shoulders and I pull her to me and kiss her, bobbing together in the warm river water. I feel her hand inside my boxers and I rise to the aquatic occasion and ease her wet shirt open then her bikini up to reveal her lovely breasts, but we hear the throb of a boats engine approaching. "Damn!" I say pulling her bikini down again. A boat appears behind us and we hold on to the Sandpiper watching it trying to moor up. It's a young family. Mum Dad and two young kids. We watch them for a minute and it becomes obvious that they are having problems mooring up so I exit the river to give them a hand. I take the fore rope that the woman throws me and tie it to a mooring point then squatting again I tie the rear line up. "Ok, I say, you are secure." and wonder why they are looking at me in a strange way. I return to Sandpiper to see Romilly laughing her head off at me, tears of laughter on her face. "What's up?" I say mystified. "Check below decks shipmate." she giggles looking down at my nether regions. My boxers are wide open where she had undone the two buttons in the river and I have just treated the unsuspecting family to an unsurpassed view of my wedding tackle as I helped them tie up their boat. "Oh shit." I think. Romilly is absolutely cracking up by now; the tears are rolling down her cheeks. "I think you are in with the Mum." she laughs. I go below to hide my embarrassment.

Chapter 19. In the Pub.

After I get over the embarrassment of flashing to the young family in the next boat we get showered and get ready for the bright lights of Loddon. It's a sleepy little town, lots of pubs but we eventually settle on a nice friendly little hostelry and settle in for the night. A jukebox, a dartboard and some old Norfolk boys playing dominoes. Romilly is still taking the piss about my flashing of the family jewels to the young family, but I take it in good humour asking her if she really thinks I could be Ok with the mum? This comment of course earns me a good natured slap from Romilly and we soon get chatting to a few locals and we are having a great night. I can see the locals are captivated by her ready smile and chat. I'm talking to some guy who spent time in the Fleet Air Arm. I did the same in the very early 1970s. Three years of extreme drinking and servicing Her Majesties' helicopters and a few wrens too along the way. Great times the 70s I think. Romilly has got involved with a couple of local lads in a dart match. I know about her experience at darts and duck as one flies past narrowly missing my head. "For Christ's sake be careful ya dipstick." I say smiling thinking she's as bad as Elaine with the arrows. The Fleet Air Arm guy introduces me to his Dad, an ex naval man too. He has to be 80 at least and we have a good giggle together telling each other old sea stories. My new friend nudges me and tells me to watch out for my girlfriend. Shit, my attention has wandered for a moment as I talked to them and I excuse myself quickly. Romilly has gone to the loo and the two local lads have followed her out probably mistaking her friendliness for a come on. I go out towards the toilets and I see her. The bastard is holding her against the wall trying to get his hand inside her shirt. Romilly is trying to laugh it off but I can see she is getting a little out of her depth. The pratt is trying to force his knee between her legs so he is not paying too much attention to me. "Cummon darling, he is saying drunkenly. Just a little feel of your tits. You know you want to." I can hear his mate laughing from the toilet. "Don't worry. She's up for it mate. he says, Wait I'll be there in a tick to join in the fun." I walk quietly up behind the first guy and punch him sharply in the kidneys, Romilly helps by kneeing him on the way down. He drops like a stone as I knew he would and his mate walks out zipping himself up. "Your mate looks a bit sick I say." As he looks over at his friend I turn and kick him in the bollucks. His eyes bulge and he sags to the floor groaning and holding his balls. "You alright Babe?" I say pulling Romilly away from them. "Yea I'm good, she smiles, lucky you came out then though." I open my wallet and pass her a fiver. "Get the beers in will you Rommy; me and the boys here need a quiet little chat. I say. I'll be through in a minute."

She goes to get the beers in and I drag asshole number one up from the floor. He is crying in pain and I tell him that he doesn't mess with my woman if he knows what is best for him. He seems to agree so I let him collapse on the floor again. Asshole number two tries to slug me when I drag him up, so avoiding his wild swing I give him a little reminder by way of a little tap on the chin. His lip is now bleeding as I remind him to be a gentleman with my woman, and I let him sag to the floor to join his mate. I stand there leaning against the wall watching them and light a cigarette. Asshole number two looks up at me, blood on his face. I flick my ash and look back at him. "About time you were leaving I think don't you unless of course you disagree?" He and his mate help each other up and exit as quickly as they can from the rear entrance of the pub. Its life I think to myself, you stand up for your friends or you get the piss taken out of you. I join Romilly back in the bar. "Everything Ok Matt?" she asks me, a worried look on her face. "Yep we're good

Rommy, the boys decided it was past their bedtime and they decided to go home."

Apart from my little chat with the boys we had a great night and we leave the pub about 11:00pm. I take her hand and we walk back to the boat. I keep a weather eye out for our friends from earlier in case they try to jump us on the way back to the boat but all is quiet. They seem to have learned their lesson. We leave our clothes outside the bedroom area. I pick her beautiful small body up and carry her into the bedroom. My earlier violence seems to have aroused her and we make love with such passion, with her calling my name out as I whisper in her ear about how much I need her. How much I want her. How much I am looking forward to her being my wife. We climax together tight in each other's arms, her lovely legs wrapped around me trying to pull me deeper into her. And that's how we fall asleep. Locked tightly together, in a sweaty ball of bodies and bed sheets kicked awry. Her breathing is getting slower in my ear as she relaxes into a gentle sleep murmuring "I love you Matt" one last time before she drifts off.

Chapter 20. Getting Romilly Drunk.

About 3:30 in the morning I awaken to hear the rain pattering on the Sandpiper's roof just as she starts to have another of her nightmares. I am dozing and still holding her close when she sits up with a jolt. Her eyes are closed and her legs start kicking me and trying to push me away from her. She starts telling me to go to hell and tries to grab my face and bite me. I hold her close and stroke her hair. She struggles like a wild animal seeking escape from a trap but I talk to her quietly, running my fingers softly through her sweat soaked hair and eventually she settles down again, her struggles stop and a look of calm replaces the crazed hostility on her face. She falls into a more peaceful sleep again squeezing me tight. I lay there listening to the quiet of the dark night apart from the occasional pitter-patter of the rain on the roof and wonder what is causing her these nightmares. Is it a symptom of our crossing over to this timeline? If it were then surely I would be having them too, wouldn't I? But as far as I knew I was sleeping perfectly soundly at nights. I gently unwrap her arms from me. She stirs a little and murmurs something incoherent, trying to pull me back, but eventually she sighs softly in sleep and rolls over on her tummy allowing me to release myself. I go out onto the Sandpiper's deck after throwing a shirt and shorts on and sit on the edge of the boat as the sky lightens to the east. I light a cigarette in the pre-dawn light and drinking coke from the bottle I think about her nightmares. It really hurts me to see the pain and savagery in her face when she has them. I think I have ruled out any psychological effect of our travelling across, but if it's not that then what? It can't be unhappiness at how we are now. This is probably the happiest we have ever been together. Life is just so damned good here together for us, we both feel the same about that. In fact earlier she had said she wished we could spend the rest of our lives together back in 1981 just cruising on our little Sandpiper forever. I had agreed wholeheartedly. Our current life just seemed to be so close to perfection together so what was causing her these bad nights? I emptied the coke and lit another cigarette. The sun was appearing now above the trees on the opposite side of the river and I could hear cars passing by on the nearby road. A white phalanx of beautiful swans with their cygnets cruised by me gracefully, looking hopefully for some bread I might throw them. I went down into the kitchen and raked out a few slices after checking Romilly was still sleeping soundly. She had shifted position since I left. She lay on her side now cuddling my pillow to her chest a small smile on her face. I kissed her cheek softly before I tip toed back up on to the deck and started breaking the bread to feed to the swans. They were soon joined by some ducks and a moorhen with some chicks all fighting for the tidbits of bread that I was throwing to them. I returned to my earlier worries about Romilly's bad dreams. So if it wasn't psychological or unhappiness about us it must be the something from her life in the 2007 future worrying her that she would not reveal to me. It had to be that. Why couldn't she just tell me? Could it so that terrible that she thought I would leave her because of it? Surely she knew she could trust me. Certainly she knew I loved her too much for that. Or did she? Maybe she wasn't sure of me after all. Perhaps all this perfection in our current life was not so perfect for her after all. The swans and ducks swam quietly away looking for more food donors when they realised I had exhausted my supply of bread. The moorhen and her chicks hung around a little longer before giving up hope and disappearing into the reeds of the opposite bank.

I went below and started breakfast for us deciding to try again later in the day for some kind of revelation from Romilly. Right! Full English I decided getting the eggs and bacon from the small fridge and putting the frying pan on the two ring hob. I actually made us quite a good breakfast I thought proudly as I took Romilly's into her. "Wake up sleepy head." I said as I entered the bedroom. Romilly's head was just visible above the sheets and I shook her gently. She slowly yawned and stretched. "Morning Spears and what have you been up to? Is that breakfast I can see before me?" "Yep I grinned. It's fairly edible too although the fried bread's a bit overdone." She sat up, still naked and looking beautiful to me in the early morning sunlight. I put the tray on her lap and told her. "Watch your boobs though, it's hot. I don't mind burned fried bread but I'm not too keen on burnt boobies you know." She playfully tries to slap me but she'll have to be quicker than that I tell her as I've been up longer and she's still half asleep. She starts to eat and asks if that was me she heard earlier on deck? "Yeah I was out chatting up some really nice birds." I grin. "Did you pull them then?" She looks at me innocently. "Yeah I did all right they were eating out of my hand." I reply. There's a twinkle in her eye as she asks me if I did alright by flashing my wedding tackle at them. "Seems to be your usual trick." she says the twinkle turning to merriment. "You cheeky git, I laugh, just wait till you get up. Your ass is grass young lady." I hear her chuckling to herself as I go out to make tea for us both.

I have planned the day while making the breakfast but it mostly involves getting Romilly pissed to try and prise her secret from her reluctant lips. The getting her pissed part won't be the hard job though I think. We set off early and cover quite a few miles along the river before lunchtime. We head back towards Reedham and find a nice little riverside pub to stop at for our lunch. I visit the nearby shop as Romilly gets ready for our meal. I top up our supplies. More bacon eggs bread and a few bottles of German white wine, some salad and some nice Norfolk ham. Returning to the Sandpiper I see Romilly has really made an effort. My heart almost stops beating when I see her. She is looking.... ravishing, simply ravishing. She is wearing a short white summer skirt, well above the knee and a simple low cut lilac top displaying her ample cleavage. Matching white high heeled shoes and just a touch of make-up, she looks stunning and I want to take her and make love to her there and then. She can read my mind and wags her finger at me laughing. "No way Spears. Not till later and anyway I want my dinner first you randy git." I put on a sad face and whimper pitifully. She grabs my arm and tells me. "Come on before I change my mind and lose out on my lunch."

The pub is lovely. Old roof beams and wooden furniture, there would be a roaring log fire if it wasn't a scorching hot day outside I think and we make for the bar to order our lunch. I get us a beer each as we wait and the landlady asks us if we want our meal indoors or out? We settle for an inside table as its cooler and I think to myself a lot handier for the bar too. We both have the homemade steak and kidney pie followed by apple pie and ice cream and I make sure her glass is kept well topped up throughout. The meal is delicious and as we leave I notice happily that Romilly is a little tipsy. We make our way back to the boat, Romilly laughing at everything and anything we pass. "Spears you bastard you've got me pissed, she laughs tripping over a tree root, if it's because you want my body then you are in luck you naughty boy." I help her on to the boat resisting very hard the urge to rip her clothes off there and then and make love to her. I have ulterior motives as I mentioned earlier. Making love would sober her up and that is not what I want, not at all. The Sandpiper is moored on a bend of the river amongst some beautiful old weeping willows and I pull the awning down so we can sit in the kitchen area 'al fresco' as it were. I sit her down and fetch the nicely chilled wine. I put the cassette player on. Something nice and laid back. Bob Dylan's 'Blood on the Tracks'. I fetch us two glasses and pour the wine. "Isn't this just perfect Matt? she asks me taking a large sip from the glass. I want this to last forever here with you. I just love you so bloody much." She leans against me and her hand is unbuttoning my shirt as she looks expectantly at me. I can see the swell of her gorgeous breasts under her low cut top and her lips brush mine gently. Now this is the hardest thing I have ever done but I resist the urge to return her caresses and leaning back I say, "No let's just talk for a while Rommy." She looks disappointed but sits back and slurs "Ok I don't mind. What about?" I top her glass up and tell her. "How about us? More specifically how about you." She looks at me a bit warily but then shrugs and says "Ok." I light us cigarettes and place hers between those Oh so inviting moist lips."Tell me about your husband, I say, and why did you divorce?" I think the liberal measures of booze I have been giving her have worked as she starts to tell me about her life after leaving me for the first time. Haltingly at first but then she grows more confident. I suppose I hear what I had expected all along. She wanted to forget me after leaving and start a new life and before she could think she had met him married him and given him his expected children to order. Before she knew it her life had lost a lot of its sparkle. But she took to motherhood and the husband made his way up in the world. She was content with motherhood but in the back of her mind something was always missing. She wasn't unhappy just something wasn't there. I keep her wine glass topped up as she continues sadly. I suppose she thought she had found the end of the rainbow only to discover there was no pot of gold awaiting her there. Probably the husband felt the same way as well. His lovely little Rommy at home with the kids while he is out in the world making a name for himself. But isn't there more to life. And so they both look for the 'More to Life'. I know the feeling myself only too well I think. So eventually the loving died to be replaced by acceptance and happy diversions. They had comfortable lives. Privileged even I suppose. The husband is doing very well. Material comforts. Education for the kids but yet still something was missing. That old 'Pot of Gold' I think. And then the husband goes too far one day and finds another easy going little wife. Blonde like Romilly. Beautiful like Romilly. But younger unlike Romilly. Oh well she thinks after the divorce. Life isn't too bad, I get the kids and the alimony and I'm free again. Life goes on. Till you realise you have a boring repetitive life of young lovers and evening cocktails becoming afternoon cocktails. Then the solicitor's letter from the husband seeking custody of the children for a lovely new wife. A barren lovely new wife. Now I know Romilly is a fighter. Always has been and she fights, but the wrong way, probably the same as I would. The husband starts a custody battle for the kids and she falls apart. Meanwhile has she totally forgotten me? I could be dishonest and say I was always in her mind but it's obvious that I wasn't. I was long forgotten. A barely remembered memory. That rebellious little shit she used to be married to. The occasional moment or snatch of a song might remind her of me but nothing more. Nothing more than a teenage memory to a nearly forty year old woman. I'm sad but I understand. Its life it happens. I was older and so the memories of her lingered on with me. I never forgot her. Always thought of her. Always have Always will I think sadly.

I notice the silence and looking at Romilly I see she has fallen asleep probably from the effects of the drink. Her hand has found its way into mine and I help her up and take her to bed. All of the urge has left me now.

She just looks like a poor sad misunderstood child now to me and I feel such sadness for her and for me as well. But for all she has told me I think it isn't reason for her nightmares. Even though my alcoholic version of the truth drug hasn't given me the whole truth I think sadly. There's just not enough there for her nightmares. There must be something more. Had to be I think sadly. She just isn't telling me the whole truth.

I have been holding off the on the alcohol that day with my plan to interrogate Romilly but now I hit it with a vengeance in my unhappiness. I get the scotch out to start some serious drinking. I just don't know what else to do. I have tried everything. The sky starts to cloud over and a few drops of rain start falling so I pull the boats awning up again and sit alone at the kitchen table. Romilly is flat out on the bed snoring lightly when I look in on her. Why the hell won't she tell me I think for the hundredth time at least. I leave her and go back to sit at the table. The rain is lashing down now and I continue with the scotch my mood sinking lower by the minute. I put the Bob Dylan tape on again. I totally missed it the first time around. As the afternoon passes by I must pass out from the scotch and an overdose of melancholia, but I am awakened by Romilly shaking me. "Matt wake up. Come on darling. Wake up please." I stagger uncertainly to the door and throw up over the boats side. I have a stupid thought and look round at Romilly who is rubbing my back. "Will the ducks eat it I ask as my vomit floats off along the river." "Not unless they want to get monumentally pissed." she smiles. An old couple are walking their dog along the riverbank as I continue dry retching into the river." It's Ok, Romilly assures them, I think he has eaten something that disagreed with him." The dog, a small black poodle, barks at me but they just continue their stroll ignoring us politely. The sun is setting, a gorgeous red orb over the reeds to the back of us and I ask Romilly the time.

"Nine o'clock." she tells me. "Damn the last thing I remember it was pissing down." I say.

"I suppose that getting me tipsy was your pathetic attempt to pump me about my future? She lights us cigarettes as I finally finish retching. You are just so obvious Spears, she laughs passing me the cigarette, it might have worked in the real 1981 but not now." Romilly was always the brighter of us two and I nod sadly. "Was worth a try though don't you think?" I say inhaling the smoke. "But why do you keep trying when I told you that I will tell you when I am ready?" She goes and puts the kettle on and spoons ample measures of coffee into two mugs. I sit quietly smoking my cigarette and she puts two mugs of steaming elixir on the table. I'm still pissed and scald my mouth taking a sip. "Ok, I begin, you probably think I am doing this out of curiosity or something but I see the nightmares you have been having for the last couple of nights. I am suffering with them too you know. I still have the scars, and I show her the marks on my shoulder where she fought me in bed that morning in her last nightmare, believe it or not I think we have been offered a unique opportunity here to actually start our lives again and I am so very grateful for that. Who wouldn't be? But I have had to deal with your nightmares now Romilly. I see the fear in your face and it hurts me so badly. Romilly finds my hand and squeezes it. I don't know what is causing them and don't deny that you are having them Ok? I know that you have to let me know what is causing them before we can ever have a chance of happiness here. I can't marry you with this hanging over us don't you see? I am so sorry."

As we have sat there talking the night has almost come and I put the light on. She is sitting there hands together in her lap, her coffee undrunk in front of her. I can hear the old couple walking past on the return from their evening walk as the dog yaps at our boat on its way past. I sit down next to her and lifting her face I stroke her soft cheek with my hand. "For Christ's sake Romilly I am doing this because I love you darling. Why can't you see that?" She kisses my thumb as it caresses her lips and looks back at me sadly. "I know you are Matt but if I told you then you would leave me I know. I know you care for me and want to help me. But I have to be totally sure of you before I tell you. You cannot imagine how bad it is and yes I know I do get the nightmares, I've been having them ever since I first came back here to 1981 not just with you and I know what causes them but I hope they will go eventually. I am sure that being back here with you will cure them." She looks sadly at me and slowly lifts her left hand and pulls the engagement ring off. "This is yours I think." she tells me handing it to me. I take it in my open hand and wrap it in my hand; it is warm from her finger still. Then she stands up and pouring her coffee down the sink she heads off to the bedroom in tears.

As I sit there finishing the coffee she made me I hear her moving about in the small bedroom as she gets ready for bed. I can see that I have drunk almost three quarters of the scotch but I feel relatively sober now and pour a large one into the last of my coffee and go outside to sit on the end of the boat. I kick off my shoes and socks and dangle my feet in the river thinking about her. Perhaps I should return to my 2007 timeline and forget all this 1981 nonsense. Forget it even happened? But the cool river water flowing against my feet reminds me that this is real. Not a dream. Not a hallucination. It is real. So real. More than my life in 2007 is. How could I forget it? So I pour the whiskey and cold coffee into the river and go back inside the boat and lock the door. I turn off the light and enter the bedroom in darkness. Sitting on the edge of the bed I dry my feet on my jeans and strip off my clothes.

Climbing quietly in bed beside her I put my arm around her. She feels so warm. Her back is toward me and I kiss it and then the back of her neck. I can feel she is naked under the covers and my hand moves around to stroke her tummy. She turns her face to me in the dark and kisses my cheek a small sigh escaping her lips. I feel for her face and pull her lips to mine and kiss her hungrily. I start to kiss her all over. Her face and neck and ears. Then her breasts and tummy. Then her legs and calves and feet. "I love you Romilly." I tell her. I kiss her toes and then her fingers. "I love you so much." I tell her. Then I kiss her lips again. I run my fingers lightly over her stomach and down between her legs. She opens them slightly and I spend time running my fingers through the soft hair there before stroking her so intimately there. I insert my finger tip into the wetness stimulating her gently for a while and then raising my finger to my mouth I kiss her wetness from my finger and put it between her lips. She runs her tongue over my finger tasting herself on me. "I love you Romilly and nothing will ever end that. Do you understand that?" I feel her head nod yes in the darkness. She feels my hardness against her leg and slowly and deliberately opens her legs more for me. I enter her so slowly feeling every millimetre of myself entering her as her arms wrap around my neck, taking my tongue into her mouth she bites it gently and nibbles my lips. "Just never ever leave me." She whispers in my ear. "You know I couldn't." I whisper back. We lay there kissing each other with my hardness deep in her and I feel her internal muscles caressing my manhood gently like small lips kissing me there so intimately. I raise myself above her, my hands resting on the bed either side of her head, and slowly make love to her. Her slim legs wrap around my back as I lower myself and kiss her lips again pushing my tongue into her mouth in time with my pelvic thrusts. I am sure I see fireworks as I reach my orgasm at the same time that she does. Romilly never ceases to amaze me. Every time we make love it is like the first time all over again and we lay there afterwards totally spent, me holding her to me tightly in the darkness of the boat. As we drift off to sleep together I tell her again that I love her and I can almost see the smile on her face as she says "And I will love you always too Spears." "Look. I tell her softly in the dark of our boat. I think you need this, hold out your left hand." She does so and I slide the ring back over her finger and holding her finger I kiss it and the ring. She starts to speak but I put my fingers to her lips to stop her. "Just three words Ok Romilly. I love you. Totally." I feel her arms around me pulling me closer to her and she kisses my lips before saying. "That's four words you fool."

Chapter 21. Last Night on the Sandpiper and Alan.

The final night of the holiday came too soon. We were sad at the holiday's imminent finish but decided to have one last meal out and as we were back in Reedham we found a nice little pub and settled in for our meal. Romilly and I just wore jeans, hers with a plain pink T-shirt and me with my loud red checked shirt. We had fish and chips again as we had on the first night in Acle and talked about the holiday and our future life together in our new 1981. "Romilly I just hope we don't make the same mistakes again sweetheart." I say holding her hand across the table. "Naaa Spears we will be Ok just have faith yeah?" We laughed about our wonderful days aboard the Sandpiper and even the night in Loddon with the local lads getting a little bit too frisky. "We sorted them though didn't we Matt. What a team we make eh? Just you and me together." I squeeze her hand gently and tell her. "That we do mate." It had been a lovely last night but it came to an end eventually and we returned for our final night on the Sandpiper together. We had already packed earlier on and so we sat there for a last hour just holding hands and talking of the things that lovers talk of together while sharing a glass of white wine. Then it's time for bed as Rommy starts to yawn tiredly. I know I am shattered as well especially after a week of broken night's sleep due to Romilly's nightmares and so we fall into bed together. We don't even make love that night due to our tiredness and I think that I was asleep before my head even hit the pillow. But joy of joys. That night was the first of the holiday that I wasn't disturbed by one of Romilly's terrible dreams. Perhaps they were coming to an end after all?

The holiday ends and we are more in love than ever and we are ready to plan our wedding, but I remember how badly our original 1981 holiday had ended but this one has been idyllic apart from her nightmares, and so we say goodbye to the Sandpiper, our own little Sandpiper, and with lots of sadness as we start our trudge to Reedham station for the journey back to Cardinals Stratford and our new reality. And that night I return to 2007 again.

It's a lovely afternoon back in 2007 and so I take Pepper for a walk down to the park. So I'm sitting in the little bit of park near the house. Pepper is sitting with me his tongue lolling out in the heat of the afternoon. I suppose I am thinking about the past as my mp3 player is playing an old Eagles album. 'Desperado' and I love it. I am trying to detach myself from all that is happening to me and I love just sitting back on the bench soaking up the rays. No pressure. A young couple walk past. I suppose they are in their late teens and I can see the love between them. They are so involved that they don't even notice me and my dog at first. Their love is so wonderful to watch. He has his arm around her waist and she is smiling into his eyes. I know what she is thinking and it is just Oh so beautiful to see their young love. His arm is around her protectively and they stop briefly to kiss. I can see the lovelight in their eyes and I have to hold my tears back at the beauty of the scene in front of me. The girl stops and bends down to stroke Pepper and the guy says Hi to me. Pepper loves the fuss being made of him as she strokes his head and ruffles his ears. "How old is he?" she asks. She looks so gorgeous and so innocent and I tell her he is only two. Her guy bends down to join her in making a fuss of my dog. "He's a lovely boy. We are looking for a dog as friendly as him." We talk for a while about dogs mostly before they stroll away arm in arm and I am left alone again with my thoughts.

I think sadly of our original holiday in the real 1981 and how we had broken up after the arguments. I even remembered telling my mum to tell Romilly that I wasn't there when she rang me that Saturday evening of our return. I had never done that before. I knew I had really wanted to talk to her but my sad 1981 self had just ignored her and so she found someone else because of my stupid stubbornness. I thought I was teaching her a lesson but instead good old Romilly taught me one. Oh yes she really taught me a lesson I thought. I remember the following Saturday after our holiday in the original 1981. My old mate Alan picked me up and straight away asked me where Romilly was. "We have split up." I tell him sadly. "Don't talk daft; he tells me, you two are so good together. You are made for each other." People were always telling me that it seemed in those days. I tell him it's over and to take us to the Crescent Moon. We need a good night out. So we get a little pissed on lagers washed down with neat gins in the Crescent Moon and then we end up in The Three Ways by 9 pm and my Romilly isn't there I notice sadly. By now the drink is starting to affect me and Alan tells me to cool it a down a little. Always a good mate was Alan. He was always a bit of a bad lad and we had done a few dodgy things together over the years and I remember with a smile a dark night in 1977 forcing our way into a local country vet's to nick the speed from the medicine cabinet. They use them I think to make male greyhounds sexy and ready to mate he had told me but I laughed and told him I thought he was talking bollucks as I knew speed had the opposite effect on me. He acted as look out as I forced the window trying not to make too much noise and wake the neighbours. But it was mostly good stuff together. I always had taken him as a pussycat but that night he surprised me completely. Good old Alan. Good old pal. I was getting close to the state known as legless and was chatting up an old flame in The Three Ways entrance lobby. Alan came out and I smile at him as I am chatting up a rather luscious looking and willing old girlfriend. Lesley I remember her name was. I know I am on a certainty as she whispers in my ear that she will see me back at hers later if I want, her hand stroking my shoulder.

Alan walks out and sees what is happening and smiles at me it seems in collaboration but the next thing I am seeing stars. He has slugged me one, the bastard and I am lying on my back with the lovely Lesley beside me screaming at Alan to leave me alone. He pushes her away and kneels beside me. "You are a stupid shit he tells me. If I had a chance with Romilly I would take it and yet you...Yes you are pushing her away you fucking twat." I can feel my nose pumping blood and try to hit him back but he grabs my fist. "Listen to me he tells me. That girl loves you and yet you push her away you asshole. Now you sort yourself out before you lose her Ok?" I am left laying on the foyer floor with the taste of blood in my mouth and a sobbing Lesley beside me trying to ease the blood flow with some toilet paper. I'm feeling groggy but I ease myself up and go back into the bar, Alan hands me a pint and I smile at him. "Am I that much of a pratt I ask him?" "Oh yes. Most definitely" he tells me. And then Romilly comes into the bar. I had never seen her like that before, she looked so self assured and confident. She nods Hi to me and Alan and goes to the bar sitting on a free stool and accepting a drink from the landlord. She is wearing a smart black skirt and a new silky blue blouse. A new black jacket is draped over her shoulder and she is wearing high heeled shoes and looks so beautiful. "Fuck her." I tell Alan belligerently. "So do you want to lose her? Do you?" He asks me. "I don't care." I reply but he grabs me by the shirt and looks into my face. "You are going to if you carry on." he warns me. And I see her at the bar; her lovely slim legs crossed as she is talking to the barman and laughing. I suppose then that I saw the light and got up.

So I go up to the bar and stand in front of her unsteadily. "Hiya." she says uncertainly. I'm still a little drunk although the punch I took from Alan has sobered me up considerably. I lean forward to kiss her but she pushes me away. "I thought we were finished Matt. I've got a new boyfriend now." she tells me looking around uncertainly. "So who is he?" I ask her. "Why do you care? she replies. You wouldn't even take my calls." That old Romilly petulance shines through and it turns out she is with the landlord of The Three Ways. Now I was twenty seven then and ten years older than Romilly but he must have been in his forties at least, not particularly attractive but she told me that he treated her really nicely. "He's bought me loads of clothes too." she told me. I had asked her if it was all over between us and she smiled and told me evasively that I was the one who finished with her. "Ok Romilly I know I made a mistake. I know I am stupid. But if you want me back then, well. Oh shit Ok I love you and I'm asking you to forgive me." "And if I do then what am I going to tell him?" she replies. In the end she tells him nothing and we leave The Three Ways together with Alan and head out of town to Harbury. We kissed and made up in Alan's car on the way to a pub there with Alan looking on with a big grin on his face. Romilly seemed happy to be back with me and I know that I certainly was. As we sit down with our drinks Romilly asks if I've been scrapping as theirs blood on my shirt and I am wearing a sore nose as well. "This bastard decked me." I tell her pointing at Alan and laughing. She leans over and shakes Alan's hand. "Good for you Al, he deserved it." she laughs.

Two different worlds I think sitting back on that 2007 park bench with Pepper beside me remembering the original and the new 1981, two totally different worlds so alike but so very different. I sigh and get up to return home, the dog trudging along behind me.

Chapter 22. The Car Crash.

So far on our trips to 1981 much had been the same with our lives historically but that was all about to change that August evening. Romilly and I had enjoyed a nice evening out at a restaurant in Old Harbury. We had talked about our old lives in 1981 the first time around and we talked about our wedding plans while enjoying our meal of steak and chips washed down with a couple of cold lagers. It was cold and wet that night, the good weather we had been enjoying was a memory now as the rain teemed down, squalls of wind rattling the deluge against the restaurant windows. It seemed more like October than August. We left about 10:30 pm and I held Romilly close sheltering her as we ran across to the Cortina in the car park. I let her in first then ran around to get in the driver's side. "You're getting very gentlemanly in your old age Spears." she laughs her hair soaked by the rain and plastered to her face. "And you are looking disheveled but very beautiful Romilly." I say stroking the wet strands away from her eyes to kiss her. There is something about sitting in a car in the dark with the rain lashing down that I love so much, it makes me want to just lay back and listen to it and I have done that on a few occasions in the past. The music on but turned down low and the sound of the rain on the roof and the heater gently blowing warm air into the car. I just wanted to snuggle up to Romilly and enjoy that moment and I suggested it to her. "Awww you are so soppy Matt and so sweet too." she grinned sweetly at me and squeezing my hand she kissed me gently on my cheek. We lay back for a while to enjoy one of those personal magic moments together that were now so much a part of our relationship, just being close and holding hands was enough for us at that moment. Listening to the rain together, hands linked, fingers entwined.

After a while I sit up and say to her. "Oh well babe, I suppose we better leave while the windscreen wipers can still cope, and you need your beauty sleep too." I joke. She cuffed me gently on the cheek and laughed, "Well so much for the gentleman tonight then." "Yea I can't let you be having too much of a good thing now can I, I smiled, or else you'll expect it all the time from me and what a letdown that would be eh?" "She squeezed my leg enough to hurt and said, "Just get me home before I whack you ya wally." "Ok, you're the Boss." I replied to which she told me. "That's right and don't forget it my lad." I turned on the cassette player and put an old David Bowie tape on, and putting the windscreen wipers on full blast we turned out of the restaurant to make our way back to Cardinals Stratford in the pouring rain as Ziggy Stardust and his Spiders played softly on the stereo.

The rain didn't seem to want to ease up on the way home but we didn't mind, we were dry, in the warm and listening to great music. Then it happened, the unthinkable. We were just about a mile from Cardinals Stratford with the rain bouncing off the road ahead of us in the beams of the headlights, when a car pulled out in front of us from a side turning. Romilly screamed as I jerked the steering wheel hard to the right to avoid it and then seeing we were heading off the road I slammed on the brakes. The road was so flooded that the car just skidded and spun out of control and we shot across the road missing the car that had pulled out in front of us narrowly but careering down a bank by the opposite roadside. We hurtled out of control down the bank and I saw a tree in front of us then a came the terrible lurching bang as the car ploughed into it. The windscreen exploded into a million fragments as a bough of the tree punched through it narrowly missing us. And then silence apart from the rain which was lashing my face through the broken glass. My chest hurt terribly and I could hardly breathe, every intake of breath was agony. I looked around at Romilly but she was lying back in the car seat unmoving, blood streaking her beautiful face and the wind blowing her hair into disarray. I tried to reach out to her but a searing pain hit my chest. I sat back trying to ease the pain and I smelt the strong smell of petrol. I tried again to reach out to Romilly but the pain was excruciating. "Must get out of here." I muttered to myself and I started to struggle to undo our seat belts. My hands didn't seem to want to work properly and I think I passed out a couple of times briefly with the pain but the smell of petrol kept coming back to me forcing me back to a groggy consciousness. I finally managed with difficulty to undo our seat belts, but by now I could smell a strong electrical burning smell as well as the petrol fumes. I struggled to push open my door and I literally fell from the car into the mud, the rain lashing my face helping to keep me conscious. I could hardly stand but managed to drag myself around the car slowly to the passenger door. Come on Spears I said to myself you need to do this and quickly. I pulled myself upright against the front passenger door and tried to pull it open. It was stuck. Crumpled, my barely conscious mind noticed. I could see Romilly inside, her head back, eyes closed and a trickle of blood running down her face. The tree's branch had narrowly missed her though thankfully I noticed. I tried the door again but it was wedged shut tightly. Leaning against the car for steadiness I moved to the back door. It too was unopenable. Damn it's locked I thought. The smell of burning was stronger now, and I could hear the crackle of sparks as the rain continued to fall. I moved back to the front door and turning my back to the car I mustered all my strength and rammed my elbow back into the glass. Nothing. I tried again. Still nothing except a painful elbow but I tried a couple more times and at last it gave and smashed, showering Romilly in more glass. Sorry baby I thought. I reached my hand through the window and unlocked the back passenger door. Using the car for support I managed to drag the back door open and leaning across the back seat I pulled the front seat recliner lever so that Romilly's seat slowly lowered towards me. The pain was almost unendurable as I pulled her unconscious body out of her seat and out of the car through the back door, the smell of burning spurring me on. I pulled us both out into the mud and rain, the pain in my chest now so intense I could not stand. I crawled away from the car dragging Romilly through the mud on her back. I could see flames now licking around the car's interior and with a last effort I managed to pull us further from the car till we rolled down a small bank and I lay on top of her to protect her. I heard a muffled boom and saw the surrounding muddy grass light up with an orange glow as the petrol tank exploded. I could feel the wave of heat pass over us then the smell of burning hair and singed clothes. Looking back the car was now a fireball, barely recognisable. It lit up the wet night sky and I could hear the hiss of the rain landing in the fierce flames and feel the heat on my face. Looking down at Romilly's face I tenderly wiped the mud and blood from her and rested my cheek against hers. Her face was wet and so very cold. I could hear the sound of a siren in the distance, but all I could do was lay there in the slimy wet muddy grass cradling her small body in my arms and praying for the pain to stop. I heard voices and the sound of people running through the mud. Then all descended into darkness as I passed out.

Chapter 23. After the Car Crash in 2007.

I jolted awake in a cold sweat of fear. It was dark and I couldn't feel any pain. I felt my chest, it was Ok it seemed. Then the realisation that I was back in 2007 and totally uninjured hit me. I was in my lounge chair and panicking I fumbled for the light switch beside me. Switching it on I looked at the clock to see it was only 3 a.m. I had been back in 1981 for days but only about 4 hours had passed here. My half drunk glass of scotch was still beside me and my pack of cigarettes. I downed the scotch in one and lit a cigarette. Pulling deeply at the cigarette I poured another scotch to steady my panic attack. My shirt was soaked in sweat and I noticed my hands were trembling. What the hell had happened? I remembered the car wreck and dragging Romilly to safety and then no more after that. Oh my God had I died back there? Why had I been catapulted back so quickly I thought? I was frantic with worry about Romilly and I back in that muddy 1981 roadside field beside the burning Cortina. I swore loudly to myself and poured more whisky. For Christ's sake I must get back there now I implored the God that I didn't believe in, and make no bones about it I would have implored the Devil too if he would help to get me back this instant. I had never been pulled back this way before, so quickly and in the middle of the night. Something dreadful must have happened I thought as I remembered Romilly's cold wet lifeless face and the terrible pain that I had felt in my chest after the accident. I broke down in tears at that moment crying like I never have before. I thought the worst thoughts imaginable, that either Romilly or myself or both of us were lying dead in the aftermath of that terrible event. I just couldn't know, nothing like that had happened in the original 1981. Apart from a few minor shunts I had no major accidents back then. Another instance of our lives creating a totally new timeline and bearing less and less similarity to the old one with each days passing. But surely it couldn't all be over? Could it? Had it all been ruined by some bloody idiot pulling out in front of us on a cold rain swept night back in our new 1981? All our new hopes squandered in one blink of an eye.

I cried for a while longer, all the time swigging my scotch, but eventually the tears stopped and lighting another cigarette I lay back in my chair to try to sort out my situation. There was only one realistic thing I could do. I had to get back as soon as possible if I still could. It had been relatively easy lately to get to 1981 lately for me; just close my eyes relax my mind and sort of drift across was how I would explain it. But I had never returned before so quickly after a previous visit. It was 3.50 am so I had been back not even an hour yet, would it work? And the terrible thought that if I had died back there then I would never be able to go back again. The End? Finis? But I was too shaken up still to relax my mind and so I just sat there drinking my whisky and chain smoking one cigarette after another until I heard Elaine stirring upstairs and I gave up for the time being and decided to take the dog out for a walk to try to clear my mind a little. I shouted up to Elaine that she could have a lie-in while I took Pepper out for his early morning constitutional.

And so with my mouth tasting foul from the whisky and the smokes, I stepped out into a chilly but bright 2007 summer's morning. It was just after 6am and the birds were singing, the sky was blue and dotted with small white fluffy clouds and a light cool breeze was blowing from the East. It was so peaceful. Sunday morning and no-one about yet I thought gladly. I headed towards the top field, the dog seeming to want to stop and personally autograph every tree on the way. We walked for miles that morning me and Pepper.

Past fields full of that summer's golden wheat crop. Through woods so full of life, edged with bright summer flowers and pigeons cooing in the leafy tree tops. We passed a couple of young girls out on an early morning ride on their horses. I think they said hello but I was deep in thought and only realised after they had passed me by. We walked for almost three hours, getting home about 9am. Elaine was up and dressed. "You've been gone a while?" she said. "Yeah I needed to clear my head." I mumbled." I'm not surprised. Have you seen how much scotch you drunk? Nearly a whole bottle." she answers her own question. "Yeah sorry babe just got a lot on my mind at the moment." "Are you ok? She asks looking concerned. "Yeah I'll be Ok I just need some sleep" I answer. "Ok you go up to bed; I'll bring you a cuppa up in a minute."

I wake up at six that evening unhappily from a deep almost dreamless sleep. Just a few flashbacks of the crash. The skidding car, the bang as it hit the tree and the orange glow of the fire. Holding Romilly to protect her from the worst of it. But that was it. No visit, just a few dream memories. My tea from the morning is still on my bedside table untouched, its stone cold but I am parched and so I drink it in one. I've slept for over 8 hours so at least I feel refreshed. But almost at once the fear returns. Why have I not gone back yet? Did we die back there? Is it all over before it could begin? Lying on my side in bed I light a cigarette and try to get a grip of myself. It was as if I could hear Romilly telling me, "Spears for God's sake pull yourself together and sort this one out will you ya wally." "Ok Babe I will, don't worry." I found myself whispering to thin air.

Pulling on my dressing gown I stumbled downstairs, still only half awake. Elaine was sitting watching the T.V. "Haha it lives." she said sarcastically." "I need tea and right now." I groaned. "Ok Ok. Sit down pisshead

I'll make you one and your dinners in the microwave, its roast lamb." There was no way I could eat so I satisfied myself with the tea. "Look Matt, said Elaine, you are acting very strangely lately, what the hell is going on. Will you tell me if you have found someone else?" She takes of her glasses and polishes them slowly, awaiting my answer. What could I say? I had met my old love from 23 years ago in another timeline? I'm sorry babe I'm with an ex love from 1981? Naaa I had to stall. "No Elaine its work getting me down, I lied, I'm not sure if I want the responsibility and it's getting me down a bit." She looks at me for a while before turning back to the T.V. I sip my tea putting my feet up on the arm of the sofa. Elaine laughs at her programme then looks back at me. "Are you sure Matt only I've never seen you like this before?" "Don't worry babe I'll be ok." I smile weakly. I normally hate Elaine leaving me to go to bed so early but tonight I must admit I'm glad as she makes her excuses and goes to bed. But she looks around the door before leaving and says, "We have been together for 23 years Matt and I know when you are not being straight with me you know, and I think you are not telling me something. I just know it, Ok." Before I can answer she has gone and I relax back into my chair sighing.

I suppose I am in love with two women in two different realities and I do not want to hurt either of them I think finishing my tea. But my immediate problem is what happened back in 1981 after the crash. I have to get back I must get back. I turn my attention to the TV and start watching it. Heartbeat is on and for a moment I get wrapped up in its gentle 1960s humour, I just love seeing the old cars and one of my favourites that keeps turning up in it is an old Mk 1 Cortina just like my first car. Dark green as well, the same colour as my first car. My son comes in and asks if he can go on the Xbox 360. "Yea go on then Jamie I'm not really watching this anyway mate." He fires it up and I watch him playing Gears of War for a while, but after he's killed his 900th alien I get bored and decide to go on the computer. I go on MSN but no-one I know is on. I search Friends Re-United aimlessly again for Romilly knowing that I won't find her, and eventually Jamie gets bored of blowing up aliens and goes up to his bed. I've downloaded a John Peel programme from 1981 and put it on. Donning the wireless headphones I migrate to my chair to listen to New Order and Killing Joke circa 1981. I doze but I can't get back to 1981. It's now 11 pm and I'm starting to think the worst. I must have died back then. It's all over. It must be.

I get up not knowing what to do in my sadness. Back to the computer and sign into AOL. I put an old favourite album of mine on, The Verve and Urban Hymns and then I go into the chat rooms but it's the usual arguing and crap between people who would not behave half as badly if they met you in real life. By about 1 am I start talking to some girl I have never met before. She is from North Wales in Colwyn Bay and she is called Jen and seems really keen to talk to me. We chat about our lives and before long I am telling her about what is happening to me with my trips back to 1981. I just know she will think I'm completely crazy but who cares? Not me. This is the internet and just perhaps I have found a kindred soul who is not just into the cybersex. We laugh about it and she lightens my mood a little. We exchange pictures by Email and I see she is a nice looking lady but knowing the internet I am always a bit dubious so I give her my spare mobile number and we chat on the phone for a while. In the meantime my dinner is still in the microwave and I have attacked a bottle of Elaine's Australian white wine from the fridge so I am feeling a bit high. "Look mate, she says, if it is to be then it will be you know. True love and all that? It never runs smooth you know." I agree with her hoping that she is right. We chat on for a while longer and then I say goodnight to her after agreeing to talk again sometime. I put James Morrison on after hanging up and settle back in my chair slowly. Its 3 am now 24 hours since I last left 1981.I start analysing it again. The crash, the cold wet night and before long my eyes are closing. And then thankfully I slip back at last.

Chapter 24. In Hospital After the Crash.

I awake to a terrible pain in my chest. So hard to breathe, every breath hurts and my eyes seem as if they are stuck together with super glue. I struggle to sit up but feel a hand on my arm and a familiar voice urging me to stay still and take it easy."He's awake", I hear Romilly's worried voice saying."Shhhhh baby take it easy." She calls out. "Doreen, he's awake." Doreen is my Mum and I hear her calling, "Nurse, Nurse he's awake. Quick." I can hear the sound of chairs moving and my arm is held to take my pulse. I try to open my eyes but all I can see is a blur so I give up and close them again and drift away into my darkness again.

I awaken again later, just briefly, alone. I can open my eyes a little and see blurrily that I am in hospital. My hearing is Ok and I can hear nurses talking and the clatter of a trolley before dropping into oblivion again. I must regain consciousness briefly a few times as I can remember hospital smells and see a nurse looking at me and telling me to rest. I sleep, full of questions unanswered. But I am so happy; I must still be alive in 1981 at least and so is Romilly. Finally I regain full consciousness. I see my Mums face looking at me and my Dad behind her. "Romilly?" I croak. "She's ok my mum says, better than you in fact." "Thank God, I say relaxing back into my pillows. Where is she?" "Shhh Don't worry Matt she's just gone to get us a cup of tea." smiles my mum. You are quite the hero, she says squeezing my hand, and you probably saved her life you know." I see my Dad looking over her shoulder and I think I can see a look of pride in his eyes although I didn't think he'd ever admit to it. I squeeze my Mums hand back. "I don't tell you two this enough I know but I love you both." My mum chokes up and stands up to hold my Dad. She leaves, and my Dad and I are alone. "Look Matt he says, I know I've not been the best father but what you did makes me so proud. You saved Romilly's life and you were lucky to come away with your own life?" I know he finds it hard telling me this and I respect him for it. I try to reach out and embrace him but I feel the pain in my chest and try to laugh it off. "Dad I love you mate, and for your information I've not been the best son either." He squeezes my shoulder gently but it still causes me a great deal of pain but I just smile and he says as he sees Romilly coming in, "I'll leave you two alone shall I then?"

Romilly enters my ward. White blouse, blue jeans and my heart seems to jump at the sight of her gorgeous smile. She has a few scratches on her face but otherwise looks fine. She gives my Dad a plastic cup of hospital tea as he passes her and he wrinkles his nose up at it and winks at her. "Be gentle with him." he laughs. She pulls the plastic hospital chair closer and sitting down takes my hand. I see the lovelight in her eyes as she says; "You saved my life you know?" "Had to, I croak, aint got you insured yet." Her face lowers till we are eye to eye. "I mean it Matt she says tenderly without you I'd probably be dead by now. You had three broken ribs and a punctured lung and you still managed to pull me clear while I lay there like a lemon." "So what, I say, was I supposed to do, leave you there then?" "No but you protected me from the blast you idiot and that's why I still have hair and you are missing some." I remembered the smell of burning hair and realised it must have been my own. "Told you I'd protect you, I smiled, but now you owe me a haircut." Her head lowers to my bandaged chest and she suddenly dissolves into tears. "Awww Romilly I say, its Ok baby." I notice the scars on her face from the glass. I take her hand and lift her chin till her tear stained face is looking at me. "Are we going to be Ok this time around Rommy?" I ask. She looks at me and says, " You bloody idiot, you didn't think twice about saving me from that, you put yourself before me, after all that effort saving me you still protected me. You didn't give a shit about yourself you bastard. You have put me through hell. You've been unconscious for two days and I thought I'd lost you at one point. How could I ever look at another man when I have you, you stupid fool." "Yeah, I say, but you are only 17 here." "Spears. She tells me, I'm 43 and you bloody well know it too." "Yeah I forgot that." and feeling the pain I pass out again. I wake a few times after that and Romilly is always there beside my bed and holding my hand.

Chapter 25. Coming Home From Hospital.

After a week of hospital care I'm allowed out although still bandaged up and with lots of painkillers. I've been told to rest and have a month off work to recover. Romilly comes with my Dad to take me home. They help me into my dad's car. "No nookie for you for a while Spears." she whispers in my ear so that my Dad can't hear her. "Dunno about that Rommy I smile back, I'm sure I'll find a way." She goes to poke me in the ribs but stops herself at the last moment thankfully for me. "Have they found out who was driving the car that caused our accident yet?" I ask my Dad. "Nope not a sign of them yet, my Dad replies, so it looks like you will lose your no claims bonus on your insurance. "Damn it, just what we need." I say to Rommy. "Don't worry about it Matt at least we are both still alive." she replies squeezing my hand gently. We drive back to my mum and dad's but on the way we pass the place where we had the accident that stormy night. "Slow down Dad I want to see." I say. I can feel Romilly watching for my reaction, her fingers gently stroking my arm. "Are you sure Matt?" she asks me. "Yea Babe I want to see it." I can see the tyre marks in the muddy field where the Cortina left the road, I can see the tree we ploughed into, its trunk and lower branches scorched from the fire but the car is of course gone. A few bits of burnt wreckage and a large burnt patch in the field are all that is left of my old Cortina. I'm determined not to break down but I feel the pain in my chest as a sob escapes from it. Then another and then Romilly is cradling me in her arms as the floodgates open and the pain in my chest and the pain in my heart mingle as my tears soak the front of her blouse where her breast is against my face comforting me. "Shhh Matt It's Ok darling, we are both going to be Ok. Shhh Don't worry I'm here with you." Her hand rubs my back as I tell her how I was so afraid we had died in that muddy field when I couldn't return from 2007 and how I wanted her so much and feared I had lost her again. My dad drives on and slowly my tears stop. I look up to kiss her lips and see she has been crying too, small tears on her soft cheeks, so I kiss them away first, look into her eyes and tell her."This time Romilly we are together for good, I'm not going to lose you this time." I see a small flash of fear in her eyes before she kisses me and then we arrive at my mum and dad's house.

They help me from the car and into the house, my dad and Romilly on either side of me. My mum is at the door waiting to usher us in and they leave Romilly and I alone in the lounge as my mum finishes of preparing lunch. "You can eat but then its bed for you Spears. No arguments." Says Romilly firmly. "Sounds good to me. I laugh, best offer I've had all day." Romilly cracks up with laughter. "You get worse you know. There will be none of that till the bandages are off my lad." I feign disappointment as I know she is right on that score, but the thought of it is nice though. "Ok you tyrant I'm in your evil clutches till I'm better, I laugh, but you just watch out when I am because you will be the one then needing the bed rest you know." "I hope that's a promise." she smiles sexily as my mum walks in bringing two plates of shepherd's pie. "Ok you lucky ladies I say, who gets the honour of feeding me then?" My mum laughs as Romilly picks up a spoon and puts it in my hand. "Feed yourself stupid and if you weren't injured you would be wearing that shepherd's pie Ok?" My Dad brings the beers in as we all tuck in hungrily. It's delicious after a week of hospital food and I ask for more. My dad pours us a beer and says. "We thought Romilly might like to stay tonight in the spare room. If her parents don't mind that is?" "I'm sure they won't." Romilly replies and goes to ring them straight away. That night turns into a week and by the end of the third day Romilly is sharing my room and we are looking forward to the wedding arranged for the following week. At least I won't need to take holiday as I'm still on the sick.

The only thing that continues to mar our happiness is her nightmares. They don't happen every night but the on the second night of my return from hospital as she sleeps in the spare room next to mine I awake to hear her crying out for me. I move as quickly as I can to be with her and opening her door I see her thrashing about in her bed. She is fighting the covers and pleading pitifully, "Matt. Matt, please get him away from me. Please. I hate it. Please Matt." I lean down to comfort her, trying to avoid her wildly swinging arms. I grab her and whisper to her that I'm with her and will never leave her. Slowly she calms down as I talk to her softly and eventually she returns to normal sleep but I daren't leave her and wrapping my arms around her so gently I climb in beside her and that's how we stay until early the next morning when my mum opens the door quietly to pop her head round. I think I may have some explaining to do but my mum just whispers, "It's Ok Matt, we heard Romilly last night. Was it a bad dream?" I leave the bed as quietly as I can and leaving the room I shut the door behind me. "It's not what you think mum. I was only there comforting her. She woke me up." I start to explain. "No it's Ok Matt your father and I heard her and then you going in and talking to her. Does she have them often?" "Yes now and again, I tell her, but she is Ok if I am with her to calm her down. I don't know what causes them. I wish I did." My mum goes back to her room and I decide to go downstairs to make tea. It's only a quarter past six but it is already light out and I sit on the back step drinking a large mug of tea listening to the dawn chorus from the woods behind the house. Then I hear a footfall behind me and look around to see my mum standing there. "Hiya mumsie want a cup of tea too?" I ask her trying to sound cheerful. "No you are Ok Matt I'll make it. Would you like another?" she asks me to which I say yes of course. I come in and sit at the kitchen table to have a cigarette with my mum. "Look I've just talked to your father and we both think it might be best if Romilly moves into your room if it helps her, and besides you will be married soon anyway." "Awww thanks mum, I tell her, that makes me so much happier and I'm sure Romilly will be too. As soon as we are married we will try to sort this out Ok?" I kiss my mum's cheek and make Romilly a large mug of sweet tea before ascending the stairs to wake her with the good news from my mum.

And so that night Romilly is with me sharing my bed and seems to sleep peacefully. Leading up to the wedding she still has her bad nights and I am there by her side to comfort and calm her, but I know that this is not the answer to her nightmares. We really do have to sort this out and I tell Romilly so. She will still not tell me about them but assures me that they are not so bad now and she will tell me more after we are married. But I am starting to doubt her now. I just get the feeling that she doesn't want to tell me at all and will just keep on putting me off with her excuses. But what can I do. I love her but I think that trying to force her to tell me will only be counter-productive so I just let things be for the time being.

Chapter 26. The Wedding.

So this is our marriage in our new timeline. Cardinals Stratford registry office at midday. Things are going well and our wedding day is just so perfect. Even the weather is on our side and the sun shines down from a clear blue sky. How proud I was as she entered the registry office waiting room in her beautiful white wedding dress. I have never seen a woman look so beautiful or so happy as Romilly did then, and I must have had such a stupid grin on my face as she walked up to me and holding my chin kissed me tenderly saying, "Well Spears this is it. We are doing it again yeah?" I was wearing my hired grey morning suit and I thought I cut a dashing figure in it especially with the cravat and top hat. Eebie was the best man again and even his jaw dropped when she entered and kissed me, such was her self assurance and beauty. She pulled away from my lips and I felt her hand squeezing my rear and she whispered. "Damn you do have such a great ass Spears." We entered the registry office laughing and duly did the deed together no-one knowing this was our second time around but us. I remember thinking, am I committing bigamy as I am still married to Elaine in 2007? But if I was then I didn't care in the slightest, no one was going to find out after all. I was still very stiff from the car crash but I got all bendy outside the registry office for pictures after we made our vows and we have some great pictures of ourselves in the gardens across the road virtually identical to our original wedding pictures. Parents and friends looking happily on and confetti flew everywhere in the light late summers breeze. We had decided to do this all differently this time around and so the reception was at my mum and dad's. No reception in the Crescent Moon or the Golf club and I think it was so much better. We had loads of food and plenty of alcohol to keep the guests happy. We wanted to keep it simple and it was so much better for that.

And so we started our second marriage in comparative bliss, so close but then we shared a secret from 2007 that no one else could possibly know....Except Bazza. He was at the wedding and even made a small speech afterwards at my mum and dad's. He sidled up to us at the reception and pulling us aside asked us how 2007 was going? I wasn't worried as anything he said would be laughed at but he warned us again to be careful. "You two are just so perfect together. He told us, Just don't ever forget that Ok?" Good old Bazza. He was really worried about us after all. We were still at my mum's place but we were buying a small one bedroom maisonette on the new Thurley estate. Not the one from our original timeline. The Pipkins hadn't been built even yet and would only hold painful memories anyway. So we eventually went to bed tired and very drunk but most of all so very very happy as husband and wife again. We even managed to make love despite the pain it caused me but Romilly was really gentle with me and so we sealed our new life together. We talked together in bed about our hopes and desires and I tell her how so deliriously happy I am at having her as my wife again. She held my hand in bed. The hugging was still out for a while yet but as I drift away to sleep I feel myself being pulled back to 2007. At first I want to resist the urge to go back but then I think tipsily, "What the hell. Oh well let's see what's happening there." as I return.

Chapter 27. Elaine. The Row.

I arrive back to another Saturday evening at home in 2007. Elaine is stretched out on the sofa and we watch some crap on TV, me in my usual chair. I'm about half way through a nice bottle of Cotes Du Rhone and I have a nice buzz as we watch the TV. I'm lighting a cigarette when Elaine looks round at me and tells me. "When are you going to give those things up? You know I can't stand the smell anymore." "I will babe. Soon." She goes on, "You always say that but you just seem to smoke one after the other now." "Got my reasons babe." I shrug. "O yeah and how about letting me in on the secret then." she replies, "I know you are seeing someone else, and don't give me the crap about worrying about your job. I know that's all bullshit. I know when you are hiding something. Just be straight with me you bastard." She's looking pretty pissed off with me and I know I can't hide much from her, It's written on my face with Elaine, she knows me too bloody well after all these years. So Ok I start to tell her what has been happening over the past few weeks. I pour a fresh glass of wine and stubbing my cigarette out in the ashtray, I give her lock stock and barrel. How I started going back to 1981 and met Romilly again. About the holiday, about the car crash. Just about everything. Even about making love to her, the 24 year old Elaine in 1981 in my car, but I don't mention the wedding obviously. The TV programme is forgotten as she listens to me in stony silence at first then stops me by raising her hand. "But I would have remembered that. I remember going to the Crescent Moon for a night out on my friend's birthday in about 1981 and I know for certain that you weren't there. Try a bit harder Matt eh you lying git." I go on to tell her about my thoughts on parallel timelines and how this happened in another timeline, how time is fixed in each timeline and it had not happened in this one. She is looking more incredulous by the minute and eventually waves her hand and stops me. "Look you lying bastard I don't know where you dredged this story up from but it is the most amazing load of bollucks you've ever made up. I think you need help. You have always been in love with Romilly. I know that but this is getting a bit out of control now. Romilly is in the past, she left you over 20 years and you have to forget her can't you see that?"

Perhaps she is right I think, maybe this is just an obsession. Just an obsession fuelling itself as I go along gaining strength and vitality and realism. We all dream about the past and how we would love to recapture our youth. Maybe I am just living that obsession and turning my desires into an imagined reality, but it can't be can it, it is all too real. Perhaps I do need my head read. Elaine turns conciliatory, concerned even. "Look Matt if it's getting to you that badly why don't you try to find Romilly in real life. Perhaps if you see she has her own life now and you are just a distant memory it might cure you of these dreams. Just try to let go before it destroys you. You've got me and the three kids for God's sake. Just concentrate on us, let this ......I don't know. She searches for a word. 'Madness'. Yes madness. Just let it go." I light another cigarette and tell her of Romilly's fear of me finding her in 2007 and of the promise I made to her in the Old Crown not to search her out here as we return to watching the TV and I pour the last glass of wine from the bottle. But Elaine doesn't let it go. Oh No not my Elaine. She looks at me sadly and says "I think you ought to leave if this carries on. I can't take much more of you like this. I don't know if its lies or some elaborate plan to hide an affair you are having, but I want you to go." I shrug again, what else can I say to her?

Chapter 28. Leaving Home for the Flat.

And so that was the start of the break up with Elaine? Well I suppose that it was always going to happen even before my trips back to 1981. A Tuesday evening of all times, I always thought it would happen on a weekend. An argument between Elaine and myself about something trivial as usual escalating into a full blown row and the next thing I know is that I am walking out of the door shouting at her, "That's it we are finished, I'm leaving." "Bloody right, she shouts back at me, go and find your darling Romilly and see if she will have you." I take the car and drive. Anywhere I don't care, I want to just get away and think. I've no plans but of course I end up back in Cardinals Stratford. I drive past my old haunts, bringing back only sadness and tears at the memories, dry dusty dead memories scattering like dead leaves in a bitter winter wind before me. I even drive past Romilly's parent's house just to see it. And I wonder where Romilly is in 2007 and what she is doing at that moment. Perhaps that's why I am hanging about still in 2007. I want to know the 2007 Romilly. With tears of the past in my eyes I return to the source of memory. To Capfield forest in the miserable dark of a sad night on my own. I park the car and zipping up my jacket against the cool night air I start to I walk off my frustration. Leaves and twigs crackle softly beneath my feet. I walk aimlessly through the dark wood imagining I can hear Romilly's voice calling my name plaintively, but it's just night sounds, maybe the hoot of an owl somewhere nearby. I can hear the answering whisper in the breeze stirring the dry autumn leaves on the trees. I eventually end up back at my car and the exact spot that I had returned to the first time in 1981 in the forest, our favourite spot, where we had made such glorious love on a hot July afternoon. I can hardly see it in the dark of night but just standing there alone drawing on a cigarette is so poignant in the dark emptiness. I imagine I can hear a young couple's laughter and joy at being together after so long but its only night sounds again. I flick the cigarette end away, a glowing firefly arcing through the dark trees, and I get back into the car. I drive back home in a melancholy mood knowing what I have to do. What I must do.

The house is dark when I get home, Elaine and the kids are in bed, and so I fire up the computer and try to put my thoughts into words. My life in 2007 is so negative and I look back at my life and think of my mistakes. I know that I have caused my own sadness. Every time I find something beautiful in my life it seems that I have to destroy it. I always have, it's the story of my life I guess. Find something that has the essence of beauty and crumple it up between my callous waster's hands. Find a love and promptly destroy it before it can take root. I seem to revel in my own sadness. Perhaps it's my Irish heritage perhaps it's a personality defect, I just don't know. I rub my hands against the stubble of my unshaven cheeks and think, why do I have this urge to destroy all that could be good in my life? I look at my original time with Romilly and realise now that I destroyed us. I tried to pass some blame on to her but it was always me. I should have understood her feelings and not tried to make her to understand mine. I should have realised my mistakes but as I said life is full of 'if only's' and now I bear the full effect of my own gross stupidity. Can I overcome this given my second chance or will it only end in heartache and despair yet again? I open a new bottle of scotch and pouring a large measure I tried to work out some kind of rationale to my situation. It's no use. I can't so I work my way through several more large ones till half of the bottle is drained. I must have dozed off in a drunken blur but I awake to find that I have written something in a word document and I blearily read my own depressing words on the screen.

I am Death. As I lay my hands upon life it withers.

I am Completion. All I start is finished.

I am Finality. The end is in everything that my cruel fingers touch.

I am Armageddon. The final reckoning for all that is love.

I am Execution. In all young things I see their demise.

I am Destruction. I can turn love to hate.

Feel the end in this in my cold dry kiss.

I love two women but I seem to want to destroy one of them. Why? Whatever I do will cause pain to one of them now. But I know I have to leave my Elaine to get any sense of perspective, and so I arrange my departure, Romilly needs me more. I find the flat in the local paper the next morning after leaving the house before Elaine wakes. To be honest it's a shitehole above the local shops but it's a good size and cheap so I take it on straight away. It's furnished, sort of so I do my best to smarten it up a bit. It needs a good clean and so I get busy with the job of turning into a place I'd want to live in for a while at least. I clean it from top to bottom and arrange some broadband over my mobile. I can't do without my window on the world now can I? Finally I pop back to the house while Elaine is at work to pick up my stuff, well enough to set me up at least. My computer and a portable TV along with my clothes and other bits and pieces. The computer is the main thing I need. Seems my life is on that hard drive and I smile at that thought as I lug it into the new flat.

At last it all looks fairly presentable. I sort out my lounge, placing a picture of my kids on the unit above the gas fire. My Pc takes pride of place on a small table in the corner and I set up the speakers before firing it up to check for problems. I've no broadband yet, that will take a few days but I temporarily use a slow dial up connection for my internet. At least I can check my Email and surf the net albeit slowly. It's better than nothing I think to myself. After 20 minutes or so everything seems to be working reasonably well so I put some old Brian Ferry and Roxy Music on and sit back on my sofa to think and admire my handiwork while listening to 'Avalon'. I ring Elaine on my mobile and tell her that I have left and where I am living now and it's not so far away, only a five minute walk away in the local shopping square. She sounds unsure and even asks me to consider coming home. "We can sort this all out Matt." She tells me quietly although she doesn't sound so sure. "No Elaine I need to get away for a while, just to sort myself out. It will do us both some good. Maybe I will come back but not just right now Babe."

I had rung work that morning pleading personal problems telling them I needed the rest of the week off, and so I spent the rest of the evening just tidying up and doing a lot of thinking. I made up the small single bed with sheets and a quilt I had brought from home, and I visited the local Londis downstairs to stock up with a few essentials till I could visit the supermarket. Bread, beans, tea, milk and most importantly a nice bottle of scotch. By 9:00 pm I think that's about it for the day and sit down to relax and generally unwind to the sound of the Editors playing on the hard drive helped along with a scotch or three. Before long though my eyes start to go and I am away back to 1981 and I awake there in pain.

Chapter 29. Finding Out About 2007 Romilly.

I have returned to where I last left in 1981. In bed after the wedding night with Romilly and she is having another nightmare. The pain is caused by her pulling my hair and dragging my head from side to side. She is shouting at me to just hurry up and get it over with as she needs to sleep. Her poor face looks so pitifully vulnerable beside me. At least she isn't hitting me I think gladly, I don't think my ribs could take it yet and I gently talk to her as I tenderly release the vice like grip she has on my hair and start my usual ritual with her in these situations. "Shhhhh baby. It's Ok. It's me. I love you. Shhhhh calm down now. I'm here with you now. Please baby don't worry." I continue just reassuring her gently and eventually she calms down and returns to normal sleep as I lay beside her stroking her face and shoulders. I can feel the tension relaxing from her muscles and kiss her sweat streaked cheek. I check my watch and I can see by the luminous dial that it's 1:35 in the morning.

I ease myself slowly from the bed so as not to disturb her and picking up my cigarettes and lighter and finding my shirt and shorts I tiptoe from the bedroom to head downstairs to the lounge. It's still a bit of a mess from the wedding party but I find a glass and pour myself a whisky and coke. I hear movement on the stairs and I think its Romilly at first until my dad enters the lounge in his old stripey pyjamas. He looks at me with a concerned look on his face and asks if everything is alright. He can probably see from my face that it isn't but I smile at him and comment on his pyjamas. "I bet the girls loved those in the 1920s, I laugh, so very sartorial." He takes one of my cigarettes and lights it. Then he joins me with a drink and sits beside me on the sofa. "So are you going to tell me what's going on between you and Romilly or are you just going to take the piss out of my pyjamas?" "Nothing dad, I say, I can handle it myself, Ok?" He takes a sip of his drink and looking me in the eyes he says, "Look Matt sometimes talking about it helps and this isn't the first time we have heard Romilly in the night is it? Something must be wrong for her to be like this. Are you sure you have done the right thing here in marrying her?" I can see what he is thinking and shake my head, "No you have it wrong Dad. It's not me she is shouting at, it's in her sleep." I open up to him and tell him of her nightmares, of the terrible dreams she is enduring. How she won't tell me about them. I can't tell him the truth about our real situation. He wouldn't be able to handle that God bless him. "She goes to sleep Ok but wakes up in the night attacking me and saying such awful things." My dad is the first person I have confided to about this and I watch as he slowly digests what I have just told him as he draws slowly on the cigarette. "Have you considered getting her some kind of professional help? he eventually asks me, it might be the best thing for her." "No way would she even consider that. I tell him. It's for us to sort out Ok?" I know he is only trying to help me but I can't tell him the whole story. "Could it be because of the car crash? It could be delayed shock you know." He asks. I tell him it has been going on since before then and tell him about the holiday on the Sandpiper. How she had them there also well before the car crash. He goes and pours us both another scotch with a splash of by now warm coke in mine. I offer him another cigarette and light it for him as he leans closer to me. "Look son in my experience nightmares usually have a reason behind them. Find the reason and maybe you can cure them." I tell him that it's a bit more complicated than that but I can't explain anymore to him yet. "Ok perhaps you know what you are doing Matt, he says stubbing the cigarette out in the ashtray, but your mum and I can see something is wrong and believe me you DO really need to sort it out. We can see in both of your faces how much in love you are but if you don't get to the bottom of this I really think that this will destroy you both. But we will keep out of it for the time being. Just remember that we are here if you need us Ok? And remember what I said. Sitting back and hoping for the best isn't always best. It might be the easiest option in the short term but if you really love her then you need to do something before much longer. Just don't let it slide." He pats my hand and gets up to return to bed. "Night dad. I say. And thanks for listening Ok. You may have helped more than you think you know." He smiles sadly at me and tells me to get back to bed and look after Romilly before going back to bed himself.

I sit there for a while longer thinking of the conversation with my dad. I also think of Bazza's words about being careful as Romilly's and my love for each other could end up destroying us and I decide I that I have given Romilly ample time by now to tell me about her future life in 2007 and about how much I was beginning to worry about her nightmares. Something was badly troubling her about her future but as much as I reassured her that nothing could ever destroy my feelings of love for her, she would not open up to me. Even after we had arranged our marriage she would tell me nothing, always fobbing me off with some delaying tactic. I told her that she was as much a part of me as my heart and that I would sooner tear that out than be without her but she would argue, shout even that it wasn't my business and even sink into a non communicative silence if I tried to probe too deeply. Nothing I could say or do would change her mind. I could see the pain in her eyes sometimes and I had also seen her fear in the nightmares she was having. I remembered that when I had awoken her from them she had held me so tightly almost crushing me as if she is afraid I am going to leave her. She denied that her nightmares were anything other than that, just stupid bad dreams that she had forgotten when she awoke. She even put them down to the car crash the same as my dad but I knew they had been occurring since before that. She had admitted as much on the Sandpiper. I noticed as well that the pain in her eyes was at its most intense after the bad nights. The final reason that decided me in favour of breaking the promise I had made to her was in knowing that finding out was not for my own benefit now. It was no longer just to satisfy my own curiosity. It had gone way beyond that now. I had a real fear for my Romilly's state of mind and health and so I decided that as soon as I was back in 2007 I would break my promise to her and try to learn the truth. As my dad had said, "Find the reason and maybe you can cure the nightmares."

I knew that at any time my ability to cross over could end completely and having decided that my life now lay in 1981 with Romilly I realised that I would have to do this sooner rather than later or risk being stuck back in 2007. It was so ironic I thought how on my first visits back to the alternate 1981 it had seemed so much of a foreign place to me but now it felt like my home in fact it was my home now and 2007 seemed a cold and forbidding place, full of my middle aged heartache and arguments. I did not even miss its modern distractions anymore, not even my internet and besides I had them to look forward to again in the future of my 1981 life I hoped. So draining my scotch and after stubbing out the cigarette I made my way back up to bed. Romilly was still sleeping peacefully as I slipped into the bed beside her. I lay there for a while watching her features in the slight glow of the light from the landing, thinking how much I adored this woman but wondering about what could be causing her distress. She murmured quietly, incoherently in her sleep and I felt her pull herself closer to me and drape her arm over my chest. I could just make out a slight smile on her face as she muttered my name and ran her hand over my chest and up to my neck. She looked so content then to me as if the nightmares had never happened. So peaceful lying beside me. And that moment of contentment in time finally made up my mind for me. I would not let us end this time around but I had to fight for her. I knew that. I suppose in a coarser moment I'd have called it, 'Shit or Bust'. But I think that just about summed it up. If she wouldn't take the initiative then I would have to. For Romilly and for me also.

And that was how it happened. My mind was irrevocably made up and I dozed off beside her willing myself back to my cold inhospitable 2007. I returned to wake up on my sofa in the flat back in 2007. I had made my mind up so I'd better get on with it I told myself and so I stretched my 54 year old bones and pushed myself upright to visit the kitchen and my welcoming kettle. Sipping the tea I sat down at the computer and lighting a cigarette I began by carrying out a little internet research. I track down Romilly's old home number so that I can phone Will, Romilly's father, and he is still in the phonebook at the old address. I knew I'd probably get rebuffed as even when Romilly and I had been together I had definitely not been his or his wife Naomi's favourite person. The usual crap. I was not good enough for their beloved daughter and our age difference only made it worse to them, but at least I had to try to find out something about my mysterious modern day Romilly before I returned for the last time I hoped to 1981. I hadn't seen my ex in laws for 23 years and wondered how time had treated them. I smiled to myself as I remembered flannelling them back in 1981. Will was a tall slim guy with a mop of dark unruly hair and a glint in his eye that lead me Romilly and our friends to call him Mad Will, he and Romilly's relationship was volatile to say the least. Naomi was a small plump woman, something of the Sunday school teacher look about her, which was very apt as they were both practising Christians, they probably still were. I thought I'd leave contacting them till the evening after finishing of my moving into the flat and working out the best way to approach them.

So anaesthetising myself with a scotch on that lonely 2007 evening alone in the flat and with much trepidation I picked up my mobile and dialled their number. I recognised Will's voice as soon as he answered, it had hardly changed a bit, "Err Hi Will, look I know it's been a long time but it's Matt," "O yes?" came the wary reply obviously waiting for me to explain why I was ringing, I hardly knew where to start, I mean we hadn't spoken in 23 years and then not even in good circumstances. "Err. Well it's about Romilly, I blurted out feeling like a schoolboy explaining some prank to the Head teacher, I just called to see if she's ok, err, and what she's doing now." At least he hasn't put the phone down on me yet so that's a result at least I think. "O yes and why would you want to know that then?" he almost growled. Where to begin I think. "It's a long story Will but I am genuinely concerned for her and would like to think I could count on you helping me to help her." I said. "What would you know or care about her after all these years?" he replied sounding irritated by now. "Will, I said, I can't explain this to you but I am being totally serious with you. I need to know what is happening to Romilly. Will you please help me?" "Not a chance." he shouts and slams down the phone on me. Putting the now dead phone down and with my mind in turmoil, I pour a large and I mean LARGE scotch, splash in some coke to taste and retire to my chair to think over the outcome of the call. All I wanted was, I don't know, Explanations? Enlightenment? Anything at all, out of Romilly's dad. Well, I thought I'm not going to learn anything sitting here getting pissed alone in my flat so leaving my drink I went and jumped in the car. Cardinals Stratford was only a half hours drive away but although I did not want to arrive at Romilly's parents drunk, I certainly didn't want to arrive stone cold sober either. So I planned to spend half an hour in their local pub with a couple of scotches first deciding how to go about this.

I hadn't been in the Wagon since Romilly and I had split in 1984 and I noticed it hadn't changed much as I walked in, just a normal quiet little local pub. I said hallo to the landlord and ordered a scotch, he was obviously having a quiet night and we chatted for a while, while I polished of a couple more before leaving. "Cometh the hour Cometh the man, I thought to myself as I left the car in the pub car park and crossed the road to Romilly's old house. Walking up the drive I thought that, well the old place aint changed much and I wouldn't have been surprised to see Will's rusty old Vauxhall Viva from 1984 parked on the driveway, but I saw he had updated to a newer car. It was a cold wet evening and I shivered as I knocked at the front door as much in anticipation as cold. I noticed a face looking out from behind the front room curtains at me briefly. The door opened and I came face to face with Naomi, Romilly's mum. She takes one surprised look at me and calls out to Will who quickly appears beside his wife. "Can't you take a hint Matt; we are not going to talk to you? he says raising his voice to me, It's none of your business, now please just leave us alone for Christ's sake man." He goes to shut the door in my face but I quickly put my foot in it to stop him shutting me out. "Look Will, I sigh, knowing that shouting at him in return won't help my case much, I can't even begin to tell you how I know this but I believe..... No in fact I know that Romilly is in some kind of trouble and if she is then you probably know about it too." I notice that Naomi all of a sudden seems to be listening to me although Will is just standing there glowering at me. I continue in a conciliatory tone. "Now you probably will not believe me but I am probably the only person who can help her at this moment in time, BUT first I do need to know what the hell is going on. Now I am going to take my dainty little size seven out of your doorway and you can chose to shut the door on me, in which case I will sit here until you do decide to talk to me or get the police to remove me or you can invite me in and we can talk reasonably now." Will looks like he is going to explode at me but Naomi takes his arm and says to him. "Will I have a say in this and I think we should let him in, it can't make things any worse after all can it?" Will looks at her and then at me and finally grunting he grudgingly opens the door to me and beckons me in. "Good old Naomi." I think gratefully.

Chapter 30. The Truth about Romilly.

As I follow them into the lounge I realise this is the first time I've been in this house since March 1984 on Romilly's 20th Birthday; it doesn't look too much different from how I remembered it though. I decide that the old saying "Faint heart never won fair maiden" applied here and so seeing Will sit down at the table I sat down opposite him and said, "OK Will, what's going on?" "Why do you want to know, he says, it can't matter to you about her anymore?" I felt like telling him to cut the crap, but I decided perhaps a bit of civility may be in order here as well, so I replied "I'm fine Will I hope you are Ok too." After sizing me up for a few seconds Will sighed and asked me if I'd like a drink. I asked for a Scotch and Will duly asked Naomi to fetch me one. "You'd better make him a large one and I'll have one as well." he added. Will looked his age I supposed about mid 70s, his hair a lot thinner and gray now. What he had lost on his head seemed to have been replaced by the hair sprouting from his ears and nose. Naomi had not changed much, and still looked pretty sprightly for her years. Her hair was still the mousy blonde I remembered and her watery blue eyes still seemed to search your soul as you talked to her, much as her daughters could.

The scotches arrived and it was nitty gritty time. "Will, I said taking a large sip of my scotch, we haven't talked in, let's see, 23 years but we seriously do need to talk right now." This brought a smile to Will's face. "But why, you haven't been in her life since she was little more than a girl?" he says sipping his scotch." Will can you please cut the crap and tell me what the hell is happening with Romilly's life please?" I say with an exasperated sigh. A cloud seems to darken Will's face, "We'll talk of that in a minute, but bear it in mind that we are only talking to you because Naomi thinks it can't do any harm. Personally I wish you would just leave us alone. Now what do you know of her since your divorce?" "Not much, I replied, I heard she had kids, married her boss from the tax office and ended up in Swindon via Peterborough but not necessarily in that order. And that's about it I'm afraid." I leave out the stuff I had learnt from Romilly in our new 1981. "Well it's a long story, so we best make ourselves comfortable." says Will moving over to the sofa and pointing me towards a rather uncomfortable looking armchair with his whisky glass. "Naomi, you had better bring the bottle and sit with us too. Well I'll begin at the beginning, Will said sitting forward on the sofa and sipping his scotch. Romilly went a bit wild at first after you two first split as was to be expected and she went out with a few men but she met someone else very quickly and married him and had 3 lovely kids. She moved about with her husband over the years first to Peterborough, then to Swindon. He goes on to tell me about Romilly's life and upward rise and family for about 5 minutes. I knew about that from our chat on the Sandpiper. Then things started to go wrong about 6 years ago." he says. I was all ears now as I was in so called uncharted territory and maybe the vital answer to my questions and Romilly's nightmares. I knew little of Romilly's recent past obviously. "Go on." I tell Will. "Ok I'll just top you up" said Will leaning over to fill my glass. "Would you like one too Naomi?" Naomi nodded and fetching a glass joined us. "OK where was I? says Will. O yes about six years ago or so she found out her husband had been having an affair. She didn't seem that worried at the time as I think their marriage was unhappy but then he moved out with his new woman and decided to fight Romilly for custody of the children. That did upset her as she loved her children and for whatever reason she started drinking. This led to a series of unedifying events that we won't go into, which the husband obviously used against her and won the custody battle." He must be talking about Romilly setting fire to her ex husbands car I think to myself. Will continued. "Romilly was devastated. I knew about this too but I knew there had to be more. She got herself a flat in Swindon after the divorce was finalized, but her drinking got worse and I fear she started taking drugs as well, she got so bad that her ex-husband banned her from seeing her children at all. Then her debts built up and she took to less savoury ways to pay her mortgage and... I stopped Will at that point. "What do you mean by less than savoury Will?" Naomi touched my arm and took my hand, "He means she became a prostitute Matt." Will looked daggers at Naomi and continued "Yes Ok she started selling herself to pay her bills. We tried persuading her to move back home with us especially after her family moved abroad to the States, but things were bad, her kids would have nothing to do with her or even talk to her, something in her had died." Naomi started crying then and I noticed she was still holding my hand, and the news that they had told me was leaving me close to tears too but I held them back. "In 2004 she lost her flat because of the drugs." he replied a look of desolation in his eyes. She..." He takes a drink of his scotch and his head drops and he starts to cry without continuing.

Naomi takes up the story as Will sits dejected on the sofa. She takes my hand again as she notices the tears on my face too. "Her children meant everything to her Matt and losing them seemed to tear her soul out, but even she admits they are better off without her now." "I can't believe that of Romilly." I say aghast. "No she's right in that respect Matt, continues Naomi, she has sunk so low now. Oh she pretends she is Ok when we talk on the phone but Will and I hired a private detective to find out what was happening to her a couple of months ago." "But why." I say. "Because she would tell us hardly anything about herself or what she was doing, even if she had a job or not. We just got a pack of lies from her. It was the only thing we could do Matt." My mind is in freefall now, and I ask Naomi what they had found out. Will starts sobbing again and downing his scotch in one gets up and leaves the lounge in tears. I hear the front door slam as he leaves the house. "I worry about him, Poor Will he has taken it so hard." Naomi sighs softly. "The private eye?" I say wanting Naomi to continue. "Ok well she is working as a prostitute in Swindon to be blunt; she has no money left as she is using it all for drink and drugs. She is in a bad way they said... Oh but Matt I think she is killing herself slowly and painfully and I can't see her coming back from this can you?" Her small face looks at me pleading for an answer that I just can't give her.

Naomi sits back in the chair and I hear small sobs welling up from inside her. I pour another glass of Will's scotch for her and one for myself. "Shhh Naomi, here drink this. I say softly. Now do you have her address?" She gets up and rummaging in a drawer brings out a beige office folder. "Here you might as well have it; it's only brought us pain. " Naomi sobs. It is the private detectives report I see and I sit back in the chair and sipping my scotch I proceed to read the cold dispassionate words it contains. Not really much more than Naomi has already told me already. Romilly's full name, I notice she is using her maiden name again and aged 43. Date of birth etc etc. It has her address which is in Swindon, a bedsit in a seedy area. The dates seen and the observations made by the detective company. Her pimp and pusher or should that be pushers, she has more than one. Drug of favour is heroin I notice, but mostly I look at the photos. They are of a Romilly I have never known. The photos are obviously taken from quite a distance but through a powerful lens and they show a sad looking woman who seems more 53 than 43. Her hair is long, lank and dyed blonde. Her face is haggard and careworn. But most of all I see her eyes in the one telephoto blow up. My 1981 Romilly's eyes are full of life and sparkle but the eyes I see in the blow up are cold and dull. Eyes waiting for death, I think to myself despairingly.

And so now I finally know the reasons for her nightmares. I suppose I start to understand her refusal to tell me about this. Her terror of me finding out about her in 2007. Maybe shame even. But I can't understand it even now. Why did she think I would leave her over this? I never would have. Perhaps it is shame? No it must be more than that. Perhaps she just wanted to start all over again in 1981 with me afresh and wants to forget this. I don't blame her. Maybe my finding out will mean that I will carry the memory back there alongside her. Forever reminding her of her downfall as it were with my mere presence. But I am now certain that sadly her terrible nightmares will never stop unless she exorcises these dreadful memories. Covering them up, sweeping them under the carpet? I have a horrible feeling that it just won't work unless she confronts them in some way in 2007. The memories will just continue to haunt her AND me there. As I said earlier, a festering sore between us that needed some kind of surgery and not just merely trying to ignore it and hope it will get better on its own.

Chapter 31. Deciding To Rescue Romilly.

I left Will and Naomi's house in a state of near shock that night clutching the slim beige folder under my arm and after picking up the car from the pub car park I headed home in a confused daze. I most definitely knew what I had to do though and that most certainly did not include returning to 1981 immediately. And so on my return to the flat I had a couple of scotches and read the meagre information in the folder again over and over but mostly I studied the photos. Romilly at her door talking to her pusher, a small bag of heroin changing hands. Romilly looking into the face of her pimp with a questioning look on her hard face, her hands pushed deep into her jacket pockets. He was pointing his finger at her and obviously telling her something forcefully. Mean looking bastard too, I thought. Another of her in a bar on a bar stool wearing a short skirt her still shapely slim legs crossed smoking a cigarette and smiling unkindly at another pusher. Another of her obviously touting for business on a dimly lit street, wearing the short skirt again but her hair in a severe looking ponytail this time and a low cut revealing top under a short leather jacket. I closed the folder and sat back lighting another cigarette. I felt like crying but I was out of tears and just a few dry sobs escaped my sore throat. To be honest I felt like I had been kicked in the stomach, my mental pain taking on a physical feeling at that moment. I was devastated at the news I had received. I just could not take the immensity of it all in.

No wonder she didn't want me to know about this. No wonder she thought I might leave her if I found out about this. How could she tell me about this? I could imagine the conversation."Yeah Romilly I'm a boring factory worker, married with three kids in 2007." "Really Matt? I'm a drug addicted whore working the streets of Swindon for a tenner a blowjob." End of conversation as I collapse on the floor stunned? But then again I think that do I bear part of the blame for all this? Am I in a small way to blame for her present situation? I introduced her to drugs I suppose back in 1981, not heroin, but certainly cannabis and speed. Did she in her downfall remember the highs we used to have and decide they were a way to forget her misery? Did she look back at our hard drinking nights and remembering the fun we had try to lift her spirits with spirits if you like? Perhaps I do need to share the blame I think dismally. But the most painful thing to me is that she didn't believe me when I said I would stay with her forever whatever happened. That she thought that I could stop loving her over this. It is a lot for me to handle at this moment but how could she doubt me. How could she? Why couldn't she just have had the faith in me to tell me all about this? Now I know I have to prove to her that I am there for her totally, no matter what has happened. I go to bed resisting the urge to go back to 1981 and knowing that I need my sleep ready for the next morning. But still I visit briefly.

I'm lying back on our bed at my parent's house in 1981. It's early morning and I am so comfortable and I watch her lovely outline as she prepares for the day ahead. She is brushing her hair in the mirror paying full attention to every detail. I admire every sweep of her hair as she removes the tangles of our lovemaking from it her face examining herself slowly contemplatively as she brushes her honey blonde hair. She examines her face as she leans closer to the mirror. She thinks I am asleep as she pulls her stockings on. Black and slinky she rolls them up her long slim legs and I hear the static of them as she pulls them fully up turning sideways on to admire her profile in the full length mirror. I can see her look of appreciation as she smoothes her knee length black dress down against her legs. Then she applies her makeup. A little blusher and mascara followed by the peach coloured lipstick. She doesn't need much; her face is so beautiful without it. But that's women for you I think lying back and enjoying my voyeuristic peep show. She stands up in the glow of the bedside lamp and straps her shoes on. Then she turns to me and thinking that I am asleep runs her fingers down my face and says. "I love you babes, sleep for a while longer. I love you." I open my eyes a little and she smiles at me and bending over kisses my eyelids tenderly. I roll over lazily and yawn. "Good luck with the interview." I tell her only half awake. She is trying for a new job that morning and she looks stunning. I know I would employ her on the spot. At least it's not at the tax office I think but at the local Lloyds bank. She finishes buttoning up her plain white frilly fronted blouse and squeezes my hand in reassurance. "See you later Matt. You can take me to lunch when I get back." She bends to kiss me on the cheek and disappears out of the door. I doze off again and force my way back to 2007.

Chapter 32. To Swindon and Charley.

I wake up the next morning about 6am in 2007 feeling every single ounce of the burden I am taking on. Willingly I know, no-one has forced me to but I want to do this for Romilly and myself. Getting up I dress in my old jeans and selecting a Fila hoodie from my wardrobe I am almost ready. A quick cuppa, a bit of toast whilst checking the internet for some numbers to program into my phone and make a flask of tea and some sandwiches. The sky was leaden, but it wasn't raining at least I thought as I prepared a few extra items I thought might come in handy if I was to be Romilly's guardian angel today. I left my place at about 6.30 am with a heavy heart. I stopped to fill up the car and draw some cash from the cash machine, then taking the M11 I headed south in the Berlingo. By the time I hit the M25 the rain had started to pour down relentlessly and the traffic slowed to a crawl through the sheer volume of cars heading to work. It took over an hour of stop/start driving before I reached my intended exit. The M4 heading west. Next stop Swindon I thought grimly. I put the Editors on the car stereo and turned up the volume and finally eased the car up to 70 for the first time since I had left the M11. The miles flew by as I was against the traffic flow now and could maintain a decent speed at last. The rain had turned to intermittent showers and the sky brightened a bit ahead of me as I reached the turnoff I wanted. I stopped to fill up with petrol again. Welcome to Swindon I thought grimly. I knew that I wanted Corporation Street and following signs to the bus depot I found it and a place to park. Five minutes' walk later and I found myself in a street of old run down three storey town houses. Destination, I thought. The street reminded me so much of the Spijker Kwarter from Holland in 1980 and I even remembered my visit to a prostitute there myself in the far distant 1980 as a dare from my friends.

Pleasures of the flesh for 50 guilders a time. Well actually there wasn't much pleasure, the girl, a gorgeous looking oriental, was very welcoming as she smiled at me through the red lit window and was very eager to take my 50 guilders but as soon as I had paid she just wanted to finish me off as quickly as possible so as to move on to the next punter I supposed. Not much of a turn on and I never bothered again. Some of these houses must be drug shops I thought remembering my days from Holland. The two usually go hand in hand.

I walked up and then back down the street slowly getting to know the area. I had seen the place that I recognised as the address mentioned in the detectives report. It didn't look any better than it did in the photos. As shabby as the others with peeling paint and a front garden overrun with weeds and containing an old rotting mattress dumped against the overflowing bins outside. Loud rap music blared out of the top window of the next door property and I could hear an argument between a man and a woman in there. Pulling my hood up I walked twice more past the house before returning by a different route to get the car. This time I drove back to the street and parking down the street a little way from the house I locked it up and walked to the pub on the street corner. It was a dive to be honest, very rough and ready but the landlord seemed friendly enough, chatty even, as I ordered a large scotch. I took my drink and sat by a murky window where I could observe the front of the house. I had to make sure Romilly was living there before I could do anything else. She could have moved on for all I knew but my patience was rewarded after an hour when I saw her, in a housecoat leave the house with a black bin liner of trash to throw it against the rotting mattress and bins at the front then go back inside after briefly looking up and down the street. From the report I knew she lived on the first floor at the front, but on my first reconnaissance the curtains had been drawn tightly. I could see they were open now. I also knew from the report that the place was run more or less as a brothel with several other women living on the premises and making a poor living from sexual services. I had noticed a few men coming and going while I sat nursing my scotch and wondered if any had been punters of Romilly's. Or Amber, as she called herself now, according to the detective's report. Yes Amber! How the hell had Romilly thought that one up? The report neglected to tell me if the pimp lived on the property or not but I hadn't noticed anyone resembling him around the place yet but he would most definitely be a regular visitor and probably not on his own either going by the photographs.

It was now late afternoon and I notice the front door of Romilly's house open and some old guy walks out of the house and towards the pub whistling happily. The pub door opens and he enters all smiles. He looks to be about 60 and none too fastidious about his appearance. Old stained jeans, scuffed boots and a grey belt up raincoat all topped off by the grubbiest oldest flat cap you have ever seen. "Hello Jack." he says jauntily to the landlord. "Hello Charley, replies the landlord, usual is it?" I walk nonchalantly up to the bar to hear any conversation with my empty glass seeking a refill. "Yea pint of Guinness Jack" says Charley. "Coming right up says Jack, and looking at my empty glass he says, I'll be with you in a minute sir." "Been having fun with your little friend Amber again today then Charley?" laughs the landlord pouring Charley his pint. "Sure have, says Charley she's not the most exciting bunk up but she don't get too busy nowadays and I get extra time for free. Twenty quid all in, literally." he grins coarsely. The landlord laughs along with the joke and passes Charley his drink and turns to me."Scotch please." I grin and looking toward Charley I join in the fun by saying "Old Charles here sounds a bit of a goer eh?" "He sure is, says Jack, the randy old git still has his brains in his ball bag, has to pay for it now though as he's lost his boyish good looks." Charley sups his pint and cackles to himself. He don't smell too good neither I think to myself realising that Charley and personal hygiene walk separate sides of the street. "So what's this brass like then Charley I smile, she can't be too particular if you are a regular eh?" "Oi you leave my Amber alone, he smirks, she is Ok. As I said she's not the best bunk up but she gives a pretty good blowjob and she is cheap. She keeps the lights low as well so she doesn't look too bad neither." We all laugh at this and turning to me Jack says, "It's a shame but most of the brasses round here are on smack or crack. Going on the game is the only way they can pay for it." "Well I'm enjoyin' her while I still can, says Charley, she doesn't get many punters now, she's getting too old to be on the game for much longer, and it's all teenagers nowadays. She won't be around much longer; less if the drugs get to her first. I'll be sorry to see her go though." Funnily enough I think my new friend Charley is quite fond of his Amber. My Romilly. "If there's ever a woman whose days are numbered it's my Amber." says Charley sadly as he rolls a cigarette between nicotine stained fingers. "Where's she work from then mate? I might just pay her a visit later. I haven't had me end away in weeks." I say grinning lewdly. "Just down the street at number 22 mate, you can't miss it; it's the one with the mattress outside. Tell her Charley Maloy sent you, I might even get her for half price next week." he smiles. "And I might get a discount too." I answer and all three of us laugh at this and I buy us all a drink being as we are all good old pals now. We sup on our drinks and I say, "Yep I think you've whetted my appetite Charley I might go and pay my respects to your Amber as they say." To much ribald laughter I ask for a bottle of scotch and 40 cigarettes to go, and finishing my scotch I decide to make my move and thanking the landlord I pull up my hood and leave the pub shaking Charley's grubby hand on the way out. Heading down the street I prepare to meet Romilly for the very first time in 2007.

It's getting dark by now and as I walk down the ill lit street I try to think how Romilly will react to seeing me after I promised her I would not try to find her in 2007. Oh well Spears I muse to myself using her old name for me, you are about to find out at last I suppose. Walking up the broken steps to the peeling front door I see a column of bell pushes beside it. I can just about make out the name Amber on one and with trepidation I push hard on it. Somewhere above me a bell rings. Then? Absolutely nothing. I ring again and then again, still nothing. Damn it have I come this far and missed her. Frantically I push the bell push again this time keeping my finger on it. Eventually I hear a cold dispassionate voice asking me. "Who the hell is it?" over a tinny distorted intercom. Deepening my voice to disguise it I say "Oh Hi you don't know me but Charley Maloy recommended you to me Amber." "And I suppose he thinks he's up for a discount does he, the dirty old git?" I am momentarily speechless at hearing Romilly's voice. It is most definitely her, older, harder but most certainly her. "Well don't hang about on the doorstep. Come up. First floor, turn left, third door." she informs me in a businesslike manner. I hear the door buzz and push it open to enter a dilapidated entrance hall. The place looks as if it hasn't been decorated since Queen Victoria was a lad, mouldy wallpaper curling off the wall and a wet rotting carpet underfoot. The place smells bad, really bad, of old cooking and urine. The stairs are covered in old cracking linoleum and creak as I make my way up to the first floor. The stair rail feels greasy to the touch but I take my chances using it to guide my way up the poorly lit uneven stairs. Turning left at the top I find my way along to the third door and with my heart in my mouth I rap on the old brown painted wooden door. "Come in, it's unlocked." I hear her shout.

The door creaks as badly as the stairs as I push it open to enter a small room, lit dimly by a red table lamp, and I remember Charlie's comment back in the pub about her liking to keep the lights low. The room is neat but functional. No pictures or ornaments. No personal stuff at all that I can see. No Romilly either, till I hear her voice shout, "I'll be out in a tick. Its fifteen quid for a blowjob or thirty quid for the full works. " I settle myself in the small armchair, that apart from the double bed and an old Formica table with two rickety chairs which supports the rooms only dim light seems to comprise most of the room's furniture. I hear a toilet flush and a door opens opposite me. And there she is, at last, My 2007 Romilly. She stands in front of me in a well worn short red skirt and black stockings, a diaphanous almost see through white blouse, no bra, and her nipples vaguely discernible beneath the thin fabric. On her feet are a scuffed pair of black stiletto high heels. Her lank dyed blonde hair hangs loosely around her heavily made up face. She looks dirty and unkempt, a veritable fallen Madonna indeed. She looks at me dispassionately, the way you might study a kipper on the fish counter at Sainsbury's, but then I see a just the tiniest look of uncertainty cross her face. "Don't I know you?" she says. I slowly pull down my hood showing her my face. "Hello Rommy, I say, or should I be calling you Amber?" I look her straight in the eyes waiting for a response.

Chapter 33. Meeting Amber.

I watch expressionless as the emotions cross her face. Confusion, disbelief closely followed by fear and even a little anger. Then at last slow recognition. "Matt???" she asks, incredulous. She stands there immobile as I get up and opening my bag I slowly place the bottle of whisky and the two packs of cigarettes on the cheap stained Formica table. She follows my movements in disbelief as I find an ashtray and two tea mugs. I place the mugs on the table and motion for her to sit down opposite me. She moves around to unsteadily sit down opposite me her eyes never leaving mine once and I can see the heroin in her eyes, the cold craving. I look back into those dead eyes and unscrewing the whisky I pour us both a large slug. She takes a large swig and then breathes, "Why?" I say nothing and unwrap one packet of the cigarettes. Taking out two, I light them, and passing one to her I can see the tremor of her hands. She sucks hungrily on it and repeats, "Why?" but more firmly now. I just return her look and blow my smoke out in her direction but she doesn't lower her eyes. "You promised me. You promised me that you wouldn't try to find me you bastard." she says huskily. I lean forward and taking a slug of my scotch I say, "Yep but you were never going to tell me about this were you, so I joined the club and lied." She starts to stammer "But I never..." I cut in and tell her bitterly "You never lied to me babe you just omitted to tell me the truth. Didn't you? Same difference" For the first time I see her sad eyes drop.

"So Amber, and I accentuate the Amber almost spitting the name out, why didn't I deserve the truth?" Her hand rises from her lap and she starts to toy with the material of her blouse. I notice her bitten painted fingernails and look questioningly at her. She looks back at me, a look of defiance in her sad eyes and takes another deep drag of her cigarette. "Why the fuck would I want you to know about this." she says indicating the room. I notice the pack of condoms beside the bed and seeing that I've observed them she says in a small sad voice, "How could I ever have expected you to understand my life? How could you expect me to tell you about this bloody abysmal existence" "You could have tried you know, I'm pretty big on understanding, surely you know that. Did all the times I told you I that I loved you mean absolutely nothing. Did what happened between us mean nothing to you at all then. Was all that I said to you that worthless?" I say sadly. "So how did you find me then Matt. After you promised me you wouldn't?" "Your parent's, I answer, they used a firm of detectives. They know all about this too so I hope you are pleased to know that you are destroying them as well as yourself. Your dad is distraught." "They know?... Oh Christ. I didn't want that, I swear I never wanted that." she cries. I lean over and take her hand in mine, she doesn't resist, and raising the sleeve of her blouse to reveal the needle marks on her thin pale arm, I say, "And this. Didn't you want this either?" I pull her sleeve down again and let her arm go. It drops lifelessly into her lap. "It helps a little." she mumbles rubbing her arm where I just touched her." "It doesn't help anything Romilly, I say using her real name, it's killing you. Do you understand that? I can see it in your bloody eyes for God's sake."

As my words sink in she visibly shrinks and laying her head on top of her arms on the tabletop she starts to cry softly her tears wetting the arms of her blouse. Then looking up at me with tears streaming down her over made up face, she says, "Maybe that's what I want, that's what I knew you wouldn't understand, couldn't understand. I have nothing to live for anymore. I might just as well be dead." "So Romilly, I ask her cruelly, why didn't you just do it quickly. Why the long drawn out guilt trip. If your life is that bad why this slow descent into degradation?" The look of defiance returns to her face. Her makeup is badly smudged now and she looks a mess in her cheap whores outfit. "Because my life is a complete fuck up Matt, two failed marriages, my kids won't even speak to me anymore. I'm just another old brass addicted to jacking heroin. So why should I do it quickly. I want the pain, perhaps it's my penance. Can't you see that? Allow me that at least please." Her eyes bore into mine. I look back at her and I smile just a little. "One failed marriage." I correct her. She looks confused and I pour us both another scotch and light us another two cigarettes. I place one between her lips and watch as she takes a draw between her lipstick painted lips, scrutinising me from under hooded eyes. Exhaling the smoke she asks, "One? What do you mean one?" I take a swallow of the scotch and leaning closer to her I whisper, "Your first marriage never failed did it, and I'm still here......Romilly."

She looks back at me in shock. "But why? You can see how I am now. You should be off like a shot. I wouldn't blame you, I'm not your sweet little Rommy anymore am I for God's sake?" "Thought I told you, I smile, I'm big on understanding and I told you before that I love you no matter what happens. Always have, always will. I thought that you knew that?" I stand and walk around the table and taking her arm I lift her unresisting body slowly from the rickety chair. I raise her face gently with my fingers and kiss her lips, tasting the waxy taste of the lipstick on them. Then sitting her on the bed I strip the whore's clothes from her and searching her wardrobe I find some jeans and a simple white T-shirt. I put them on the bed beside her. I take her gently by the hand and take her into her shower. I start with the lank dyed blonde hair by lathering some shampoo into it. Finding some scented shower gel I wash her body all over starting from her face and working down to her feet. She looks at me listlessly as I wash her. I scrub the whores' makeup from her face. She ties to kiss me but I say "Wait." And I push her away. I turn her around in the shower and tenderly wash her slim back. I lead her from the shower by the hand and spend some time drying her with an old smelly towel I find hanging behind the door. I can see the needle marks on her thin arms and legs and I kiss them feeling her pain between my lips. I dry her and take her to her small bed. I lay her down and taking the packet of condoms I throw them out of her window. "Lay back Romilly, I say, I'm here and I am taking you away from this if you want me to. But only if you want me to." She tries to pull me to her but I resist. I am not going to make love to her in this room. No way. This is her past and I want to be her future. "No. First I need you to tell me." I find an old pyjama suit and put it on her. I take her thin little hand and hold it and stroking her face I watch as cries softly in my arms. I sit there beside her guarding her from her demons as she sobs. "Well? I ask her again. This life or my life?" "Are you really sure about this?" She asks me. "Stupid question. I tell her, you know I am." "Stupid answer then she smiles between her tears. You!"

And so at last now I have found the reason for her nightmares from our new 1981 in this small flat in the bad part of town as she tells me of her life. The drunken men who visited her just to abuse her and use her for their brief gratification. Totally loveless sex for money. No wonder that in her nightmares she tried to push me away and fight me. In her violent dreams back in our 1981 I was just another of them in her poor sad nightmares. Another punter using her body just as a vessel for their lust in her dreams. I had been telling her in 1981 of my great love for her and popping back to my boring unfulfilled life in 2007 and she had been coming back to me from this. Hell on earth for her and I feel shame at the way I had bullied her to tell me the awful truth about this life. But I knew I had done the right thing in finding her and I think she knew that too now. It hurt her terribly to know I had found her like this but I think she felt relief at not having to lie to me anymore. She went on to tell me of the two abortions she had to have. The heroin is not the best aid to remembering that you have to take your pill after all. And about the beatings she received at the hands of the drunken punters. And I sat beside her in that sad lonely room as she told me all about her life of drugs and abuse. As she tells me in a pitifully sad voice of her recent life I take her hairbrush and start to brush her hair gently, slowly removing the wet tangles from the shower. "I'm not a person to them, she tells me angrily. I'm just a bloody receptacle for their lust. Something to come into apart from their poor bloody wives on a Friday night. I tried to blot out the things they did to me with the heroin and do you know what Matt? She turned to look at me. After a while I didn't care. I really didn't care. As long as I can blot it out with this, she points to the needle scars on her arms; I really don't care at all. I have lost my children. So why should I care anymore?" She sits on the bed beside me and a sudden flash of pain crosses her features as she collapses against me sobbing. Taking her in my arms I ask her what's wrong. "It's ok she replies it's just a few stomach cramps from the heroin. Just don't worry about me Ok?" I finish brushing her hair and start to put her to bed then I sit beside her in one of the rickety chairs as she tries to sleep off her stomach cramps. She eventually passes out into a kind of sleep as I hold her thin hand, still full of her own personal demons but at least she is no longer alone.

Chapter 34. Saving Amber.

Slowly the dark night outside turns to a grey murky daylight and I start to prepare myself, shit or bust I think. A few items from by bag go into various pockets. I was only briefly a boy scout, I remember. I got drummed out unceremoniously at thirteen for inappropriate behaviour with a girl guide, I didn't care at the time as I think back in pleasure that they were the first female breasts I had felt. But I had always believed in being prepared. Romilly sleeps on occasionally turning over with a small moan of pain. She needs it. And so do I but I'm running on adrenaline by now. I daren't sleep. Six o'clock comes and I make myself tea and toast in her small kitchen. I make her tea as she awakes and she pleads for her needle. I help her to jack up the heroin. I'm not going to deny her that now. "What time does he come?" I say as she lays there amongst her heroin paraphernalia sipping her tea and pulling the belt tourniquet tight to feed herself the heroin. As if in answer I hear a loud knock on the door, she looks at me with fear in her eyes again. I supposed he would call early on his women to get any cash before they spent it. I unlatch it and her pimp barges in. He is a big lad I think to myself, smartly dressed but still he looks a thug. He looks at me dismissively. He looks at Romilly still in bed. He looks a tough bastard but not half as hard as the thug who follows him in. This must be his minder I think. He is dressed in denim jeans and a leather jacket and has a neck as thick as a gorilla with a face that is just as ugly. "Amber get your useless flabby ass out of bed." shouts the pimp. I sit on one of the chairs and wink at the ape. "Come on you slut get your ass up I need my dosh." shouts the pimp again. "How much did you make? he asks her, only you owe me loads for the smack." Romilly sits up and looks at the pimp blankly. "Amber you owe me three grand now baby, he says, and you just aint turning the tricks anymore. How are you going to pay me babe?" He sits down heavily beside her on the bed scattering her gear on the floor and grabs her face cruelly with his hand. "You little fucking whore, he spits, where's my cash?" I'm still sitting and make a move to stand up. Like lightning the ape pushes me back into the chair his fist against my chest. Damn he's quicker than I thought I think. I see the pimp slapping my Romilly's face threatening her relentlessly and I relax back into the chair and watch what happens next although not taking my eyes off of the ape. "So you fucked my bitch last night did you? he says turning to look at me menacingly. How much did you pay her?" "Nothing at all, I say, she paid me so I reckon you are the one that owes me some dosh shit for brains." I smile sweetly at him and receive a slap from his minder for my trouble. He looks at me incredulously as I wipe a small trickle of blood from my lip and then turning to Romilly he says, "Who the fuck is this joker. Is he on the shit as well?" She looks at me a small smile on her lips and then back at him and says. "He is my husband so just leave him alone Ok." Both of the men are looking at Romilly in amazement and so taking my chance I pull the small canister of mace tear gas from my pocket and leaping up I give the ape a blast in his fat ugly face. He collapses on the floor clutching his face in agony. The pimp looks on astonished wondering what is happening so I advance on him quickly. I can see just a little fear in his face but it's enough to make my heart sing. I give him a little taste of the spray too. He collapses to floor rubbing his eyes, worst thing you can do that, it just rubs it in and makes the irritation more intense. "Grab his keys Romilly, I shout and anything else useful, phones cash anything." The ape is starting to recover so I take a small fruit knife courtesy of Sainsbury's from my pocket and punch it into his fat ass. He squeals like a woman. I rifle his pockets and after emptying them of anything interesting just for old time's sake, I kick him in the head to quieten him a little. I presume it works as he groans and goes silent. One advantage of my works protective steel toe capped trainers I think. "Ok Rommy, make it quick." I say. The pimp is still down moaning and holding his face and I sashay over and give him a little slap to the face. Just to keep him docile as it were. Romilly dresses quickly in the jeans and T-shirt I had laid out then grabs a bag and throwing some stuff from the bedsit in it, we are out of there in a jiffy. The ape tries to rise as we pass by so giving him another swift kick to the stomach on the way out we disappear out of there in double quick time. I know the mace will hold them for only a couple of minutes but that's enough for me. We exit the house quickly running down the stairs in a rush to escape and out of the grotty entrance hall but I stop her briefly and say. "So are you sure you want to say goodbye to this babe. Do you want to?" She grabs my arm and says, "Only if you really still want me? My arm wraps around her and I kiss her lips. "Do you doubt me?" At last I see some fire in her eyes. "No never again." she says firmly. "Ok let's move it. Have you got his keys?" She places a bunch of keys in my hand. I ask her which car is the pimps and she points rather obviously to a rather nice looking BMW parked a short way down the street looking extremely out of place among the other tatty vehicles on the street. "Duhhh. Black BMW. Pimpmobile?" I smile. "And his stash? She looks at me evasively. Now." I shout. She hands me a large pack of smack. "Wow. I say. There must be a couple of grand's worth here at least. I pocket it and pass her my car keys. "Ok it's the mauve Berlingo I say pointing down the street. Put your stuff in the back and start it up. Get ready for a quick getaway Ok?" I run to the pimps BMW and opening it I look inside. Mm very nice I think inhaling the scent of expensive leather. I hide the large bag of heroin under the back seat, and then before lifting the bonnet to pull a couple of wires loose I have a quick rummage through the motor. I memorise its registration number as I run back to the house and throw the keys back into the hallway. Then as I hear feet coming down the stairs I run like hell to my car. Romilly is sitting in the driver's seat looking questioningly at me from the open window. "Drive NOW , I shout as I jump into the passenger seat, as fast as you can. We want the M4." I look behind and see the pimp and his muscle running towards us, the ape is limping badly and no way is he going to catch us but the pimp seems pretty nippy still but then Romilly puts her foot down and I hear the wheels burning rubber as we shoot away from them. I see them stop and run back towards the BMW. I can see with enormous satisfaction a large bloody stain on the back of the ape's jeans. "Don't worry they won't be going anywhere, I assure Romilly, now head for the M4 and pass me the pimp's phone." Copying one of the numbers from my phone into it I make a call. Romilly is laughing as I tell the Swindon Constabulary of a gang fight and I think they have drugs and I give them the BMW's registration number and where to find it. Declining to give my name I ring off after telling them to hurry before the thugs get away and I think they have guns. I wait until we reach the M4 and are cruising at 70 before I open the window and chuck the phone out of the window to see it smash into hundreds of pieces on the hard shoulder. "Ok Romilly I am totally shattered, I say reclining my seat, wake me when we get to Cambridge." She squeezes my hand and then I'm gone. Out like the proverbial light. The last thought I have is that maybe we have done it. Perhaps we have just done it.

Chapter 35. Return to the Flat.

I wake up with a stiff neck and the car has stopped. We are at a petrol station and Romilly isn't there. I sit up and rub the sleep from my eyes wondering where she is. It is raining and I can hear the sound of cars whooshing past on the wet road outside. She appears from out of the garage and swinging herself into the car passes me a sandwich, a can of coke and a Mars bar. "Thought you might be needing this." she says smiling at me. I glug eagerly on the coke and as we leave the garage I light us a cigarette each. "She looks just about all in and I guess she must be getting close to needing another fix soon. "Ok Rommy take the next right and carry on for 12 miles, not far now."

We arrive at my flat just before midday and grabbing her bag from the boot I lead her in. I see her looking around the small flat, running her finger along a picture of my kids examining it sadly. "How do you feel?" I ask her. "Totally and utterly shattered." she says tiredly. I lead her through to the bedroom and help her into my small single bed. I stroke her face and see her drop into almost immediate sleep. I put her bag beside the bed and leaving her to sleep I go back into the small living room. Looking back on the events of the past day and a half I pass out also on the sofa to my own dreamless sleep. I come to about 8 pm in darkness just the orange glow of the outside streetlights lighting the room. Switching on the light and drawing the curtain, I go and look in on Romilly. She is still sleeping soundly so I jump in the shower and then put on some clean clothes. I tidy up quickly and then nip out to the chip shop across the square; I am famished and return to the flat with our evening meal. I can hear the shower running and knock on the door. "Grub up." I shout through the door. Going to my small kitchen I arrange the fish and chips on plates and take it through to the living room along with a nice bottle of red wine, Montepulciano d Abruzzo, one of my favourites. She enters a few minutes later smiling at me and wearing my grey dressing gown and I have to admit that she looks a lot better in it than I do. "Awww I thought I smelt fish and chips, it reminds me of our holiday. Do you remember Acle Matt?" "Less salubrious surroundings though." I tell her."Don't knock it Matt it's a lovely little place I love it, she grins, and it's better than where I was before." "Eat up babe." I tell her pouring us some wine. Romilly and I both eat ravenously and before long the plates are empty. I get up to clear them but her hand pushes me back into my seat. "No you sit there Matt and I'll wash up. It's the least I can do." She insists firmly.

I switch on the Pc and shout to her, "Any music you fancy?" "No you choose." she calls, so I put on Snow Patrol in honour of our first meeting in 1981. She appears from the kitchen and grabs me pulling my face to hers, kissing me softly. "You bastard I really love this you know." She says between kisses. I lead her to the sofa and fetch the wine and glasses. She takes a pack of cigarettes and lights two for us, putting one between my lips. We lay back on the sofa and all that remains is the talking. So I talk to her. I put my arm around her shoulder and tell her that this place is hers too. She looks stunned but I tell her. "It's not a lot but if you want it it's your home too. I will have to get us a bigger bed and we need a bigger wardrobe too, BUT, this place is ours Ok? No arguments. She pulls me closer to her and squeezes me. "Shit. Matt I don't know what to say." "How about welcome home handsome." I say grinning. She pulls back a little and scrutinising me says, "Well I dunno about handsome but you don't look too bad for 54 I suppose, a bit crusty around the edges though." "For God's sake Rommy, I laugh, I rescue your sorry ass and straight away you are insulting me. Seriously though we need to ring your folks." I say picking up the mobile. I place the call and hear Naomi's voice at the other end. "Hi Naomi, it's Matt, I tell her, I've got good news, someone here wants to talk to you." I pass the phone to Romilly and sit back listening to the conversation, Romilly telling her mum she's Ok, and not to worry as she is with me. Then she is crying over the phone telling her mum that she loves her and not to worry. Then she is talking to Will telling him the same." "Tell them we'll be down tomorrow." I butt in. She ends the call to her parents and melts into my arms, my 43 year old Romilly. "You know what? I say to her softly. You still are my little Rommy after all." She digs me in the ribs while she snuggles up closer to me. I get up and put an old Bon Jovi album on that I find on the Pc. It's a best of and we sit back listening to 'In These Arms Tonight'. We sit together but I can see that she is starting to get twitchy and so I go to fetch her gear. I cook the smack and applying an old belt as a tourniquet I help her to inject her fix. She holds her arm out as I inject the shit looking at me with pain in her eyes, "I'm sorry." She tells me sadly. I clean up after her and see a soporific smile appear on her face after a few minutes as the heroin reaches her brain. Tenderly I hold her. "I want some too, I say, just to remind me of the old days." She passes me the kit but as I said before I hate needles so I lay some out on the coffee table and using my penknife I break down any lumps till I have a nice fine line. Using an old tenner from my wallet I sniff the line of the stuff up one nostril in one go. It's the first time I have touched drugs in many years. Within 10 minutes I can feel it hitting the spot and relax back with her. She smiles lovingly at me and squeezes my arm looking so happy. "Do you remember back in the original 80s after we married and lived at the flat Rommy? We had that glass topped coffee table." Romilly laughs and says, "Yeah I remember we snorted a few lines off of it too babe didn't we?" It is great to see her smiling and laughing after what has happened to her in the last few years. I know she is going to find it hard forgetting the pain but I vow to do my best. I fetch the scotch from the kitchen and pour us generous measures as we talk about the old times together.

We both have a pleasant buzz by now from the smack and she pulls me up from the sofa and leads me to the bedroom. She pushes me back onto to the bed and stands before me looking down at me with lovelight in her eyes. She crosses her arms and lifts the T-shirt over her head. She unsnaps her bra and throws it into the corner. I see her breasts have sagged a little with age but still look fine; I can see the needle marks on her arms. She releases her jeans and they fall to the floor along with her knickers. She still has the lovely slim legs I see and she kneels beside me unbuttoning my shirt kissing my nipples and unhurriedly removing the rest of my clothes. I feel her take my hardening manhood in her hand and stroke it gently with her small slim fingers. She kisses its sensitive tip and then she works her way up my body kissing it along the way. Her tongue is in my navel then on my nipples and eventually my mouth, kissing me hungrily. I reach behind her and stroke her back and run my fingers along her spine pulling her tightly to me. We look into each other's eyes and know this is the way it should be, her caressing me, and I feel her mount me, her sex sliding down on my hardness. Drawing me into her fully I can feel her muscles caressing me. She starts to rock gently on me, soft moans escaping her. I roll her over and make love to her, tears coming to my eyes with my emotions. I look down on her, legs spread wide and me deep inside her. She opens her eyes and looks at me. "I love you so much Matt, how could I have ever doubted you?" I stroke her face and hair in reply and eventually feel my climax building and then I feel myself cumming inside her releasing myself in gorgeous waves of pleasure. We lay together afterwards as I feel myself softening inside her. She is stroking my face and telling me she loves me and this time its forever. I look at her face in the light from the living room shining in through the bedroom door. "We need to talk." I tell her. No point in dressing. We aren't going anywhere so we sit back in the living room on the sofa together naked. "I want you to give up the heroin, I tell her. I see fear in her eyes briefly but I carry on. It will kill you and I don't want you leaving me again Ok?" She nods her head uncertainly and lies back against me. "I know it's not going to be easy babe but I will be there every step of the way for you Ok?" We listen to more music, 'Styx', and I ask her about the nightmares she was having in 1981. "Were they about your life in 2007? "Yes she tells me and a shadow of fear crosses her face momentarily, obviously I couldn't tell you about them then but they are really horrible, full of pain and hurt, full of monsters and death. Don't ask me to go into detail Matt. It only reminds me Ok? Besides they might stop now that I'm safe and with you. I agree to that and then I take her hand in mine and squeeze it tightly as we lay together on the small sofa together. I watch her as she slowly passes into sleep as 'Babe' plays softly in the background and I feel so happy that she sleeps soundly beside me without her nightmares that night after I lift her small body from the sofa and carry her through to my.. No. OUR bedroom.

Chapter 36. First Day of Our New Life.

I awake early the next morning with the dawn and the first thing I see is Romilly's tousled sleeping head nestling against my shoulder. Her dyed blonde hair is there to remind me of her recent past and sadly I stroke my fingers through it while still holding her tightly to my chest. She has slept without her nightmares I think happily as I look at her peaceful sleeping face, pale in the mornings light through the window curtains. I lightly kiss her lined but still lovely face and slip out of our small warm bed. It was a damned tight squeeze in there I think not unpleasantly but we will have to get a bigger bed as soon as possible. I raise the roller blind in the kitchen and fill the kettle from the tap for our tea. As it boils I light a cigarette and plan the coming day ahead. Taking the mugs of tea through to our bedroom I sit on the bed and rouse her slowly. She awakes looking briefly confused but then realising where she is she smiles happily at me and says, "Mornin' Spears is that tea I can see?" "Yep babe, I laugh, drink up and get that sorry chubby butt out of bed, we have lots to do today." "Oooh I love it when you get all masterful." she grins sipping the tea. She pulls my face to hers and kisses me and I feel her want as our mouths meet. I can smell our previous night's lovemaking in the bed and soon we are at it again. I slide in to the small bed beside her and my early morning hardness slips into her so easily. Her arms are around me caressing my back as I make love with her, gently this time with no hurry, savouring each other's nearness and touch. Feeling each other's need and joy at being together at last in our joint 2007. After our lovemaking we shower together, soaping each other and laughing under the warm spray. She makes us breakfast as I dress, tea and toast and loving kisses. "Ok Romilly, I say, time for your new life but first I think you need some clothes and we most definitely need a new bed as well." She is wearing the jeans and T-shirt I had put out for her the previous day, the only clothes she now owns. We hit the shops and buy her some new kit, jeans skirts blouses, lots of underwear. The pimp's money pays for it all of course and there's plenty of it, almost ten grand most of which was in a brown envelope that I found under the seat of the BMW, he won't be needing it where he is going I guess. Then makeup and all the basics, soap, toothpaste, shampoo. And last of all a double bed for the flat. Next stop is to be her parents and as we make the short trip to Cardinals Stratford she has her fix in the car as I drive. Her parents are overjoyed at seeing her and after much hugging and kissing Will takes us out for dinner. I can see the happiness on his face as he hugs his daughter, shaking my hand too. He actually looks pleased to see me which must be a first. "What are your plans he asks us?" "Just to be happy again, says Romilly squeezing her Dads hand, just to be normal again." Naomi pulls me aside as Romilly is talking to Will and asks me how I had persuaded Romilly to come back when they had tried to without success. "Naomi, it is a very long story and one day I may tell you but I warn you now that you will probably not believe me." I tell her. She looks at me not understanding but after a few moments she smiles and says, "Well Matt I will look forward to your story but it doesn't matter really. All that matters is that she is back and out of that terrible place, and what's more she actually looks happy. This is the first time I've heard her laugh in years you know it is so wonderful and... Well... thank you." I give her mum and dad our address and our phone number before we leave telling them to visit us anytime, and we arrive home to await the delivery of our new bed. Its late afternoon and we sit in the lounge listening to the Editors together and talking. "So how's your new life going Romilly, is this for you?" I ask her. "Don't be daft Matt you know I am so happy now. In just 48 hours you have given me a reason to live again. I can face my life again now that I have you and don't have to lie anymore." She squeezes my hand. "And how about the smack, how much do you have left?" I ask. "Three days if I'm careful." she says. I ask if she is ready to stop taking it, knowing that it's not going to be easy. She looks sadly at me and tells me she is as ready as she will ever be and knows that it will be hard. But she knows I will be with her to help her through it all. So I tell her that I will book us in at the doctors and after a short phone call I arrange us an appointment for the day after tomorrow.

The bed arrives shortly after and it takes me about half an hour to assemble it after I struggle getting the old single one out of the door and down the stairs ready for the council to pick up. When I finish assembling it Romilly brings me a mug of tea and then she finishes the job by putting on the bed linen. We admire our handiwork then sit down with our mugs of tea in the kitchen. I reach for her hand across the table and stroke her fingers lightly and I see the lovelight in her 2007 face as she smiles back at me across the table. "Hungry?" I ask her and she tells me yes. Now I am not much of a cook so I rustle us up a couple of microwave meals, spag bols, with crusty French bread slices and a nice bottle of Cotes Du Rhone to wash it down. We sit in the lounge eating it and watch one of my favourite films on DVD. The Bourne Ultimatum with Matt Damon. Romilly washes up as I uncork another bottle of wine and we settle back down together on the sofa to listen to some music before christening our new bed together. I put on our old favourite from 1981. Dan Fogelbergs 'Netherlands' and we talk of all that has happened to us in 1981 and 2007 since we shared that wonderful first reunion in Capfield forest together but before long Romilly is yawning and we decide to go to bed. I stand up and take her hand and lead her to the bedroom. We stand in the doorway for a few seconds first admiring our new bed together in the soft glow of the bedside lamps, arms around each other's waists and then we sit down on it and I take her face in my hands and kiss her lightly. I start unbuttoning the buttons on her blouse but she stops me and tells me she has a surprise for me but I have to leave the room first and no peeking. "Mmm sounds interesting." I laugh and leave shutting the door behind me. After a few minutes I hear her call out. "Ok Matt you can come in now." And so I re-enter the room and see her laying on the bed on her side smiling seductively at me. "Wow!" I say. "And?" she asks me. "Just Wow again." I tell her. She must have bought it on our shopping trip earlier that day when I wasn't looking I think as I admire the beautiful silky pink nightie that she is wearing. It follows the curves of her small body perfectly accentuating all of her curves. I walk towards the bed admiring her and start to undress unable to take my eyes off her. After all the years and at 43 years of age she is still so beautiful to me. Despite the needle marks and the lines appearing on her face and the cheap blonde dye in her hair I can still see the beauty of her and my heart is hers at that beautiful moment in time as I lie on the bed beside her and gather her into my arms. We kiss and I can feel the flimsy silky material that is the only thing between us. It just feels so wonderfully erotic. We start to make love together gently feeling our excitement growing by the minute but all of a sudden I feel her stiffen and opening my eyes I see a flash of pain on her face. I pull myself from her and ask her if she is ok. She has pain etched on her face but tells me not to worry at all; it's just the stomach cramps from the heroin. I go out to the kitchen after throwing on my shirt and shorts and make her some warm milk and return with it and some ibuprofen to try to ease the pain. "I'm so sorry Matt I've ruined the evening haven't I?" she tells me still holding her tummy in pain. "No you haven't Romilly I tell her giving her the tablets it isn't your fault. And it has been a beautiful evening, now take these and drink your milk it will help Ok." And so I lay beside her holding her in bed gently in my arms as she writhes in pain beside me clutching her painful stomach, until eventually I suppose that the painkillers kick in and she passes into a fitful sleep beside me still in her lovely silk nightie.

Chapter 37. Rhiannon Jamie and Beth

The next morning she awakes beside me still in some pain but a lot better than the previous night and I get up telling her to stay in bed and take it easy. "Don't worry babe I will make you some tea just stay in bed and rest." I make us mugs of tea and take her some more painkillers in. I start tidying up and when I look in on her she has gone back to sleep, so I write her a note and prop it up against her glass of orange juice so she will see it when she wakes telling her that I have gone shopping. I have my daily shower and leave the flat quietly taking some of our ill gotten gains from the pimp. I daren't pay it in the bank; we will just have to use it to live on. Oh well at least I can have a good spend up at Sainsbury's I smile to myself. As I am driving there I see my daughter Rhiannon walking out of her flat in the Junction so I toot the horn and pull up beside her. She jumps into the car beside me and asks me where I'm off to. Sainsbury's I tell her. "How are you off for shopping?" "The usual Dad. Skint and foodless." "Same old story then, I groan, Ok you better come shopping with me then. " We have a pleasant expedition and I blow lots of the pimp's money on her getting her some new clothes along with her shopping and a new mobile with lots of credit on it for her. I tell her I've left mum and where I am living now and ask her to pop round later to meet Romilly. I do worry so much about her lately, she is such a dreamer and needs to grasp life by the balls and do something but it's pointless telling her that as I would just get lots of abuse back in return and so I drop her off at her place and bung her some cash for treats.

Returning home I find Romilly is awake and looking so much brighter now than when I left. "Awww you look a lot better babe." I tell her as I walk in. She is sitting in the kitchen drinking tea and I bend down to kiss her.

"Yea it's ok I get the pains sometimes but they pass."
She smiles at me. Her heroin gear is on the table and I
ask if she can put it away as my daughter might be
coming around some time. I fetch the shopping from
the car and unpack and tell her we have a treat. "Yep I
am cooking you a steak dinner my little friend I tell her.
Chips, veggies the whole works. Sit back and prepare to
be amazed Ok?" "She looks at me for a few moments
and then tells me to chill out as she will cook it for us.
"Might avoid me getting food poisoning too Spears." she
grins impishly. Well as I said I am no Jamie Oliver in
the kitchen and so figuring it might do her good I let
her get on with it and I pack stuff away as she gets on
with our dinner. Apart from that I know that Romilly
was always a good cook, certainly better than I ever
was. So I go through to the lounge and stock our drinks
cabinet with some particularly nice malt whiskies that
the pimp has treated us to. Then I sit down on the Pc
and check if we have our broadband yet. No such luck
and so I put some music on, Amy MacDonald's new
album. Romilly surpasses herself with our meal. Not a
single microwave item in it and I gobble it down
hungrily telling her that she is a star. Rhiannon turns up
that evening about five. Rhiannon is my eldest daughter
and this is the first time she has met Romilly. I watch
nervously as they meet. They say hello. This is
Rhiannon's first visit to our flat and she looks around
the room curiously and shyly. I think to myself privately
that Rhiannon is sixteen and a half now. Three months
younger than Romilly was when I first met her. Lots of
similarities in that Rhiannon couldn't wait to leave home
either. She can't seem to live with Elaine and me, just a
clash of personalities and teenage angst. But Romilly
was a lot more worldly at that age I think as I study
Rhiannon. Another failure I suppose in my life I think
sadly. She seems to be heading nowhere but I hope she
will eventually find her niche in life. Surprisingly her and
Romilly seem to hit it off and are soon talking like old

mates. "You know my Dad talks about you sometimes and he is always looking at your pictures on our computer. He thinks that I don't know but I do." she tells Romilly. "Really?" says Romilly smiling at me. I go to make the tea after I laugh and tell her not to give any more of my deepest secrets away. When I return from the kitchen Romilly has found my old artists pad and is drawing with a pencil she has found somewhere. I put an old Dire Straits album on and Rhiannon talks about her latest expectations. She's living at a local place called The Junction now that is supposed to help disaffected young teenagers but it doesn't get my vote much in that department as Rhiannon still seems to be doing nothing. Romilly carries on drawing, her tongue out in concentration as we all talk and laugh and eventually Rhiannon asks to see the drawing. Romilly has always been a wonderful artist and holds up her pencil sketch for us to see. It is truly beautiful, a sketch of Rhiannon smiling, that look of mischievousness shining through her young face. It captures her in every way. "Wow that's great, Rhiannon cries, I love it. Romilly you are such a great artist. Can I have it?" Romilly smiles at her obviously pleased at the compliment from my daughter and says, "Yea Ok but first let your Dad scan it on to our PC first." Rhiannon loves her sketch so much and I must admit it has really caught her in a moment in time. Rhiannon impatiently goes to scan it onto the PC. "When we go back, whispers Romilly I will do it again for you to remind you. We can take something back after all you know?" I kiss her inviting lips but Rhiannon looks round from the computer and feigns sick making gestures. "Dad you are so embarrassing." she laughs.

After Rhiannon leaves I talk to Romilly about the sketch. "That is such a beautiful idea I tell her, we can't take photos back but I never thought of sketches. I will have to get Jamie and Beth round so you can draw them too. At least I will have something to remind me of them when we go back for good. Do you mind Romilly?" I ring Elaine and ask her if the kids are there. I get a little abuse at first as she taunts me about me leaving her and the kids but I know she is probably happier at this time with me moving away from her and it sounds like she has had a few as well. "So are you coming home?" she asks me bitterly. "Not at the moment. I reply. I have things to sort out first." I hear her put the phone down on me so I ring Jamie's mobile and ask him to bring Beth round to visit us. Romilly is watching me intently as I have this conversation, and she smiles at me in sadness as I put the phone down. They turn up about half an hour later. Jamie full of curiosity and Beth looking warily around as I ask them in. "So how's Mum." I ask Beth. "Being a pain as usual." she smiles. "Come on in then." I tell her ushering them into the small lounge. "Rhiannon was here earlier." I tell them and Jamie asks me when I'm coming home. I tell him I can't at the moment and then Romilly emerges from the bedroom. She has obviously had a fix and looks so laid back as she welcomes Jamie and Beth in. "Ok gang meet Romilly." I tell them and they say hello shyly to her. Jamie seems nonchalant as usual but Beth seems quiet and withdrawn as she usually does with strangers. I go out to make the tea yet again as they get to know each other and I return with chocolate biscuits and opened cans of coke. Always the way to their hearts I think smiling to myself. I ask them how they are doing at school as Romilly settles down with the art pad in the corner seat to begin sketching. I bring the picture of Rhiannon up on the Pc to show them but they don't seem that interested. And I can see Beth's face start to crinkle up and the small tears start to run down her cheek as she suddenly grabs me and hugs me tight. "Dad please come home I miss you." she whimpers. "Darling I will soon Ok I just need to sort things out first." I tell her wiping the tears away. Jamie looks on disdainfully at his sister's tears. "Come on I tell them cheerfully I have more biscuits, chocolate ones too." Beth looks a bit happier at last and takes three of the proffered biscuits. Jamie follows suit and sits there stuffing himself. "Have you got an Xbox Dad?" he asks me hopefully. "No, only the Pc." I tell him much to his disappointment. I must admit they don't seem too enthusiastic about Romilly and they leave after snaffling all the biscuits. Oh well what did I expect I think sadly, at least they came. In the meantime Romilly has drawn two lovely pictures of them which I admire before scanning them to the Pc. You can see the happiness in Beth's face and the cheeky couldn't care less grin on Jamie's. Romilly is in pain again with stomach cramps by now so I usher her into the bedroom and tell her to rest for an hour or so while I sit back on the sofa and pour myself a large malt whisky courtesy of the pimp. I then get a vituperative call from Elaine later telling me how much I have upset Beth by introducing her to my whore. I laugh at her use of the word whore thinking she doesn't realise how perceptive she is being right now. Elaine has obviously had a few as she starts to plead with me to come home. "Babe I am home I tell her." The phone goes dead on me again. I suppose I knew this would happen but what can I do. I love Elaine so much but I love Romilly also and at the present time she needs me more.

Romilly spends a couple of hours sleeping, but walks through to the lounge looking sleepy still at about 9:30 that night. I have Daniel Powter's album playing quietly on the hard drive, listening to 'Bad Day', and savouring my scotch. She is wearing a just a long T-shirt and my flip flops. "How are you feeling mate, are the tummy pains any better?" I ask her taking her hand and sitting her down on the sofa beside me. "They have almost gone now, she smiles, and I think the ibuprofen helped." I put my arm around her to comfort her and ask her if she is hungry. "A little." I ask her if she fancies some cheese on toast and she nods wearily, stifling a yawn. I make my way out to the kitchen and warm up the grill and put the kettle on. Slicing some cheese I shout through to her. "Red or brown sauce?" She tells me red would be lovely and I take the toasties through to her with a large mug of tea to wash them down with. I sit back down beside her as she enjoys my cuisine, laughing at the faces I have drawn on the toasties with the tomato ketchup. A smiling face on one and a sad face on the other. In between mouthfuls she asks me which one is hers? "They are both you, I tell her, the sad one is you before you came back here and I hope the happy one is you from now on." "Awww Matt, she smiles, that is just so sweet." Then she asks me what will happen to us here when we go back to 1981 permanently. I think to myself for a while and then tell her, "Well Romilly I must admit I haven't thought that much about it so far but I would hope we will be together here. I don't know perhaps if you sort yourself out you will move on from me. You know? Start your life afresh." "Romilly looks at me in astonishment for a while and then replies. "Matt you can be really stupid sometimes. Of course I will stay with you. I have no intention of leaving this time. I do love you so much in 1981 and here in 2007 as well you idiot. After all that has happened? How do you think I could ever leave to ....What was it you said? Start my life afresh? This is starting my life afresh and I do want to be back in 1981 with you but it would make me just so incredibly happy if I knew I was here with you in 2007 also." I lean forward to the woman I am so in love with and wiping some ketchup from her lip I kiss her. "I love you." I tell her. We sit having a nice smooch for a while and then I ask her what she thinks of my kids. "Jamie is the most like you, she says. He's all bravado upfront but he hides his true feelings you know." I think of what a little git he can be sometimes and smile. "Do you think so; I always thought Rhiannon was the most like me?" "Well yes she is like you but she shows her feelings more than you ever did." I think about this and ask her about Beth. "Mmm replies Romilly She is a hard one to call. I think she will go the furthest in life. She knows how to wind you around her little finger for a start." "So how about us then when we go back?" I ask her pouring us both another scotch. "That's going to be down to us Matt isn't it now but as far as I am concerned you are the only one for me back there after all this. She snuggles up to me on the sofa and takes my hand and kisses it. I relax back on the sofa with her but after a while I can see she is crying softly. "Awww babe why the tears?" I ask her. "Because I never trusted you and I should have. I should have told you about my life here I know that now but something always held me back. I almost told you on the Sandpiper when you got me drunk that afternoon but I just couldn't. I even almost told you that day back at my parent's house when I asked you to marry me but I kept thinking of how you were back in our original timeline and how I wouldn't have trusted you then and could I trust you now, but I can see now how much you have changed. You have lost the callousness you had sometimes then and and....... Oh it's so hard to explain.... Ok I'll try. You are a complete person to me now. Before there was something missing in you. I always got the feeling that I couldn't trust you completely. I loved you yes most certainly but there was always that doubt in me that you were really mine. I always thought you would leave me for someone else and so I suppose another reason for deciding to leave you then was that I decided to get out first before you did. Do you remember that day towards the end in 1983 when I told you I loved you but didn't like you? Well that was it. I suppose I loved the person you could become but I hated the person that you were then. If only I had stayed Matt If only I had given you a chance. But I didn't. I was young, you know that now. But after all we have been through recently together? Well what else can I tell you? Three little words? I love you... Totally." I kiss her dry lips tasting the ketchup on her mouth and lean back and smile. "That's four word's you dipstick."

Chapter 38. The Doctors Appointment.

We arrive the next morning at the doctors early, a first appointment. Romilly has not had her morning fix and had given me the last of her heroin and her works the evening before. Looking at the small bag I had doubted if there was more than a day's worth left. We have to sign Romilly up as a patient first. The doctor is a lovely young thing of about 25 I notice and looks sympathetically at us as I tell her of Romilly's addiction and other problems. The Doctor goes on to explain to us all about heroin addiction. Nothing much we didn't know already. There are two choices basically. Going cold turkey with help from painkillers and withdrawal drugs or the methadone route in which case you are swapping one addictive drug for another but aim to wean yourself off it slowly. I hold Romilly's hand and ask her which it is to be and she chooses the cold turkey way. The doctor agrees but looking over her glasses tells me it is going to be hard for both of us and am I going to be there for her in her bad moments? "Of course I am." I tell, her that won't be a problem. And so the doctor takes blood tests and signs her up to a clinic for drug addiction in Cambridge. I also tell the doctor of Romilly's stomach pains but the doctor tells us not to worry as it could be the heroin and we may know more after the test results come back. She jots down a few more notes and we get a prescription for the medication and leave the surgery together.

Romilly hasn't looked well through the whole consultation and I take her thin body in my arms and help her into the car. Getting in myself I ask her if she's ok. "Yea I'm great, she smiles, just a little cramp in my tummy. I'll be Ok as soon as we get home." We stop at the chemist's for her medications on the way home and I help her out of the car and into the flat. I can see she is in a lot of pain and so I suggest she goes back to bed and I will make her some warm milk to wash down some of the new painkillers. As I take them through to her I can see the pain is causing her some distress as she screws her body up in the bed hugging her abdomen. "Shhh babe I'm here." I say stroking her cold clammy forehead after putting the mug of warm milk on the bedside table for her. I give her two of the pain killers holding the mug to her lips so she can wash them down and sit beside her on the bed tenderly stroking her arm and hand slowly, thankfully the pain recedes, but she lays there looking totally worn out, a cold sweat on her forehead. I climb into our new bed and hold her close to me. I can feel the shivers coursing through her body but she eventually drops off into a troubled sleep beside me. I think sadly to myself that this is the start of her withdrawal symptoms and will it not get any better for a while, at least a week. She sleeps fitfully and I get up to tidy the flat and make myself something to eat. I hear her calling my name and go into the bedroom. She is laying there looking up at me pitifully and I rush to hold her. She is soaked in sweat but icy cold and her whole body is shivering. "Please Matt just let me have a little I don't think I can do this, I think I'm going to die I feel so bad." She pleads, tears in her eyes and I almost cave in seeing her laying there looking so ill but I tell her that she mustn't give in. "Romilly look at me baby. We are going to fight this together darling and this is only the first day Ok? If you can make it through till tomorrow you will feel so much better, I promise you that you will. I know it's so hard for you but just give it a go for us eh?" She looks unconvinced so taking her hand I talk to her about 1981 and how she looked after me after the crash. "Do you remember how you banned nookie so I could recover quickly? She smiles a little just a glimpse of a smile. Well baby doing without smack can't be any worse than that was can it? Now I see more of a smile and she seems a little happier at last. "Now, I say pulling the duvet further over her, you are going to be a good girl while I make you some soup and a tea while you lay here and rest." She smiles a little and tries to punch me playfully but I take her fist and opening her small hand I kiss her fingers one at a time.

I prepare her some vegetable soup with some nice fresh bread and butter and a large mug of strong tea and take it through but I see she has dropped off and seems to be sleeping peacefully so I leave her be as I reckon the sleep will be a hell of a lot better for her at the moment than the food, so I put it away for later and drink the tea myself. I even doze a little myself on the sofa for a while. When I awake I can hear her in the kitchen moving about. She smiles as I enter the kitchen and see her warming the soup. "Hiya Sexy. How do you feel?" I ask her. She is wearing the fluffy pink dressing gown I had bought her and looking slightly better for having had a few hours sleep. "Not too sexy and I'm ravenous as well." She says. I tell her to sit at the small table and kiss her dry lips before finishing off warming her soup in the microwave. I put the bread and butter on the table and proceed to make her some tea. I make myself one as well and sit down opposite her watching her break off pieces of bread to dip in her soup. I see that her hands are trembling as she eats the soup. When she has finished I ask her if she wants more. She shakes her head, so I take her bowl and wash it up. Leaning back against the sink afterwards and crossing my arms I look at her sitting there. She looks rough, I mean really rough. Her dyed blonde hair is sweaty and matted; her thin pale leg pokes out between the folds of the dressing gown. Her face is haggard and her eyes look like mine do after a heavy late night session. I think that the old expression, pissholes in the snow would be an appropriate description of them and I remind myself how only a days before she was turning tricks for twenty quid a time in a dismal room in Swindon with the local dregs to pay for her habit.

But as I look at her sipping the tea I made her I know without any uncertainty that this bedraggled woman in front of me is the only woman that I have ever loved. I suppose I always knew that. All I want to do is rebuild her life again, and give her a reason to smile and laugh again. Whether it's here or in 1981 I will be with her always if she wants me. But will she still want me when she recovers I ask myself. Will she ditch me again? She did before so I suppose logically she could do so again. I know she had told me of her deep eternal love for me but she had told me that before in the real 1981 and as soon as things got a little bad between us she left me. Left me is probably an understatement I think. She abandoned me totally, without a thought of the pain she caused me. She took the easy option then, will she do it again. I shake my head unable to answer my own doubts. Will it be a case of, You Win Again? I think remembering the old Hot Chocolate song. Maybe I'm a fool but I know that I love her. Terminally. Always have always will, I think. But whatever happens? Well I suppose I will always love her and I smile. She looks up from her tea and smiles back at me. "What you grinning like a fool for now Spears?" she grins. "Nothing, I tell her, just thinking that I can't wait until that blonde dye grows out of your hair. It doesn't suit you, you know. Come on lets go through to the lounge we can see what's on TV."

I put the TV on for background noise and settle her back onto the sofa. She pulls her legs up underneath herself and sits back. I sit beside her and she leans into me taking my hand and stroking it gently. There is only crap on TV so I ask her if she wants some music on. She nods her head wearily so I search the Pc quickly and find something a little laid back for her. James

Blunts album. "Mmm I like this it's so relaxing." She whispers. She lays back, her head in my lap and her thin gangly legs hanging over the end of the sofa. We listen for a while without talking and I think she has dozed off until she says. "Thank you Matt." "For what darling?" I reply stroking her neck softly with my fingertips. She opens her eyes and looks up at me. "For all this of course, a home, someone with me who cares so much for me. I really thought you would run a mile when you found out about me you know. I wouldn't have blamed you if you did but instead you take me in and look after me. I just can't believe this is happening to me." Her hand runs up my chest and neck slowly till it is stroking my face. I say nothing, fearing that I will descend into tears if I do, so I just smile back and stroke the needle scars on her arm. We lay like that for an hour until I see she is asleep. I help her to bed putting a large glass of fresh orange by her bedside, and kiss her goodnight. Retiring to the lounge again I open the scotch and pour a large measure wondering what tomorrow will have in store for us. Scotch? I think. My own drug of choice nowadays isn't it. A prop or relaxation? I don't care much at the moment, I think as long as it helps me through this. I flick through an old photo album of us back in the real 1980s for a while before quietly slipping quietly into the bed beside Romilly. She is snoring lightly and hugging the pillow tightly to herself and I hope she is having good dreams for once. She may even be back in 1981 giving me hell. And I smile and kiss her cheek tenderly wishing her sweet dreams.

Chapter 39. Withdrawal Symptoms.

I suppose I knew it was coming and the doctor had warned me that it would but I have a terrible night with Romilly. She wakes up about two am in a cold sweat kicking out at me in her sleep. I think at first that she is having another one of her nightmares and I try to calm her but she is having muscle cramps from the withdrawal and terrible stomach pains. Nothing I try to do seems to help her at all. She cries out and pleads for her fix but I'm not giving in. I give her the strong painkillers from the doctor. I make her some more warm milk. I plead with her to just lay back but she is going wild, calling me all sorts of names, telling me that if I really loved her I would give her some smack, she goes as far as telling me she is going to leave me now if I don't give her some right this minute. She tells me I've always been a cruel bastard to her and why the hell did I come back into her life. "You should have left me there in Swindon Matt. Left me to die in peace you shit. I hate you." She see's that I'm not budging so she tries wheedling it out of me. "Look Matt I've almost made a day. Please please just let me have a little and I promise I will start again tomorrow. This is too soon I'm not ready for this yet." I look into her poor pain wracked eyes and get up from the bed. She follows me a look of almost pure euphoria in her eyes as I get the heroin from the place I had hidden it under the carpet. She tries to grab the small bag but I pull it away from her and go through into the lounge. I turn on her and shout, "You tell me that I don't love you because I won't give you this shit? You don't see do you. It's because I do love you so bloody much. That is the reason that I'm not giving it to you or are you just full of crap and broken promises like the first time round?" She drops to her knees in front of me and pleads for it but I walk towards the toilet. She is dragging along behind me holding my legs and rucking the carpet up with her knees. I can feel her nails digging into my calves as she sobs uncontrollably pleading for the heroin. I push the toilet door open and switch the light on, and in its cold glare and ignoring Romilly's sobs I open the bag and pour the last contents of the bag into the toilet bowl. I flush the smack away and lowering the seat I sit down. I notice the blood running down my legs where Romilly's nails have dug into my legs. She lays there disbelieving at first, then her face is against my leg wailing in heart rending despair. And she starts trying to hit me, slow weak punches to my knees and stomach, easily deflected till I slap her face. Not hard, just enough to stop her in her tracks. She lays face down on the cold toilet floor, her tears and saliva and snot against my feet. I try to lift her but she swings out wildly with her fist catching my face. I can feel the blood running down my chin from the split lip she has just given me. I grab her by the arms and pull her face to mine. "You stupid cow, I tell her, it's about time you pulled your sorry self together and try to help me help you. I feel her go limp in my arms, her eyes closed and tears running down her pained face. She relaxes a little and I release my grip slightly, then I see stars as she swings her fist against my head. Her eyes are open wide now and I can see naked hate for me in them as I hold her arms tightly again. She spits at me, "You fucking worthless bastard. You haven't changed have you? I know you hate me. Always have, always will." She mocks, the old petulant Romilly smile on her lips. Why do you think I left you before? It's because I can't stand you. I hate you so much. I hope you rot in hell you fucking asshole. Just get dressed and take me back to Swindon now." I pull her up and hold her against the toilet wall by her arms. She tries to knee me in the bollucks but I block her. "Ok get your stuff then, I shout, if that's what you want then so be it. Go flog your sad little ass to Charlie Maloy and his mates for twenty quid a pop for a fucking fix of skag, just don't expect me at your funeral when it comes Ok? And thanks for letting me know your feelings, you fucking worthless whore." My words are in anger and it seems to hit home and she sinks to the floor between my legs crying. All the fight in her has gone now. Her dressing gown is wide open from her struggles revealing her breasts and thin legs and she starts to cry uncontrollably. I slide slowly down the wall beside her and pulling her to me I put my arm around her small heaving shoulders. "I'm sorry I tell her. You know I didn't mean that." Pulling her head towards my chest I cuddle her like a baby feeling her tears against my chest. Her arms wrap around me pulling me closer to her and I squeeze her tightly. "Come on let me get you to bed Baby." I lead her unresisting back to the bedroom and put her back to bed. I wipe my bleeding lip on some tissue and slide in beside her, all the time letting her feel my touch. She turns towards me and squeezing herself into the foetal position clings to me as if I'm going to leave her. "Shhhhh baby you are safe. I'm here." I tell her.

Chapter 40. The Hospital Consultation.

I wake the next morning with Romilly still squeezed into a ball beside me. She doesn't look well at all, her skin has a yellowish tinge and I have trouble in waking her. But I go through to the kitchen and make tea leaving her to sleep in peace and while the kettle boils I clear the mess up in the bathroom from the night before, the bloodstains on the floor and I wipe down the wall. I take her tea through and rouse her but she seems so listless, as if she has given up all hope. But slowly she awakens. "Are you Ok Romilly? I ask her quietly. I've made you some tea baby." She looks at me groggily and reaches out for me as if in need. "Matt I know I wasn't too pleasant to you last night but..." "It's Ok I understand Rommy we knew this would be hard and I guess we learned just how hard last night but I will be here always Ok. Just don't worry please. I am not going anywhere without you?" She relaxes back into the bed and tells me softly almost ethereally, "Trust me Matt not to leave you, or to return from following after you: for wherever you go, I will go I promise; and wherever you call our home, I will call my home: your friends shall be my friends, and your hopes will be mine also. And she lies back painfully as I take in what she has told me. I squeeze her hand and stroke the cool dry skin and smile at her with the lovelight in my eyes. "Romilly my baby, my home is your home, you will never have to follow me as I will always be by your side and I have no friends but you. And as for hopes? Well I have none, none at all. You are my hope fulfilled just being with me again." She lies back again holding my hand until I see she has drifted off into sleep again.

We get a call later that morning from the surgery. The doctor tells Romilly that some of her test results have come back and she will need her to undertake more tests at the hospital quite urgently. She has an appointment for today and we need to be there at the hospital in Cambridge for 1pm. I nod my head as Romilly asks if it's ok. She is looking worried. The doctor goes on to tell her it will involve an overnight stay at least. Now I know what the parking situation at the hospital is like and so we leave about 11:00 am. "We can grab a bite at the Burger King there." I tell Romilly. She has had a bad night obviously and is in a lot of pain still. She is also worried about the results of her tests, I can see that. I also know she wouldn't be going to the hospital so quickly if the results were not reason for concern but I keep my worries to myself and try to lift her spirits a little on the way to the hospital reminding her of the holiday on the Norfolk Broads back in 1981. "Have you been back to 1981 lately?" she asks me weakly. We are on the roundabout above the M11 as I reply. "No not since the night before I came to Swindon, but then again I haven't really tried. I've got you here now to worry about. How about you?" "I did try last night and the night before but I couldn't get there." She says sadly. I drive one handed as I take her hand in mine. "Don't worry babe, let's just get this sorted first Ok?" Miracle of miracles, we arrive at the hospital soon after and get parked almost straight away. I take her arm and we walk slowly to the concourse to visit the Burger King. I get us burgers and fries but neither of us has much inclination for eating and we both leave our food half uneaten. We look around the shops lackadaisically for a while and I get us daily papers to read. We arrive at the clinic about half past twelve and after booking in we sit down together in the bright neon lit waiting area. I put my arm around her comforting her as I know she must be going through a lot of worry right now. I can see the fear in her eyes as the nurse calls her name and she looks at me in panic. "C'mon babe let's do it." I tell her trying to smile in reassurance. We head into the consulting room holding each other's hands tightly. "Arbeit macht frei." I think to myself sadly for some reason as we enter.

The doctor is a small Indian man in glasses and he ushers us in, invites us to sit down and introduces himself. "It's not very good news I'm afraid, Mrs Spears." says the doctor getting her name wrong. I start to tell him of his mistake and but Romilly touches my arm lightly and tells me that Mrs Spears is perfectly fine by her. He clears his throat and continues, "Well we have had some preliminary test results back and they are giving us cause for concern with your liver from the blood tests. We have a very high reading of alpha-fetoprotein and also the enzyme readings which are also elevated" "What does that mean though Doctor in words we can understand?" I ask him with a note of caution in my voice. The doctor looks at me and then Romilly. "It means that results seem to indicate damage to your liver and possibly other organs but we will have to run some more tests first but due to your heroin use and the preliminary results it looks like it could be Hepatocellular carcinoma, in layman's terms that's carcinoma of the liver I'm afraid." He says sadly. "You mean cancer?" says Romilly. "Well yes it looks like it I'm afraid although we need to do more tests first before I can confirm it. I am sending you for an MRI scan later this afternoon and we will probably need to take a biopsy of your liver after it. That means taking a very small piece of your liver through a very fine needle from your abdomen under local anaesthetic for a testing. Firstly I will need to examine you though." I hold her hand tightly as he continues. "I think you need to prepare yourselves as the prognosis in cases like this is not normally very good." I am sitting there stunned trying to take it in. I had thought it might be something like this but the stark realisation of my fears still comes as a shock to me. Romilly asks him shakily. "So what are my chances then?" The doctor looks a little disconcerted but tells her. "Well unless we can get a transplant which I think in your case is very unlikely due to the drug use then about ten percent at the very best. I am so very sorry." I look at Romilly speechless but she casts her eyes downwards. "We will need to admit you immediately of course, says the doctor." Romilly agrees and the doctor asks her to get changed into a hospital gown so he can examine her. She disappears behind a screen and reappears five minutes later in a white hospital gown. "Is it Ok if I stay with her?" I ask the doctor. "Yes of course it is at least for the time being Mr. Spears." and so pulling the curtain screen back the doctor asks Romilly to lower her gown. She sits there looking so vulnerable as he checks her heart and pulse and then feels her chest and abdomen "I am just checking for any swelling to her liver." he tells me noticing the concerned look on my face as he continues his examination. He finishes the examination and asks the nurse to come back in as he fills in more notes. The nurse returns and takes samples of Romilly's blood and ushers her to the small cubicle for a urine sample, and then takes her blood pressure again. The doctor is writing out his notes while this is going on and asks me a few questions about her heroin habit. I tell him of Romilly's attempt to go cold turkey and of the problems I had with her the previous night. "How long is it since she last had some?" he asks me all the time scribbling notes in his pad. "Only a day and a half ago." I answer warily. Romilly meanwhile has finished her tests and sits back down beside me. I take her hand again giving it a small squeeze in what is hopefully some kind of reassurance.

"Ok Romilly, says the doctor, you know we are keeping you in overnight yes? Romilly nods. We need to run a few more tests overnight and we will hopefully come up with some more precise results tomorrow. In the meantime Matt has been telling me of your attempt to stop taking heroin and I think that although laudable, in the current situation that might not be the best thing for you and so I am going to prescribe some Methadone for you." Romilly nods but I don't think the bad news about the liver cancer has fully sunk in yet with her. She seems in a daze gazing down at her thin white knees that are showing from beneath the hospital gown, I can see the goose pimples on her skin. Her hands are grasping themselves as if she is praying to an uncaring God and I take them in my hand again feeling their coldness. The doctor leaves us for a while and I take her in my arms and hug her to me telling her that it will be Ok and that after all of her troubles this will be nothing at all and we can fight it together. She just has to be positive about it. Our love can conquer it. I know it can I tell her. But she hardly hears my words of reassurance and starts to cry softly to herself. "Bloody typical isn't it Matt. She tells me sadly, I finally find a bit of peace and happiness with you and now it's all going to end. Just my bloody rotten luck."

Chapter 41. Hospital Admission.

After our meeting with the doctor we go to a ward. A bored looking porter arrives with a wheelchair for my Romilly. She wants to walk but the doctor insists on the wheelchair and I tell Romilly not to worry and that I will push her and the porter leads the way for us sullenly. We are taken to a ward in the new wing of the hospital where Romilly gets her own room with an en-suite shower. "Wow I'm impressed; I tell her helping her onto the bed and trying to be cheerful for her, look you can even get the internet here." There's a small pull down monitor above the bed that delivers all of this as well as TV and a phone. I arrange payment for a day with my debit card while Romilly settles down into her hospital bed. A nurse enters shortly after with a small plastic cup containing a green liquid. Its Romilly's methadone dose. She swallows it and pulls a face. "Yuck that is sweet." she grimaces. But after a few minutes I can see she is looking so much calmer so it must help. And so here we are alone in the ward together and she beckons me to sit beside her. "Matt please hold me now." I don't argue with her and sitting on the bed beside her I take her in my arms and we sit like that for a while our arms around each other and cheek to cheek. I can feel her little heart beating in her chest against me through the thin hospital gown and I can feel her breath against my cheek. I pull away slowly and study her face. She returns my look and smiles. "Well Matt it looks like I have succeeded in killing myself after all doesn't it?" "Shhh baby we don't know that yet. You can get through this you know. Please don't just give up." I plead hopelessly. I tell her to wait for the results tomorrow but she shrugs and tells me, "It's Ok I was kind of expecting this. I've been getting these pains in my abdomen for months now. I just didn't care. And then I find you back in 1981. I wanted to hide this from you so much you big soft git. You wouldn't let it be would you? It's just typical of you isn't it. You always were so bloody stubborn. You just can't leave things alone can you. You have to keep looking for the bloody reason behind everything don't you? Why sometimes can't you just leave it be and accept it?" I try to bury my face in my hands but she pulls them away and tells me. "Look please forget me here Matt. Go back to 1981 and look after the young me and even if I can't get back, please stay there and protect her. Please. Stop me doing this again whatever you do. I know you can do it. I loved you so much in 1981. I thought you were perfect in those early days. I would have done anything you asked me to. You know that don't you? I really want you to baby. Please. You can even call the youngest Mildred if you want." She is holding my hands tightly in hers now and I can feel her nails digging into my hands. She was probably always the stronger of the two of us emotionally in spite of my bravado in a bad situation and I want to hug her but instead I feel the tears welling up in my eyes at the strength of the emotion I feel emanating from her at that moment. I release one of her hands and stroke her face gently. The blonde dye is thankfully starting to grow out of her hair now and I can see her familiar honey blonde hair appearing at the roots. Her sad eyes never leave mine though as I sigh and tell her. "Look Romilly I told you I didn't belong in 1981 but in 2007 and I stand by that baby although I suppose I belong wherever you are. But I always promised you that I would stand by you didn't I, whatever life could throw at us." She tries to talk but I put my fingers to her lips hushing her. "This for me is the real world. I'm a bloody 54 year old boring factory worker, not a 27 year old time traveller when it comes down to it. And if you are in pain and dying do you think that for one minute, for one single fucking minute that I would even contemplate leaving you to face that without me being here? She lowers her eyes. "Well do you? I am here with you till the end if it comes to that. So just give up trying to send me away ok. You are the person I have always loved. Always have always will and if the worst comes about then I will go back but the you from this timeline is my priority now and our 1981 selves will have to sort themselves out for the time being. I am not going to leave you here not knowing what happens to us. Now do you understand that Romilly?" She pulls me to her again and I hear her sob then break down crying. "But even if you go back you will still be here with me. The 2007 you will be here still." She sobs. "I know that Romilly but the part of me going back to 1981 just couldn't handle that. Not knowing how this ends and I wouldn't if I went back now." I don't let her go just pull her tighter to me. I feel the wracking sobs in her chest but I don't let her go and I tell her that for now I want to be with her now in 2007. "For Christ's sake Spears, she says between sobs. What did I ever do to deserve you? I leave you and go to totally mess my life up. I'm a loser but you still stick by me. I thought that after the past few years I knew all about men but you certainly buck the trend don't you after some of the low life's I have met." "Hey don't knock life Romilly, I tell her and remember that I talked to Charley? "Yea I remember the old git, so what." she tells me. I tell her of my meeting with Charley back in Swindon and tell her that I think that he had a soft spot for her.

We are still sitting there when the same nurse enters to take more of her blood and check her blood pressure again. "Ok Mrs. Spears we are going to take you for an MRI scan now if you would like to get ready." She informs us. I tell the nurse that I am staying with Romilly whatever happens and she points to a chair in the corner of the room. "We can get you blankets if you are cold and you are welcome to stay after the scan." she tells me. She gives Romilly something to relax her in readiness for the scan and after she leaves I pull out the pack of cigarettes and light one to share between us. I open the widow to try to lose the smell and pass the ciggy to Romilly. She pulls deeply on it gratefully and passes it back to me. I can see the pain in her eyes but she smiles conspiratorially at me as she blows the smoke out. I flush the dog end down the toilet and we sit and wait for the porter to arrive to take her for her scan. We talk together for a while about our old lives and watch some TV together but eventually I see that the sedatives are working and she is looking a lot more relaxed and so I lean over to kiss her cheek softly.

The porter arrives shortly and this time I allow him to push her to the MRI suite while I walk alongside her holding her hand. After we enter the suite Romilly is given an injection of some kind of dye to enhance the scan results and told about the process. It can be a bit claustrophobic we are told and I can see why as I look at the scanning machine. Basically it is a large enclosed tube in to which Romilly will be slid on a wheeled table. "It can be rather noisy in there too, the radiographer tells us, but you can wear these headphones and we will play some music to you to drown it out if you so wish." "Heavy metal I suppose?" I reply smiling. The radiographer laughs and gives us the lowdown on the process. It will last about an hour during which time Romilly must try to lie still apart from normal breathing. If she needs to move or communicate then an intercom connects her to the radiographer. She is asked if she has any metal implants, even a contraceptive coil as these will affect the results to which Romilly laughs, nodding her head no. Then she is asked to remove her watch and earrings and is prepared for the scan. "Don't worry Mrs Spears I can hear you through the intercom if you need me." The radiographer smiles as she slides Romilly into the machine. "See you in an hour babe. Be good in there without me won't you." I grin and narrowly avoiding a playful smack from her backhand as she goes in. And so the scan starts and they are right about the noise, it sounds like a spanner in a spin drier. I sit by the radiographer as she starts the process checking that Romilly can hear her and when Romilly confirms that she can a nurse enters and asks me if I would like a tea or a coffee while I wait. I opt for a tea with two sugars which is duly delivered and I talk to the radiographer who is called Angela between her tasks. "So how long before we get the results Angela?" I ask her. "Well normally at least a few days but your doctor wants them fast so you will probably know tomorrow. Romilly will have a biopsy after this in the room next door with an ultrasound scanner and that will be the same too." She replies. After the promised hour the scan finishes and Romilly is wheeled out of the machine. She smiles when she sees me and tells me. "Damn I was just starting to enjoy the music too Spears."

Romilly is allowed a tea before she is wheeled through to the ultrasound room for her biopsy but I am asked to wait outside for that. I start to argue but Romilly tells me she will be Ok and to go for a cigarette while I'm waiting for her. I am assured by the nurse that it won't take too long. Romilly will be hooked up to an ultrasound machine after a local anaesthetic and a very fine needle will be used to take a tiny piece of her liver for further tests. And so I leave her alone as she is wheeled in and make my way to the exit for a quick relaxing and much needed smoke. I stop by the hospital shop on my way back up to buy us some sweets, and find my way back to the ultrasound suite. After five minutes the door opens and Romilly is wheeled out. "Nice smoke? she asks, only I could use one myself after that. "Awww babe never mind I got you some sweeties instead." I tell her waving a bag of toffees at her. "Bastard." I hear her muttering as we make our way back to the ward.

Chapter 42. 1984 and Leah.

Romilly is tired after the tests and the required sedatives and she dozes as I talk about a future that I suspect will never happen now in 2007. As she sleeps I watch the small TV and try to just blank my mind to the possible outcomes of our present situation. The hospital chair is quite comfortable and before long my eyes start to close as well and I start to drift away to the warm comforting hospital sounds. It seems only a short time before I start to awaken. I find as I come too groggily that I'm still in a hospital ward, in a hospital chair but something is very different. I am in a different chair and there's a low light on above the bed highlighting the soft blue pastel wallpaper and Romilly's nails are digging into my wrist shouting at me to wake up for God's sake. I'm in a totally confused state as she screams at me to call the bloody midwife. Half asleep I jump up and I run out of the door tripping on a chair on the way out sending it clattering to the floor and I am thinking "Midwife? What the fuck? Nurse." I shout not knowing what is happening here. A nurse or is it a midwife appears and follows me back into the room and I notice this is a much younger Romilly in bed. Her hair is different. Back to its old honey blonde colour and in a ponytail to hold it from her eyes. "What's happening I ask her?" "For God's sake Matt I'm having our child wake up will you." She starts grimacing in pain and the midwife rushes to calm her. "Ok Romilly I want you to breathe deeply and push, can you do that for me? Romilly's legs are open wide beneath the bed cover and I see the midwife looking at her watch and holding Romilly's wrist as she talks calmly to her as she times the contractions. This is all happening way too quickly for me. I can see a newspaper on the floor by the bed and pick it up quickly. It's a Daily Mail and I quickly scan the date, January 25 1984? Oh my God how did I get here? Is this another timeline or the same one continuing from 1981? How the hell have I skipped three years? But I don't have time to think as the midwife tells me sharply that this is no time for reading the damned paper as my wife is giving birth early and so I drop it to the floor to rush to the other side of the bed and take her hand. "Ok Romilly darling, says the midwife keep up the breathing and push. Harder now. That's it I can feel the head. Push. Push Push. Romilly's hand is squeezing mine so hard I am worried about my blood supply and her nails are piercing my skin. The midwife is now between her legs and I can see a small head appearing there between them. "Push Darling, that's it. Almost there now darling. Push." says the midwife. I stroke Romilly's sweat covered forehead and try to calm her but I am feeling totally useless. "You bastard Spears, she cries, if I come back in another life I'm going to stay celibate, this is agony." Her face contorts and she pushes again for one last time and I can see the midwife has the baby now and cuts and clamps the cord then administers an injection in the baby's heel. "It's Ok she says seeing my concern it's just a Vitamin K injection." Wrapping the baby in a small blanket she passes the small delicate bundle of life to Romilly and says. "Congratulations Mr. and Mrs. Spears you have a baby girl. Have you got a name for her yet?" Romilly looks at me a smile appearing on her overjoyed face and I nod back grinning like a total fool. "Yes she's called Leah, I tell the midwife, and she is beautiful."

Now how can people say children have their parents' looks at birth? You just can't tell can you? This small baby has a gorgeous small wrinkled little face. Small baggy little eyes barely open. I suppose that all babies look like this. She has soft downy hair on her beautiful small head which is still wet from the delivery and my heart almost stops at the beauty of her. Her small fists clenching, her small mouth moving to an age's old yearning for feeding. She makes small mewling sounds and I gaze at her all wrapped up in the blanket in Romilly's arms in total wonderment at her tiny but strong beauty. Romilly lifts her slowly to her breast and the small mouth locks on her nipple instinctively taking the life giving milk. Our very first daughter and she is ours I think proudly. I bend forward to kiss the small face and then kiss my Romilly. "She is so beautiful, I say, just like her gorgeous mum and she is going to be so loved." I place my finger in Leah's small hand and her tiny fingers grip it instinctively. I turn my attention to Romilly from the small bundle of life in her arms. She is so tired but the smile on her face tells it all. "You know she's my number one girl from now on, you have just been demoted." I laugh softly. Then all fades out as I return to 2007. To a sad very different kind of hospital bed and in a very different kind of hospital ward.

Chapter 43. Four Weeks Left.

The next morning and I am being roused at six am by an efficient looking young Philippine nurse to take more blood and get Romilly's blood pressure. I am still in shock at my trip back. I stand up as she does and stretch to ease the kinks from my back. Another nurse enters with Romilly's methadone and asks us if we want coffee or tea. Romilly has had a good night. I realise that she has slept again without nightmares thankfully. Hopefully they are finished with now. "Hiya Sexy, I grin, and how are you today? Romilly looks rested but I see a twitch of pain as she tries to pull herself up in bed. "Oh God, it hurts Matt." she says indicating her stomach region. I find the nurse who gives her some painkillers along with her tea. I have to get my own breakfast and so making sure Romilly is comfortable I go down to the concourse to hunt down comestibles and think about the nights visit back. Was it a visit or just a dream I speculate? The cafe is open and I order a full English breakfast. I don't know why as I push it away half eaten but I wash it down thirstily with a large cappuccino. Then it's outside for a cigarette, the first of the day and I think what will the rest of the day hold for us? Should I tell Romilly about my latest visit? Was she there too? I realise that the visit was so quick and frenetic that I just didn't know if Leah's mum was the original Romilly or not. Flicking the dog end down a convenient drain I return to the ward to ask her. Its only 7:30 so I am surprised to find the doctor is there already. The same Indian guy but this time in a white coat. "Ahh Mr Spears I was hoping you'd be here for this." Make me feel guilty or what? I think. "Please sit down. He says gesturing towards the chair I spent the night in. Well we have the results and I am afraid they are not too good at all. As we suspected Romilly has carcinoma of the liver but it has started to spread to her pancreas and stomach. Totally inoperable I am afraid. You must prepare yourselves for the worst. I am so sorry." "So how long?" asks my Romilly sadly. "Maybe four weeks. He replies Maybe less. It is very hard to tell in circumstances like this I'm afraid. We are transferring you to St Nicholas Hospice in Bury St Edmunds, they specialise in palliative care in these cases." I can't help it, my mind just snaps and I run from the ward in tears leaving Romilly and the doctor alone. I find the exit and light a cigarette before dissolving into tears of fear and sadness. Passers-by look at me as I cry my heart out that chilly morning in front of the hospital doors but I just don't care about them. A passing nurse tries to comfort me but I am inconsolable. All I have done has been for nothing. I thought I was giving her a better life only to see it turn to ashes in my hands as usual. How could I have let her down so badly? And now the added complication of my visit to 1984. This is the real Romilly from my timeline and I feel I must bear the responsibility for her present state. If I hadn't met her that night back in 1980 in the Old Crown then perhaps this wouldn't be happening. All my cockiness comes back to haunt me. My introduction of Romilly to drugs in 1981 that was me wasn't it? Was it was my fault getting my mum to get her a job in the tax office where she met her next husband leading to her downfall? If I could end my own sad life myself there and then I would have done it but something held me back. A more sensible voice within told me that Romilly needed me now more than ever, how could I forget that, and so I rushed back to the ward. But what could I tell her?

Chapter 44. Hospice.

I return to the ward trying to restore some kind of order to my emotions and by the time I arrive back I'm thinking I look reasonably calm. "You look like shit Matt. You look worse than I do." Romilly says as I enter. Definitely a smile on her face although I can tell she is forcing it through the pain. The doctor and the nurse are still there but I sit on the bed and take her hand squeezing it gently. "How long before we can get her to the hospice doctor?" I ask. "We are transferring her later today, they have a room available now." Romilly tells the doctor that she wants me to drive her there and the doctor agrees and after filling in a few notes he shakes Romilly's and my hands and leaves after wishing us luck. The nurse leaves shortly after and we are alone again. I pack her few meagre belongings and after picking up her discharge note and a letter to the hospice we leave the hospital for the last time.

Romilly is in a lot of pain as I help her to the car but she fights against it gamely and we set off to the hospice. It's only a half hours drive away in Bury St Edmunds and we are soon there handing the paperwork over at the front desk. I know it well as my Dad has spent time in here as well I have to sign in and get a visitors permit as a nurse leads her away to her room. I join her after about 10 minutes and hand her my mobile. "I think you should ring your folks, let them know what's going on." I can tell she has been putting this off but she takes my phone and rings them anyway. I leave her to tell them the bad news and go to get us a tea from a machine in the foyer. She is sitting there on the bed gazing out of the windows when I return with the phone in her lap. "Well?" I ask. "They are coming straight up, she replies turning to face me, this will really destroy them you know after all that has happened lately." "Look Romilly they are both strong especially your mum and they will handle it just fine. They have no choice. And besides, at least they are happy that you are back." "Maybe." she replies sadly. Then I decide to tell her about my visit back the previous night. First I ask her if she has been back recently. "I try, she says, but nothing. I just don't seem to be able to visit now. Perhaps it's the illness I don't know." "Have you been back to anywhere other than 1981?" I ask her tentatively wondering if it was the 2007 Romilly I met in the maternity bed in 1984. "No, never, I didn't think we could." she answers. And so I start to tell her of my brief visit back to 1984 the previous night. Her face is spellbound as I tell her. "Don't leave anything out I want to know the smallest detail." she pleads squeezing my arm and I realise that the Romilly I met there was not her at all but the Romilly from the original timeline. And so I tell her about Leah, how beautiful she is. I tell her about the maternity suite, even the midwife in her blue nurse's uniform, the speed of the delivery. I tell her about our pride in our new daughter and she is by now in tears, although happy tears at least. I tell her about my confusion at finding it was 1984 and not 1981 from the date of the dropped newspaper and of almost breaking my neck on the misplaced chair. "So she'd 23 by now there?" She asks me. "I suppose so." I answer. She takes my hand and squeezing it gently asks. "I didn't tell you much about my children in this timeline did I Matt?" "No but don't worry babe if it hurts you don't need to." I tell her. "No its ok. she assures me. Ok they are Rebecca, she is twenty one now, Ross who is eighteen and Mark, he is eight and I love them so dearly but I suppose I did the same as you did to me in 1984. I made them dislike me by loving them too much. I was so upset after the divorce when their father tried to get custody that I acted so stupidly, so destructively even. The drinking started to affect me badly. I thought it helped at the time. The same as you and your drugs?

I thought I was being clever but he had me. Every time he had me. He used it all against me. I went around one day and set fire to his car in frustration. He called the police and I got arrested. They said I had an alcohol abuse problem. And all the time he was turning my children against me. So he got his custody and now they don't talk to me even on the phone." "Where are they now I ask?" "He got a job in Florida that's all I know. " she tells me sadly. "Ok give me an hour, I tell her, I'll see if I can find him. I think he needs to know what is happening I don't you?. I use the hospice computer but it is so slow and won't let me do anything so I go back to Romilly and tell her I have to leave her for a few hours. I'm popping home for a while. She looks at me. Her face is full of sadness but I tell her not to worry and I will bring her some things back from the flat when I return.

Chapter 45. Tracing Rebecca.

It's mid afternoon by now and as I prepare to leave, Romilly's mum and dad arrive looking worried, but I point them in her direction and leave after making my excuses. After three quarters of an hour I am back in our flat. The sadness at seeing it the way we left it is overpowering with our washing up still in the sink from the day before but I leave it and go to switch on the Pc. Powering up the external hard drive I put Pink Floyd on for some background music and search. I have friends who can sniff out your inside leg measurement if need be online but in this case I don't need them. I soon sniff him out myself. He has been as stupid as to leave a trail like a personal autobiography online and within half an hour I have tracked him down. First I check his name from what my friends and I jokingly call the BDSM records otherwise known as BDM, that's the register of births deaths and marriages. I got that far before and now I follow it through. I have to crack a few passwords on the way but it's mostly easy stuff. Friends Reunited gives me his workplace, the kid's names and where he lives, then LinkedIn, and Google does the rest for me giving me his address, phone number and even his mobile number. Getting curious I even hack into his work at and for a large technology company I am disappointed how easy it is to hack into his personal files, I know his social security number his pension his hobbies and most of all I confirm his address and cell phone and home numbers. "Twat." I think. I place the call and a young female voice answers. "Hiya is that Rebecca?" I ask pleasantly. "Yes who is this?" She replies. Damn she sounds like her mum so much but with a slight American accent. "Hi I tell her, in the next few seconds or so you are going to want to put the phone down on me but don't please Ok? Because if you do I will keep ringing until you talk to me." She sounds a bit confused but says uncertainly "Ok go on." "Right

Rebecca, I am with your mum, Romilly in England now and she is dying. Now no matter what your dad tells you she is not a bad woman and misses you terribly. "No way. She hates us. We know that." comes the angry reply. "So your dad told you that did he?" I ask her. Rebecca sounds bitter and tells me about her mum's drunken activities. How the police lead a sad drunk woman away as their family car burnt in the front drive. "But why do you think she did that?" I ask. "Because she's a washed up drunken lush?" she says callously. "No Rebecca it's because she loves you and was frightened when she realised she was going to lose you." "So who the hell are you?" she asks me. I tell her and she sounds astounded. Not surprising really. But she has a little of Romilly's sense and she listens as I tell her of her mums condition. I tell her of her mum's predicament. How I saved her from her life in a Swindon whorehouse and her sadness at losing her kids. Oh No. I don't hold anything back. I tell her of the life her mother lead till a few days ago. I tell her about us in 1981. I tell her that her mum is dying and only has weeks to live. I leave out the time travelling bit. And I tell her I want her to come over to visit her mum. "Use your dad's credit card if you have to." I tell her. And she needs you Rebecca." "Ok I will think about it. "she tells me sounding very unenthusiastic and then she rings off after taking my mobile number. Ok I have done my best I think and twenty minutes later the phone rings and Rebecca is on the phone telling me she has booked a flight to Heathrow from Miami and she is leaving soon. I get the flight number from her. "Rebecca how about your Dad and your brothers?" I ask her. "I haven't told them. They would only try to stop me." She tells me. I hope her dad doesn't notice the credit card transaction. I tell her I will be waiting at the arrivals at Heathrow for her and I will keep my eye out for her. Then it's back to the hospice to my Romilly. She is sleeping when I return so I leave her in peace and go out to the foyer for a coffee. I check on Romilly throughout the evening but the painkillers must have worked as she hardly stirs. So setting the alarm on my mobile phone I sit in the chair beside her after kissing her goodnight and soon I'm asleep.

Next morning I am up at five for the drive down to Heathrow. Romilly wakes as I'm preparing to leave but although she is still very groggy from the meds she asks me what I am doing. "Don't worry baby I just have to leave you for a few hours. I will be back before you know it. How did your mum and dad take it?" "Not very well I'm afraid but you were right Matt I think they will be Ok." I call the nurse and she comes in to check Romilly and ask her if she wants some breakfast. "No thanks but I'd love some tea." She tells the nurse. I kiss her forehead noticing how cold it feels and tell her that I'm off and that I will be back with a surprise for her in a few hours. She nods her head but I think the pain overrides her curiosity as she lets me go without further questions.

It's a gorgeous sunny morning I notice as I leave the hospice, the birds are singing their early morning chorus from the trees in the hospice grounds and I smile at two squirrels hunting for food amongst the hedgerow. "Morning." I say to them happily but they just ignore me and scamper up a nearby pine tree as I open the car door. The journey to Heathrow takes me over two hours, two hours of wondering what I will find on meeting Rebecca, and wondering if she will even show up. But otherwise the journey goes fine as I fight the familiar early morning traffic with my music playing full volume. Dido's albums followed by a Dutch band I love called Krezip, and eventually I find myself hunting for a parking space at the airport. I make my way through to arrivals in plenty of time for her flight. Kitting myself out with a fresh croissant washed down with a latte I wait in the arrivals lounge for the flight to be called and then eventually there she is, Rebecca. She did come I think thankfully. I see her as she walk's uncertainly through the gate looking around for someone she has never seen or met before. So much like her mother and she definitely has the beauty of the young Romilly. Long hair a bit blonder than her mums but with a fuller face. In my search for her I had found a photo of her on the internet from her MySpace page but it was obviously a year or two old as in it she was still looked like a young girl, but now I see a confident but slightly glum young woman in front of me. She is maybe an inch or two taller than Romilly but her eyes and the line of her mouth are identical to her mum's. She is wearing a dark trouser suit and carries a small overnight suitcase. I walk up to her and introduce myself. We shake hands formally. "Hiya Rebecca. I'm Matt." I tell her smiling but I don't seem to get even a glimmer in return. Oh well I think. Can't win them all as I tell her that my car is in the car park.

She follows me moodily as I take her bag. We eventually find the car and set off on our journey back to the hospice. "Did she put you up to this? " she asks me eventually as I find the M4 and start heading back. "No. I reply honestly. She didn't even know that I was planning this. She thinks that I have just popped out for a few hours Rebecca." She asks me about her mum's condition and I answer her as truthfully as I can telling her that her mum only has a few weeks left at the most as her liver is almost shot along with a lot of her other internal organs. "And it's all down to drugs?" She asks me. "Yep I'm afraid it is, mostly the heroin but the alcohol didn't help her much either I suppose." And I tell her of her mum's sadness at losing her family and how it was the long slippery slope through debt and alcohol and drugs and eventually prostitution just to feed her habit. "Damn I never knew she was that bad."

Rebecca tells me. "Well grief and sorrow affect different people in different ways. I reply I know I've been through it myself. And basically you are going to be saying goodbye to her Rebecca, just remember that Ok, she is dying so just forget how she has been for the last few years and remember her as she was when you were younger. I am sure she was a loving mum to you then?" "Well yes she was but why did she change so much?" I tell her that she had better ask her dad about that and she goes quiet for a while as we quickly eat up the miles. I eventually break the silence by asking her about her life now. She tells me about the great life in Florida with her dad and step mum as we make our way up the M25 and finally join the M11. "So what did you tell your Dad about this?" I ask her. "Easy, she replies, I didn't tell him anything. I told my younger brother though." "And?" "Well he went ballistic at first but I have always been the stubborn one of the family and he knows that when I make up my mind then it stays made up. And he won't tell Dad yet at least not till after I'd gone." As we approach Cambridge I tell her of her mum and what we have been through together over the last few days together. "To be honest I don't know if I really care says Rebecca; she hasn't been much of a mother to us lately as you know." I sigh and carry on driving putting the radio on to lighten our moods perhaps for the final few miles before the hospice. As we get closer to the hospice Rebecca asks me about the place her mum is in. "Well it's not a hospital Rebecca. There is nothing further that can be done medically for your mum and the doctor was great about getting Romilly a place in there, they only have twelve spaces for patients and we were very lucky to get her in here. You won't see much evidence of medical equipment as the place specialises in palliative care, you know? Pain relief and management." "Yea I know what palliative means Matt." replies Rebecca sadly using my name for the first time too I hear. "Ok, I continue, well it is a lovely place almost entirely run by donations and volunteers apart from the nurses who are fully trained in a very difficult job. But it is so friendly there and..." but by now we are approaching the entrance so I tell her she will see it for herself anyway in just a few, short moments.

Chapter 46. Romilly Meets Rebecca.

We pull up outside the hospice and I deposit a sulky looking Rebecca at the door as I park the Berlingo in the small car park. The young receptionist smiles at me as I enter and fill in the log in book for both of us. "So where is she?" Rebecca asks me nervously. I tell her to follow me and we walk along the corridor until we enter Romilly's room. She seems to have gone downhill a lot since I left her this morning and is sleeping but to me she is always beautiful. Rebecca approaches the bed slowly, a look of trepidation on her face waiting for a reaction from her mum. I stand back as Rebecca reaches out for her mums hand slowly and takes it in hers and I watch as Romilly stirs and starts to wake up slowly. Romilly's face takes on an expression of total surprise as she sees her daughter there in front of her. They both look at each other at first, trying to read emotions in each other's faces. Then with a sudden coming together they are in each other's arms and the mother and daughter are one. Rebecca dissolves into her mother's arms in tears. Romilly's arms are around her and her daughters head lowers to her mum's chest. "Mum?" she cries, stroking Romilly's face tenderly. And she collapses on her knees against the bed. I watch mother and daughter together hugging each other and think how alike they are. I wonder if she has the fire of her mum and I watch as they embrace. They don't know what to say to each other so they just hold each other amidst their tears. Mother and daughter re-united. I leave them as I don't think my own tears will add anything to their situation and they do need to talk alone together so I have a coffee in the foyer on my own feeling so happy for them both.

And so Rebecca and I sit outside together in the hospice foyer later as the nurses make her mum more comfortable, and administer her medication. I've bought Rebecca and me a Latte from the machine and she sips it slowly pulling a face. "So are you glad you met her then Rebecca?" I ask her knowing what her answer will be. She sits back running her hands through her blonde hair and studies me. At last I see a spark in her eyes and then a tear runs down her cheek. "I never knew she was that ill, she says, but yes I am glad I came and I am going to stay with her Ok? She is my mum and aside from all of the hurt I think she needs me?" "And maybe Rebecca you need her too eh?" I smile. I leave her alone as she is drinking her latte and walk through to see Romilly, she is sitting up in bed looking tired and she looks up at me. Her face is a picture, I think this is the happiest I have seen her so far in 2007. "Thank you Darling she says taking my hand, I never thought Rebecca and I would ever talk again before I die. How the hell did you do it?" I smile at her and tell her "She is so much like you I can almost read her and deep inside what girl doesn't really love her mum?" She pulls me to her and we kiss passionately her tongue darting into my mouth as her arms circle my neck, then we just sit there alone together embracing as she whispers in my ear how much she loves me for what I have done for her. "Really Romilly it is so great just to see you two together that's enough reward for me just for you to be happy babe. You deserve it." I tell her as my lips brush hers lovingly.

Rebecca and I find ourselves together a lot in the following days sitting in the foyer. Talking about her mum in the past. How I met her mum in the original 1980. How I fell in love with her at first sight. How much alike they are. I have come to like and respect Rebecca a lot in the last few days. She is a strong woman and she does have her mum's fire after all. Previously had I thought she was the typical uncaring American bitch but she has turned out to be Ok after all. We get on surprisingly well and we talk a lot about her mum. We sit there one night in the foyer as Romilly sleeps, talking about her two brothers. "Won't they talk to her? I ask. "No I've tried she says sadly they hardly think of her now, Mark is too young to even remember her. She lost them years ago I'm afraid." She is sitting there next to me on a large sofa bare footed wiggling her toes and I suggest it's time to check out her mum. I stand up ready to make my way through but I feel her hand on my arm pulling me back. She pulls me down beside her and kisses me. It is so unexpected that I automatically return her kiss. I feel her tongue responding to mine in the deserted foyer but I push her gently away. "Rebecca what are you doing?" She lowers her eyes and says, "Matt I'm so sorry, I don't know what happened." I see a young Romilly in her then, the same gestures the same sad smile. I go through to Romilly but she is out still probably due to the painkillers. Rebecca doesn't join me. I kiss Romilly's sleeping cheek and tell her I love her so much then I straighten her bed covers, pulling the quilt up and over her thin pale shoulders to keep her warm. Rebecca is sitting there cross legged when I return to the foyer, I can tell she has been crying and put my arm around her to comfort her. "Look Rebecca you need a base while you are here. Your mum is out for the count till the morning. You can sleep at our flat tonight and shower plus it's somewhere to keep your stuff while you are here." "Are you sure? She asks me, I mean after earlier. I am so sorry I just don't know what came over me Matt." "Don't worry about it Rebecca, these things happen. I tell her, Come on let's get your things."

Chapter 47. Rebecca at the Flat.

We drive back to the flat arriving there about midnight and as we enter the front door I tell her "It's a bit of a comedown after Florida for you I know but it was only meant to be temporary." I tell her how I found it after leaving Elaine then I say to her she that can take the bedroom and I will have the sofa. "The shower is there I point if you need to freshen up. I'll make us a drink, what do you fancy, tea coffee or something stronger." She asks for the third option and so as she showers I get out my whisky and a couple of glasses. I put on the Pc and fire up my trusty external hard drive. She comes in wearing Romilly's fluffy pink new dressing gown and rubbing her hair dry with a towel. I look at her and my breath catches in my throat. It could almost be Romilly in the room with me. The 1981 Romilly. They are so alike that I have to remind myself it's her daughter. I feel so much for her I realise as she relaxes beside me on the sofa. "Only scotch I'm afraid I tell her but I have Coke or lemonade if you like and some ice in the fridge. The computers on if you need it and the music's on the external if you want to select something. She wraps the towel around her hair and tells me Coke and ice will be great with the scotch. I go out to the kitchen and return with an ice bucket and Coke. I pour us drinks and settle back with my feet up on the coffee table. I watch as she types on the computer. I can see she has her mums lovely slim legs but push the thought to the back of my mind immediately. This is the first time I have seen her without her trousers or jeans on. "Do you want to ring your dad? I ask her; help yourself to the phone if you do. "No it's Ok Matt. I just emailed him and I don't think he's talking to me at the moment anyway after this." She is looking through the music on the hard drive and I see her select something. "Wow you certainly have a selection she says but I love this." Snow Patrol starts playing. She comes and sits beside me on the sofa. "You have the same taste as me and your mum. I smile. She is always playing this album too." Rebecca smiles and sips her drink. "So how did you find her again after all these years? She asks me. I take my feet off the coffee table and pouring myself another scotch laugh and tell her that she would never believe it in a million years. "Try me." she answers. I look her in the eyes and tell her, "No Rebecca I mean you really won't believe it. I wouldn't have myself not long ago." She pours herself another drink and smiling at me menacingly says, "Am I going to have to beat it out of you then?" "Ok Ok. But don't say I didn't warn you." I laugh. She had told me that she doesn't smoke so I light myself one and taking a deep draw I start to tell her everything from the beginning. About that boring Saturday night when I first went back to the parallel 1981 and met her mum after so many years apart. It seemed years ago now but it was only a matter of weeks. I told her of Romilly's and my astonishment when we realized we could do this and it wasn't just our overimaginitive dreams. The happy times we had spent together back in our new 1981 falling in love again. How her mum's reluctance to tell me about herself in 2007 had made me seek her out in the present day when I had worried about the cause of her nightmares. Then the shock at finding out about her descent to a life of drugs and prostitution, and how I had found her in Swindon and brought her back home. I told her how we had tried briefly to get her off heroin and then our discovery of the cancer. I talked for about an hour and the music had stopped by the time I finished but all the while Rebecca listened to me without interrupting once. "So that's about it, I told her finishing the tale at the part where I had rung her in Florida. You know the rest. Are you going to ring the men in white coats now or later?" She takes one of my cigarettes and lights it. I smile at her as she draws deeply on it and looking at me guiltily she says "Ok just don't let my mum know." I take a swig of scotch and say. "Now you are going to tell me I'm mad." She pours another drink and tops mine up too." "Well it is an amazing tale but I do believe you. It's just too damned weird to be made up. And you did all this for my mum even after she had left you so long ago?" "Well yes but I suppose I never stopped loving her even after all those years and I had to save her from herself. My repayment of a debt of honour if you like. The only thing that saddens me is that she couldn't tell me about it in 1981. She thought she would lose me if I found out." I get up and put some more music on. 'Savage Garden' for a change. As I return to the sofa she takes my hand and tells me. "My mum has been telling me how you have looked after her, how you rescued her in Swindon. If it weren't for you Matt I would never have seen her alive again." I see the tears in her eyes and give her a reassuring cuddle. She pulls closer to me hugging me tighter her tears damp on my shirt front. "Shhh Rebecca, I tell her tenderly, I know she hasn't got long but at least she is going to die knowing that she is loved, that someone cares for her and she is not going out alone in that terrible place in Swindon. She looks up at me tears still on her cheeks. "I owe her that." I tell her. "No Matt we both owe her that." she says her face betraying her sorrow.

I know what you are thinking. Did I make love to Rebecca that night? Did I? Looking back I probably could have maybe but no. For once it never even occurred to me. I loved her mum totally so why would I. We had kissed and held each other but only in our mutual sadness. And we fell asleep on the sofa together my arm around her protectively. No more than that. How could I have done that? It would have been betrayal. Romilly's daughter and Romilly's ex husband, together in our grief at the imminent loss of someone restored to our love and lives after so long. And damn it I thought she felt more like a daughter to me. I awoke at three in the morning my arm around her and her sleeping face against my shoulder. She had dribbled in her sleep down my shirt but I didn't care and I lifted her tenderly from the sofa and put her to bed pulling the quilt over her and kissing her lightly on the cheek. I had a last cigarette and finished my scotch and pulled a spare quilt over myself to get a few more hours sleep on the sofa alone.

Chapter 48. Rebecca Meets Elaine.

I'm woken at 6am by the persistent sound of my mobile phone alarm. The taste of stale whisky and cigarettes in my mouth. I shower and freshen up. Then after putting the kettle on I pop my head around the bedroom door. Rebecca is fast asleep laying there on her side facing me her lovely slim legs pulled up against her stomach and her hair is covering her face, so I leave her to sleep a little longer and put some washing on. Then I make her a large mug of strong tea and take it in to her. "Wake up sleepyhead. It's a brand new day." I tell her putting the tea down beside her. She rolls over and pulling the hair from her sleepy face says "Omigod I think I have a hangover Matt." She yawns and stretches so like her mother used to at her age. "Breakfast in ten minutes. That will sort you out." I tell her cheerfully.

I busy myself in the kitchen with the frying pan and she appears shortly after and leans against the door watching me cook. Her arms are crossed against her chest with the tea mug in her hand definitely looking the worse for wear. I sit her down at the small table and finish cooking breakfast. "Full English, I smile, putting a plate of eggs bacon and fried bread down in front of her. Eat up mate it really will make you feel better." She tucks in and tells me how great it is. "My step mums a bit of a health nut, she tells me, so it's usually fruit or muesli for breakfast back home." "Very commendable I tell her, dipping fried bread and bacon in my egg, but you need to push the boat out occasionally." "Oh yes." she grins, egg yolk running down her chin, most definitely."

As I am clearing away the breakfast things I hear a knock at the front door. Opening it I see its Elaine.

"Hello stranger, she says smiling, I thought as I had heard nothing from you I had better see if you were Ok." "Come in." I tell her, Fancy a coffee?" Rebecca is in the shower so I make Elaine coffee and tell her the story so far, the one she didn't believe. And about my trip to Swindon to rescue Romilly, I know she isn't going to believe me but I tell her anyway, she deserves it." I can see the look of disbelief on her face and she points to the shower suspiciously? "So if Romilly is in the hospice who is that is in the shower?" I tell her it is Romilly's daughter and she laughs. "My God Matt you are deranged just tell me the truth Ok? It's your girlfriend isn't it? Just tell me the bloody truth for once eh?" Rebecca has finished her shower and walks into the room casually in just Romilly's dressing gown. Elaine does a double take and then looks at me questioningly. "Ok Elaine I can explain this." I say. But she just gets up and chucks the coffee over me and leaves slamming the door on the way out. Rebecca is open mouthed at Elaine's exit. "Meet the wife." I tell her sighing.

Chapter 49. The Truth About Rebecca.

I get changed into new clothes and chuck my coffee stained clothes in the washing basket and by 7:30 we are on the way back to the hospice. The nurse tells me that Romilly has had a bad night. The pain is getting worse. Rebecca and I go through to her. I take Romilly's hand and ask her how she feels. "Matt I feel like a train has hit me. It really hurts." Her face shows her pain and every time she moves it hurts. Her face has taken on an unhealthy yellow pallor. I suppose it's caused by her liver slowly destroying itself. Rebecca is sitting opposite me holding her mother's other hand close to tears. "Mum, Matt told me all about the time travel thing last night. Is it all true?" Romilly smiles a little and easing herself painfully into an upright position tells Rebecca that it is. "This is so totally weird. How do you do it? I mean it's like something from a science fiction book." "I told you Rebecca we just don't know. It just happened; it surprised us as much as it does you." I tell her. We have to leave as a nurse comes in and prepares to take Romilly's usual tests and administer her methadone. So we go out to the foyer for a coffee and sit down.

Rebecca sips her coffee and grimaces at the taste of the machine made preparation. "Don't worry it won't kill you." I laugh. "Are you sure about that?" she answers pulling a face. I start talking about her life and she tells me about wanting to be a doctor back in Florida. She definitely has the wherewithal to do it I think. "I'm twenty three next January and I hope I will be in a medical school by then." Awww Rebecca I am so pleased for you mate and I know you will do it." I tell her taking her hand. She smiles at me and squeezes it back."You know what Matt I wish you were my dad sometimes. I just get no pressure from you. My dad is always pushing me to do better; it is so hard sometimes to live up to his expectations." "C'mon, I tell her, let's go for a smoke, your mum won't be ready for a few minutes yet." It's a lovely morning and we stroll in the grounds of the hospice listening to the birds singing in the trees, her taking my arm. I light us cigarettes and we talk about her career. "So when's your birthday Rebecca I will have to send you a card" I tell her. I just told you stupid, she laughs, it's the twenty fourth of January. I'll be 23 next year.

We walk back to Romilly's room and see she is propped up in her bed smiling weakly as we enter. I know she is still in pain but the methadone and painkillers have taken effect and she looks almost radiant. We walk over to her bed and sit down on different sides taking her hands. Rebecca smiles at her mum and tells her she is looking great. Romilly smiles and looks at the two of us."I am so glad you two are getting on so well she tells us it really makes me so happy." "Yeah mum and the nurses have told me I can colour your hair later, smiles Rebecca, I agree with Matt. That blonde doesn't suit you at all."

I smile back at Romilly and say. "Rebecca has been telling me about wanting to be a doctor in Florida." "Yep I am so proud of her." replies Romilly with maternal pride shining from her eyes. "And she tells me that she will be in medical college next year on her twenty third birthday?" Romilly's face is full of a mother's joy but then her face changes as my words sink in. Romilly seems to deflate and she looks at me in shock. "You know don't you?" she asks me. "Yep I think I do and you have done it again. Why in the name of all that's holy didn't you tell me? Can't you be honest with me about anything?" I say sadly. Rebecca looks on astonished understanding nothing. "What is going on." she asks. "I think your mother needs to tell you this." I say standing up. "Mum what's going on?" says Rebecca her face a picture of concern. Romilly lets go of my hand and takes both of Rebecca's in hers. "Matt is your father." she says. Rebecca is totally taken aback and says nothing as Romilly tells her about that last night we had together in March 1984. Making love for the last time with me in the car outside her parents house on her 20th birthday. How she decided to finish with me permanently for the new love of her life that she was already seeing. Her surprise at finding herself pregnant but hoping it was her new husband to be's child. The joy of the two of them at the small lovely daughter they had and they named her Rebecca. The marriage and then eventually the uncertainty. Then looking at the child and realisation that I could be the father. She had forced herself to forget and had succeeded until she had seen the two of us together that first time in the hospice. "As soon as you two walked in for the first time together I just knew she was yours Matt. It's not just me she is like. It's you too. You are just so alike; she even has your bloody stubbornness."

I leave the room in tears. I mean I have just become a father again now twice in a matter of days. To Leah in my trip back to 1985 and now Rebecca in 2007 or is that 1985 too, I just don't know anymore? One thing about Romilly I am finding out. Life is certainly never boring when she is around. I walk out into the grounds, lighting a cigarette and wondering what else can hit me now. I'm not displeased that Rebecca is my daughter; in fact I am so incredibly proud that this strong self assured young woman is mine. I sit down on a bench amongst the trees and light another cigarette from the glowing embers of the last one. Can I take anymore? I think of Rhiannon's joy at the picture Romilly drew of her and wonder how I am going to tell her she has an older half sister, or should I just keep quiet about it? Romilly's life is certainly catching up with me but do I love her any less I think? No of course not. Whatever she throws at me now just makes me love her even more. Rebecca joins me sitting on the bench and I light her a cigarette. "Look I told you earlier that I wished you that you were my dad and if it's any comfort to you I meant it. Ok?" she says. I put my arm around my newly acquired daughters shoulder and tell her it's Ok I love her, but it has been a bit of a surprise to me too. I look at her and laugh telling her that maybe she does look like me a bit in a good light. I know she is definitely the mother's daughter as I recover from the pain after her elbow connects with my ribs. We walk back into the hospice laughing to find Romilly looking expectantly at us unsure of the news we have just learnt. We sit by the bed and take her in our arms. Just the three of us. Mother, daughter and father together. All is forgiven and understood.

Chapter 50. Close to the End. Memories of 1981.

That afternoon Rebecca does her mums hair trying to restore its natural colour. I leave them alone and go out shopping in Bury. It takes me ages but I'm lucky and find what I am looking for eventually. I get back to the hospice to find Will and Naomi there so I leave them talking with Romilly. Rebecca is in the foyer drinking coffee and I join her. "Hiya Daughter." I say kissing her offered cheek, how's your mum? She looks at me and I can tell by the puffy eyes that she has been crying. She is shoeless again and in jeans, her arms wrapped around her knees up against her chest on the sofa. "Hey why the tears?" I ask her. "I am just so confused, she tells me, my life was so straightforward till two days ago and now it's turned upside down. All I believed in has finished. I just don't know what to do anymore. It turns out my father is not my father and I am at the bedside of my dying mother. It's a bit too much to take in." "Rebecca. I tell her softly, you father is still your father He has brought you up and he loves you. He will always be your dad. Your life is in Florida now, so when this is all over just go back and study for your doctor's exams. You will be a great doctor." She snuggles up to me. "You think so?" she sniffs. "Yeah of course babe, you are a natural, just pop over once in a while to see me Ok." "Does that mean I will get your breakfast fry ups again?" She grins. "You bet!" I say.

Eventually Romilly's mum and dad leave and we go in to see her. "I've got you a pressie." I smile producing the blue rabbit it took me so long to find that afternoon. "Awww he's so cute. He's the little guy from the first Christmas card that I made you." she smiles. "That's the fellow." I laugh placing him on her pillow. I still have that card she made me back in 1980 at home in 2007 with a painting of a happy looking blue bunny on the front. I notice that Rebecca has done a good job with her hair. All of the blonde dye has gone restoring her hair to almost its normal colour. She looks beautiful even in her illness and I fall in love all over again with her as I do every time I see her." Look I am sorry about ......" I put my fingers to her lips to silence her. "You have me and Rebecca here for you so just don't push your luck beaky." I tell her. She looks so happy at my words and takes my hand and kisses my fingertips.

  That night Romilly suffers a bad turn and the nurses are running in to see to her. I sit beside her as she cries out in pain. Rebecca is holding her other hand as we try to ease her pain. Eventually the nurse gives her a shot of morphine and her head settles back on to the pillow. I know it's not going to be long now. The next morning we have trouble getting her to come too due to the morphine and when she does she is very dazed. It's a lovely morning and I take her for a turn around the hospice gardens in a wheelchair to try to brighten her up a little and it seems to work some as she laughs a little as I joke about the wooden statues of animals in the grounds. We sit in the small summer house enjoying the warm sun and she puts on her mp3 player and listens as I hold her hand. I had found the mp3 player at home and put some songs on it for her. She squeezes my hand gently as she moves her head and lips along in time to the music and I smile at her face. Seeing me looking at her with a stupid grin on my face she turns the player off and turns towards me returning my smile. "Why are you sitting there grinning at me like an idiot Spears?" "Just because, I say, what were you listening to?" "Human League?" She replies. Do you remember we used to listen to it a lot in the car back in the real 1981?" I nod my head at the memories. I reminisced with Romilly about the time we had stayed out all night in the Cortina one summer's night back then. We had got ourselves a takeaway Chinese meal and eaten it in the car together as Human League played softly on the car stereo. Afterwards we had covered the car windows with our clothes so as no one could see in and made such sweet love together in the cosy darkness for hours before falling asleep eventually in each other's arms. Romilly laughed at the memories. "And do you remember what happened next morning Matt?" "How could I forget?" I tell her. We had awoken to a knocking on the cars window and I had wound it down to find a copper staring in at us. We had hurriedly covered up our embarrassing lack of clothes as he asked us what we were up to and if we were ok. It turned out that an early morning dog walker had seen the car with all the windows covered from the inside and thinking they might be witnessing a suicide had called the police. Seeing we were Ok and after listening to our excuses as to why we were there he left us alone with a large grin on his face telling us to get dressed and go home. "That was just so embarrassing, laughed Romilly, but at least he didn't nick us I suppose" "Well I'm not surprised. I tell her, I think he was too busy enjoying the sight of you trying to hide your boobs with my boxer shorts." We are both laughing as I push her back into the hospice. Rebecca asks us why we are so cheerful as I wheel her mum in. "Well, I smile. It was........" I get no further as Romilly has jabbed me in the leg with her elbow from the wheel chair. "Another word Spears and you are dead meat. Ok?" she laughs. And I will never forget that time we spent laughing in the hospice garden together as it was probably the last time we spent together in happiness.

And so the final days came. The cancer has spread around her internal organs leaving her in incredible pain. The morphine and methadone help but at the expense of her mind. She is hardly ever awake now and when she is she is not sure where she is or even when it is. I try to help along with Rebecca and her mum and dad. We read to her and talk to her about past happier times. But mostly she sleeps through our presence only waking occasionally in confused pain. She seems to shrink into herself as her body fights against itself losing the battle inch by painful inch.

Chapter 51. The Passing of Romilly.

And the final day came as I knew it would eventually, I am reading aloud to her that morning after we wake her, some stupid story from the paper as I am holding her hand and I feel her lightly squeeze it. She murmurs softly, I ask her if she is comfortable. I lean over to kiss her cheek. Her eyes flicker open briefly and try to focus on me and I hear her trying to say something. I lean closer "I love you so much Matt, please come back to me. Please understand that I need you back there." Then she starts to fade away. I hold her hand tighter. Rebecca is crying but I tell her to be strong for her mum. Her shallow breathing becomes laboured she seems to struggle to draw a breath and then it stops. So suddenly she just takes a last laboured breath and her eyes flicker. Her hand gently twitches in mine for the last time. Rebecca is holding her other hand and tries to rouse her mum but Romilly's face relaxes from her pain and I swear a small smile appears on her face, and then Rebecca and I are sitting there alone. My Romilly has gone. We are alone. She has finally left us in death. Her husband and her daughter beside her. I kiss her still lips and run my fingers across her cold cheeks. Her eyes are still half open and I gently close them. I look at my Darling Romilly lying on her death bed looking so free now and released from pain. I gently arrange her bed clothes and give her cold hand a final squeeze. Rebecca is curled up in the chair sobbing her heart out. I kiss Romilly's cold forehead and whisper to her for the last time that I love her. I sit like that; holding her hand till a nurse comes and asks us to leave. I get up slowly and walk into the hospice grounds in a trance but finally I find a seat and with the sound of the birds twittering in the trees I dissolve into a fit of crying. "For God's sake why, why, why, why." Will and Naomi had arrived by now and join me in my devastation; both sobbing along with me...Rebecca has disappeared in her own grief.

The nurse comes to find us after an hour or so and we re-enter the hospice with her. Romilly is lying in the chapel of rest with Rebecca beside her. She looks so peaceful, almost the 20 year old I loved so much and the nurse leaves us to our grief and we all hold each other united in our mutual loss. I leave Rebecca, Will and Naomi with Romilly for the last time together. I left the hospice then, the tears running down my cheeks and think about her death. I've told you about the lovelight before Ok? It's that look in a lovers eyes. If you have ever been in love you know where I'm coming from. That look that says, it's you I want. I will die for you. That look that says No way will I ever be happier than at this moment in time being with you. It's that look that says we are young now but I'm still gonna be feeling this way when I'm old and you are all I have left. It's that look that says we are a team. I expect nothing from you because I know you love me so much in return and my life is safe in your hands. It's that feeling that if the lovemaking stopped the loving wouldn't. It's that feeling of waking in the morning and the first thing you check is your loved one beside you. It's just that feeling. I can see it in her eyes as she looked up at me in those final days as she faced her final ordeal and I know mine is reflected back at her, 23 years apart and it's still there as if it never died. We had clasped hands as we both knew she was dying but knowing that only death can part us. We can't beat that. I studied the serenity of her face in her pain hearing Rebecca's sobs. She knew she was dying. I knew she was dying but it just increased our love for each other. No more physical love. Just the knowledge that our love is complete now. We had discovered each other anew through our past. The lies were all unveiled and at last we knew each other's secrets. We knew of our past faults and they mean nothing. Nothing at all anymore. I felt that as I held her hand tighter as she died. As her breathing became shallower and as I forlornly held her hand. She had tried so hard to focus on my face as I had felt that last tightening of her hand in mine. The last "I love you" had escaped her lips and then her breathing had quietened and I knew that she was leaving me for the last time. Her face had relaxed from the pain for the final time and I felt her life leave her. She seemed to gain some of her younger innocent beauty as she had sagged back into her pillows after the last breath had left her frail body. I had lowered my head to kiss her lips for the last time in her poor pain haunted life. But she had gone. Her lips were cold and unresponding. Her hand had still been in mine. No more squeezes, but I continued holding it, praying that she would find peace wherever she went. I put my arms around her still warm lifeless body and pulled her tightly to me. I rocked her gently in my arms telling her over and over again that I loved her until the nurse comes in and gently separates us. "She's gone Mr Spears." She had said quietly. The nurse closed Romilly's still open beautiful blue/gray eyes as I had left her in death to walk in the grounds alone, totally alone. All these thoughts haunted me as I returned to our small flat alone.

Chapter 52. The Graveyard.

It's been almost two months now since she left me after our all too brief reunion, the love of my life finally laid to rest in a cold graveyard, leaving me alone again for the final time. This time it's for real as I can't get back to 1981 anymore. I've tried many times since she died but no matter how hard I try I can't go there, and I suppose our alternate time universes have drifted apart. I wonder what I would find if I could go there anyway. I can't go seeking her out in this time. She has gone to a place that I cannot follow her to now. I stare at the sad white marble headstone and imagine her face, her voice, her arm around me, looking up into my face smiling her cheeky grin. She wasn't a great lover of flowers I remember but I have a small bunch of pink carnations in my hand and I kneel to lay them against the rain streaked marble headstone. As I bend my neck to place the flowers tenderly on her grave I can feel the rain running down the back of my jacket. Down my back like her cool fingers used to. I feel so alone in the wet winter's evening of the deserted graveyard. I touch the cold marble of her headstone as if I were touching her face for one last time, brushing my fingers against its damp coldness as I stand up. "Well Babe it's time to say goodbye for the last time, perhaps we will meet again in a better place. And I really do wish you peace at last; you deserve it for lightening up my life briefly." I put my fingers to my lips and kiss them and touch them to her headstone. "I love you Romilly. Always have. Always will." Walking away from her grave I allow my tears to escape, mingling with the rain on my cheeks. I pull up the hood on my coat against the cold rain and head back to the car and the warmth of its heater to drive back to my flat. On the way back I continually run our past over and over in my mind. Our holiday on the Sandpiper. Saving her from her way of life in Swindon. All the things she had said to me become a mixed up jumble in my mind.

Chapter 53. Back.

I gave up trying to go back to 1981 and settle down to life in my little flat. Elaine wants me to come back home but I am not ready for that yet. Rebecca rings me every Saturday evening telling me about her life and how well she is doing at her college near Daytona Beach in Florida and we laugh as I suppose a newly re-acquainted father and daughter should do. She is doing so well with her studies and I am so pleased for her. I just hope life is so sweet for her and she doesn't follow Romilly and my bad choices in life. I sit alone in the darkness some evenings holding Romilly's clothes, smelling her fading scent on them and listening to music and thinking how this could have ended differently. Why couldn't I have gone back earlier say five years before and really made a difference, but such is life? It's always ifs and buts. Perhaps if I had known then I shouldn't have gone back at all, she would have died anyway. The illness was going to kill her anyway no matter what I did. And sometimes when I doze off to sleep I hear Romilly's voice calling me and her cheerful giggle at my fuck ups, but it's only my mind playing tricks on me and I always awake in my room alone. And I know I don't regret anything about us. If we hadn't been re-united then she would have died alone in that flat in Swindon or at best in the local hospital alone without me or her Rebecca beside her and I would never have experienced that great love for her at the end. It had ended as it started. Although we had lost each other for twenty three sad years we had found out that our early promises of love for each other in that past were still valid and we loved each other anew. We found out that we hadn't stopped loving each other. Never had never would I supposed. I presume that the timelines have parted for good now and I try so hard to get back to normal. I apply myself to my job but even the people there can see my sadness. My mind isn't on the job anymore. How can it be after all that has happened in my life.

Christmas comes and I wonder how the hell I am going to get through it alone. Elaine rings and asks me to come for Christmas dinner and I reluctantly accept. Perhaps Elaine and I should get back together I think sadly. I know we miss each other but something inside stops me. Christmas was the time back in 1983 that I realised that Romilly and I were having our final days together. I lied to myself at the time but looking back it was just so obvious and so it's just a time of more sadness for me. And so I find myself on Christmas Eve alone in the flat. I talk to Rebecca on the phone and then Elaine and the kids. I put Snow Patrol on the hard drive and relax back on the sofa. I have my whisky and drain the glass before pouring another. I walk into the bathroom and I can hear Romilly's voice pleading for heroin. I walk in the bedroom and hear her voice again crying in pain asking me to hold her. Fuck it I'm never going to lose her voice so I sit back down on the sofa and pour another whisky. Snow Patrol is finished so I put Moby on and relax back to 'Why Does My Heart Feel So Bad'. I can see the Christmas lights flashing on my small tree and I can hear happy kids' voices full of the joys of Christmas outside. I remember Romilly's dying words, and how she had implored me to go back and look after her younger self.

I have written all of my goodbye letters even put stamps on them and posted them knowing that they won't arrive till after Christmas. They are to Rebecca, Will and Naomi, My Mum and Dad and Elaine and so I take the small bottle of Pethidine tablets and stare at them. I had kept them for some reason from years ago I don't know why. They are opiate painkillers. They had been Elaine's and then I slowly unscrew the top. I hear Romilly laughing at me back at Bazza's in 1981 "Yeah you druggie Spears." and I hear Bazza's words too warning us to be careful about our love. They are only small but I reckon twenty are enough and swallow them with the scotch. Too many would make me sick undoing their intended purpose. I sit back waiting for them to take effect listening to Moby's Extreme Ways. The room slowly recedes as they take effect and a feeling of contentment spreads through my body. After a while I feel my hands and face going numb and I can't move anymore. I think of Rebecca and Romilly and Elaine and say goodbye to each of them in my heart in turn along with Jamie Rhiannon and Beth. Moby's Natural Blues starts playing and I have lost all feeling now, relaxing back in a warm golden glow. Moby fades out to leave me in an inviting darkness then everything fades away. I've just burnt my boats I think. I can hear Romilly telling me to look after her. Then fading away into darkness.

Until I hear myself talking. "You know she's my number one girl from now on, you have just been demoted."I hear myself say softly as I regain consciousness back in 1984. Romilly looks at me, happiness totally lighting up her face as she cradles Leah against her breast. Somehow she knows straight away. "Spears you made it you bastard. I knew you would." I lean over and pull her and Leah to me, both of them in my arms. "Yep just me and you and Leah now, no more going back to 2007 eh?" She smiles happily at me and we both smile at Leah. I start to say "So are we......" Romilly stops me her fingers on my lips. "There is absolutely no way we are calling the third Mildred. She laughs. And the lovelight is in our eyes.

Chapter 54. Epilogue.

Firstly, the only part of this book that is actually as it happened is in Chapter One and the yearning for the past on a drunken evening. We all get those feelings. Other events may have been very loosely based back in the real 1981 but I have cast a rosier or sadder light over them than actually happened. The chapter about the time travel research although it sounds the most unlikely is actually factual. As I said Google it yourself. Parallel universes actually do exist and quantum computers are really only a few years away. I think my theories about Déjà vu and Re-incarnation are actually are quite plausible and my feelings about religion that I explain in the chapter before the holiday are truly my own and deeply felt. The people in the book are based for the most part although again only loosely on real people and I apologise but I have changed any real names in most cases. I have not used true names obviously.

I promise you that the dark side of me with a touch of violence in the story is almost totally fictitious. Well mostly. I'm a pussycat really but beware if you take the piss. You wouldn't want Matt's two finger squeeze now would you? Most of the places do exist or at least did once such as Bazza's and the Acle restaurant. The Old Crown and Crescent Moon are still going strong. Oh yes and the Sandpiper was real although I don't remember her having an awning and the pub where I get Romilly drunk is a totally fictitious place. The poem Blues Comedown was a real poem from 1980 that I still have and really does describe the feeling of coming down from amphetamines that I experienced one Saturday morning back in November 1980.

As I was writing this book my father actually died (Bless You Dad) in St Nicholas Hospice and so the descriptions of it are mostly accurate and I urge you to perhaps make a donation to them as most of their funds are raised voluntarily. And before anyone tells me that the diagnoses of Romilly's cancer and her quick entry to the hospital and then to the hospice were extremely swift just imagine 'artistic license'. I could have made it last longer if I had wanted to but I think the story didn't need drawing out that much. I do know that the NHS wheels move slower than that.

As for My Romilly? Well she is based again very loosely on a real person, bless her sweet little cotton socks, from my past and I loved her very much many years ago but I know that she is long gone from my life and I wish her well and hope she enjoys the funny side of the story as much as I did as I wrote it. And so back to the question? If you did have the chance to change things. Well would you?

As for a Part Two? A sequel? Well maybe I have already started jotting down a few ideas on my trusty old Pc and an idea is taking shape in my mind. But I will give nothing away other than the provisional title of 'Leah's Story'.

Oh and one last postscript. Me and the lovely Elaine are very much together and I think I could have made her a special timeline of her own after our meeting in the Crescent Moon in 1981 but that's another story for another day.

Be lucky.

Matt Spears February 2008